COLD
TO THE
BONE

A NICOLE COBAIN MYSTERY

Emery Hayes

CROOKED
LANE

NEW YORK

Copyright © 2020 by Suzanne Phillips

All rights reserved.

Published in the United States by Crooked Lane Books, an imprint of The Quick Brown Fox & Company LLC.

Crooked Lane Books and its logo are trademarks of The Quick Brown Fox & Company LLC.

Library of Congress Catalog-in-Publication data available upon request.

ISBN (hardcover): 978-1-64385-498-4
ISBN (ebook): 978-1-64385-499-1

Cover design by Nicole Lecht

Printed in the United States.

www.crookedlanebooks.com

Crooked Lane Books
34 West 27th St., 10th Floor
New York, NY 10001

First Edition: August 2020

10 9 8 7 6 5 4 3 2 1

For Madeleine, Ava and Lilah —You are the best of me.

1

The air stirred, and snow lifted from the trees and sprayed the icy surface of the lake. It was just after two AM and the temperature hovered at zero. The clouds were low in the sky, and Nicole felt their heaviness. Her shoulders shifted under their weight. Eight years in Toole County, Montana, and she still wasn't comfortable with the building storm systems or the swift changes in weather conditions.

She listened to the wind, the groaning of the tree branches, the sharp crunch of boots through drifts, and wished it were a better night for a murder.

Snow melted and changed the composition of evidence. The wind skittered across the lake and tossed the remains of the crime scene. And the weather wasn't their only challenge. The ME—the local family practitioner who was better suited to delivering babies and curing the common cold—had arrived an hour before and was on his knees beside the body, pulling threads from the dead girl's hair with a pair of tweezers. His ME field guide was stuffed into a pocket of his parka, and even three years into the job, he consulted it often and openly.

Forensics had towed portable lamps through the woods and hooked them to a generator stationed in the bed of a pickup truck. Nicole stood within the halo of that light and watched the ME. His meticulous care pulled on her nerves. They'd been out of time even before the investigation began, and MacAulay carried out his duties with the sedate pace of a tortoise.

She exhaled and watched her breath crystalize. She stuffed her gloved hands into her coat pockets and tipped back on the thick heels of her boots. And she stared into the shadows beyond the light. She could barely make out the pinprick of head lamps worn by her men and women as they combed the surface of the frozen lake and followed several sets of foot-prints over the rolling slopes and through a thin stand of trees. The body and the footprints were so far the only physical evidence of their suspect.

The weather, the distance to reasonable equipment and personnel, and the attitudes of small-town life were a source of constant frustration when there was a crime to be solved.

"Damn boonies," she mumbled.

"I thought we were growing on you," Doc said.

"Toole County is the best thing that ever happened to me," she returned. And it was true. She'd needed out of Denver. Law enforcement there was polluted, her personal life even more, and the worst of it was that Jordan had started feeling the pain. At only three years of age then, he'd become anxious about Nicole's return every evening and be reduced to fits of screaming and head banging whenever Nicole prepared him for the court-ordered visits with his father. Kids were intuitive. They felt things, knew things. And Jordan more than most. Her son was sensitive. He was a sponge for nature and nurture. The move had saved them both. "But it puts a crimp in my cape."

MacAulay laughed. "You thought you could come in here and single-handedly wrestle crime into the dust?"

"Caped Crusaders rock, Robin."

The doctor snorted. "Not in Toole County, Sheriff. Here it's all about cooperation—people, weather, science. It's a package. But you know that by now."

She'd joined the department as a sergeant and risen quickly to under-sheriff. Six years later she'd become the first female sheriff in county his-tory. She thought her election had had a lot to do with her Big City past, which included a gold shield and several accommodations, and her skills as a communicator. Toole County was the seat of a lot of law enforcement activity. In addition to the sheriff's department, they had the highway patrol and U.S. Border Patrol working out of their little town of Blue Mesa. With Canada serving as their northern border and three major freeways barreling through the county, it was a natural choice for command cen-ters. And it had served Nicole well.

"I know it, but I don't always like it," she confirmed.

MacAulay squinted at the fiber in his tweezers and then held it up. A young forensics tech scrambled forward with a plastic evidence bag.

"Our biggest mistakes are made when we think we can do it alone."

She wondered if the comment was a professional or personal observation. Either would apply, although she and MacAulay didn't make it obvious. No talk, no touch on the job, and other restrictions that preserved her image as the sheriff. But it had been a long time since Nicole agreed to dinner—two weeks at least.

His tone was neutral, sounding more like advice than judgment, so it was hard to gauge his investment in the conversation. He was crouched over the girl's body, peering closely into her eyes with a penlight, but he spared Nicole a glance. And she found a wealth of emotion in his gaze. Concern, warmth beyond the professional, and not a small amount of challenge.

She ignored it.

"I'd settle for an honest-to-God crime lab," she returned. A full team to back her on the field. She was a quarterback who relied on her defense. MacAulay knew that.

"And a tried and true ME to run it?"

"Yes, that too."

He stood and turned to her. His salted hair lifted in the breeze. His ears were pink. "You're losing evidence," he acknowledged. "Probably more than any of us have been able to gather for you."

"You suck at the bedside etiquette, MacAulay."

He smiled. "Just commiserating." He nodded toward the body, a young girl, underdressed for the weather. She was slender, with hair a shade darker than coffee, and was probably thirteen or fourteen years old. Nicole didn't recognize her, so she wasn't local. They hadn't received a missing child report. A lot of parents had dinner with the kids, tucked them into bed, and then hit the mountain for a little air time before turning in themselves. It was the day after Christmas, 2:00 AM, and the hotels, lodges, and resorts were packed with tourists.

"Want to know who she is?"

Always a loaded question when it came from MacAulay. Once an identity was established, the doctor referred to their victims by name. Nicole and her team had learned to harden themselves to it. MacAulay was first and foremost a physician, and a small sliver of Nicole's heart was relieved that the doctor saw people where she and her officers saw bodies. But in cases where obtaining objectivity was difficult, such as the murder of a child, even the most experienced of them softened—and that got in the way of good police work.

"She have a wallet?"

"I'm guessing there's a snow bunny ID card at the end of this lanyard." He bent and tugged at a braided pale-blue string. It was tucked under the crew neck of the girl's sweater and twisted so that the body trapped the laminated pass beneath her. Nicole stepped closer. The lanyard was complimentary and the pass doubled as a room key. With any luck, the card was still intact. "I'm ready to lift her."

Nicole knelt beside MacAulay as he slid his hands under the girl's shoulder and hip and rolled her. This close, the girl's face looked almost translucent. She had the smoothest skin Nicole had ever seen and big eyes that sloped at the ends. She was Hispanic. Her cheekbones and chin were curved and full and had beamed with health a few hours before.

MacAulay held the girl's body with one hand and turned over the slope pass with the other.

"Beatrice Esparza," he read aloud, and held the card up for Nicole's inspection.

The photo matched. She checked the print at the bottom, though the lanyard was familiar—all the resorts had them, each a distinctive color and style and easily recognizable on the slopes and in the bars. "The Huntington Spa."

"You going yourself?"

"I always do."

"That's what I like about you," he said.

"My work ethic?"

"Your respect for human life," he clarified. He lowered the body back to the snow. "Dead or alive."

The truth was, Nicole did better with people after they'd taken their last breath. She was good at fighting for those who couldn't do it for themselves. Her old CO had called her tenacious. A number of ex-lovers had been less diplomatic, and Nicole was no longer surprised when, toward the end of each relationship, her passionate nature had become a "problem."

4

"Single-minded" and "stubborn" often followed declarations of that kind. Her son, however—because Jordan was straddling those years between child and teen—was as kind as he was judgmental about her job. "It's cool," he assured her. "A little cray-cray, but you spend a lot of time with dead people."

She felt a smile spread from the inside out. Her son did that for her—he was light in a dark place.

Nicole glanced again at the girl. A child still, with the soft curves of womanhood just developing. Neither she nor the world would know her full potential. And that caused a chain reaction of emotion in Nicole, beginning with an intense sadness she knew was useless and finishing with a consuming anger that would propel her through the necessary steps toward justice.

She was looking at another mother's child. Much loved or cast away? She focused on the raven hair spread out on the ice and the gold piercings in the girl's ears—a hammered teardrop hoop with a diamond accent dangling in the center. A quarter carat. Beatrice Esparza was tended to, from her long, trimmed tresses to the tips of her acrylic nails.

"Time of death's going to be a bitch," she said. The first officer had arrived on scene at 12:22 AM and taken an ambient temperature reading. Two degrees. And she'd watched MacAulay insert a common mercury thermometer through a nostril in the victim's nose, then note the body temperature in a small notebook he kept. He'd already reconciled the numbers and given her a window of possibility, but it was wide open at four hours—sometime between 8:00 PM and midnight. Most criminals could slip through a crack in the pavement, and currently they had a crater.

MacAulay nodded.

"You can't narrow that window a little, Doc?"

"That's the best I can do, but it'll work until Missoula."

The state lab and morgue. Nicole thought briefly about having the body bagged and driven the 230 miles to the Big City and the state medical examiner, but there was nothing extraordinary about the case. Not yet. Murder by asphyxiation was about as common as a hangnail. A child victim was no longer an anomaly. MacAulay would do the prelim in the basement morgue of their tiny hospital and then move her on to Missoula, where the body would wait in line behind other murder victims for a more thorough exam.

"Sheriff?"

Nicole looked up. She had promoted Lars Solberg to undersheriff when she'd won the election two years ago. It was his job to supervise heavy crime—murder, grand theft, abduction—and the three sergeants under him worked the lighter investigative detail. Then there were eight deputies who patrolled and answered calls. Together they were spread out over nineteen hundred miles of county jurisdiction.

She had moved all but three deputies to Lake Maria. She had called in their reserves—there were only two, and she made a mental note to increase that number—and borrowed a handful of forensic techs from the highway patrol. She'd alerted them to the need for heightened watch, as was protocol when one of the related agencies was stretched thin.

She stood and gave her second-in-command her full attention. "What do you have, Lars?"

"A size-ten shoe, heavy tread. Probably a hiking boot."

Nicole looked at the girl's feet. One foot was bare, her toes painted a solid shade of pumpkin. The other foot bore a stone-colored suede boot that ended at her knee. It had a discreet half-inch heel and, on the sole, the embossed-triangle logo of Prada.

Not a snow boot. Their vic was dressed for a party, not the slopes.

Lars nodded his head. "My wife has a knock-off pair," he said, and shrugged. "Three kids, a house, and a car."

And nowhere on a cop's salary for the real thing.

"Vic's a size six," he continued. "We bagged the left boot and a knee-high purple sock seventy and a hundred and twenty yards southeast."

"Anything else?"

"A pair of gloves. Brown suede, made for a man."

"And you found both?"

"A present under the tree," he said.

"Can I see them?" MacAulay asked.

"Sure, Doc." Lars made the request through his radio, then turned back to Nicole. "There's a reason you made me lead," he informed her. "And it had nothing to do with my prowess in the box or at the range."

He was smiling broadly, and Nicole felt her lips splinter in the cold as she responded. The solemn mood of a crime scene often relied on humor.

Lars was a bad shot and every year had to repeat the marksmanship test for a pass.

"It was your ability to remain level-headed even under the esteemed accolades of your peers," she assured him.

MacAulay laughed, and Lars's smile grew impossibly wider.

"That, and assess a crime scene for motivation."

The last part was true. Nicole had already made undersheriff when Lars came around in answer to a recruitment ad. He'd had several years in Missoula and wanted a slower pace and to keep his state retirement. The man was good. He had a degree in criminal psychology and made practical use of it. And he was the only city, other than her, in the department.

"You know the why?"

"I have a hunch."

He held up a clear evidence bag. Inside were two items, individually bagged, tagged, and numbered: one unopened condom packet and a prescription bottle. "This stuff"—he jiggled the bag— "scattered but easily recovered."

"Too easy?" she asked.

"Maybe not. There are impressions in the snow, like the guy was kneeling. He's right-handed—he pulled off his left glove first, then the right, and dropped them beside him, left of his position."

"Kneeling because he dropped the condom and the pills?"

Lars nodded. "Like they fell out of a pocket while he was running."

"And he took his gloves off to try and pick them up." She smiled, following his thoughts to what was a clear break in the case. Few people thought forward to cleaning up evidence. "We'll get prints off them."

"Exactly." Lars didn't pause to enjoy the moment. "There's a third set of footprints," he began. "And they put a spin on things."

"Predator or prey?" Nicole asked.

But as usual, Lars didn't answer. He set up the scene and ran through the evidence so Nicole could form her own opinion.

"Three sets of footprints that matter to us. The vic's. This guy"—he raised his arm and waved the evidence bag—the hiking boot. His prints leave a longer trail. "After his scramble in the snow, they pick back up and end here, with our vic's body." He's our killer. He does the deed, then cuts over the slope, across the bike path, and we lose him on the Lake Road.

"The third set of prints run parallel to his, thirty yards between them, and maybe they don't even see each other," he poses. "The third set of prints are a soft sole. Maybe an UGG. Or a boot like it. This guy was trailing our vic from the beginning. We traced their prints back to the Lake Road. The vic leaves the road and cuts into the trees. Maybe she thinks she can lose the guy in the woods. And it's working. The soft-sole print is running out of steam fast, clearly can't keep up with our vic. These prints stop at the top of the slope, never make it down to the bike path and nowhere near the lake. For a minute, our vic, maybe she thinks she's okay. But she's underdressed and struggling with the weather. She's already lost a boot, no coat, hat, gloves. And now a dip in adrenaline."

"The guy in the hiking boots gains on her."

"Easily," Lars agrees. "He has a longer, stronger stride. He breaks out of the woods, barrels down the slope, and he's on her." Lars turned and walked, retracing the tangled trail, and Nicole followed until they were twenty yards out and silhouetted by light from the halogen lamps. "Right here, he grabs our vic. Her toes drag in the snow. A small struggle, because the girl is wiped out, clinging to life, but even in her last breath, she denies him." He snaps his fingers. "Then he kills her."

It felt right. If not an exact match to the events leading up to Beatrice Esparza's murder, then close. But she knew too that evidence could be manipulated by a perspective that was too narrow, by an approach that wasn't flexible.

"Denies him what?" Nicole asked.

"Sex. Love." He lifted the evidence bag and shuffled it between his hands until the pill bottle was on top. "I think that's Rohypnol."

* * *

Benjamin Kris leaned against the hood of the SUV, the engine long cold and the windows growing some serious frost. He didn't want to draw attention his way. He didn't want to answer questions, have his name jotted into some slunk detective's notebook. How many times had he watched her smile bloom on her face and felt a lightness in his chest? His heart had been like an air bubble, rising through fathoms of water to bob on the surface of a vast sea. She had done that for him, and then ripped it all away.

She had known who he was, what he was, and then later decided it wasn't enough. Or worse, that he was too much. Too much of a fuckup.

He was here to prove himself, having made it to the top. He wanted Nicole to see that he was king of the mountain before he buried her alive.

He lowered the binoculars and gazed at the scene from a distance. He knew how cops worked. Soon their tight circle would grow larger, closer, and he would have to be gone by then. He had people waiting on him, appearances to keep up. An alibi to maintain.

One more look, he told himself, because he found her obsessive. Nicole in action, tall and solid. He hated her calm, her strength, that she had once beaten him and beaten him badly. And Benjamin Kris did not like to lose.

He was tired of dangling from her string. Killing her would eliminate the threat, but he wanted more than that. He wanted to destroy her, and that took more time, more effort, more closeness. It would take striking her where it hurt most. Going for what she had been afraid of all along. Jordan. Losing him would crush Nicole. And Benjamin was looking forward to it.

2

"Two predators, one prey," Nicole said, thinking aloud as they paced back to MacAulay and the dead girl. "If they didn't know about each other, if they weren't working together, then we have separate motives as well." She gazed at the vic. MacAulay was wrapping tape around her wrists, securing her bagged hands. Her clothes were intact. Fitted jeans, a cami under the cashmere sweater. Nothing disturbed. "Our killer had an agenda."

Lars nodded. "I think he missed his opportunity."

"The girl caught on, or maybe they were interrupted and she ran." From one of the more than a hundred homes that clustered around the lake. "That would explain the absence of her coat."

"Not the first time roofie made an appearance at a party," Lars agreed.

"But the prints, they never cross?"

"Never. For close to a hundred yards, they run parallel but are separated by thirty or forty yards."

"But the soft soles, he's on the vic from the beginning? Not the hiking boots?"

Lars nodded. "The hiking boot picks up the vic in the woods. He cut in from the lake road sooner. Could be they started out together and split up to corral our vic."

"The third set of prints, the soft soles, what happens to him?"

"He stopped." And Lars turned and pointed toward the crest of a slope that overlooked the lake. "He stood there, but it's hard to tell for how long. Minutes is my guess. Long enough to watch the kill." He turned back to Nicole. "He shifted his weight on his feet—the prints overlap. At one point, he took a single step forward."

"Indecision," she said.

"Maybe in the clutch, he wanted to help the vic."

"Or the perp."

Either way, a witness to murder. The thought put an irritating tic in her blood.

She turned and focused on MacAulay's progress. Slow and methodical. But the man never made a mistake.

In a murder investigation, that was never enough.

"Make sure you cross-reference the snow with anatomy." A tech would scoop the drift and preserve it in a cooler chest for slowmelt once it was brought back to the lab. If there were epithelials, hairs, fibers under the vic's nails, there was a possibility some could be recovered in the snow.

"Of course," MacAulay agreed, unruffled. The man didn't know urgency. He had one frequency, but it was stable. It was predictable. It was even long-range. So what if his engine never kicked into high gear? MacAulay was reliable.

She turned back to Lars. His hands were at his sides, the evidence bag clutched in one.

"There a name on the prescription bottle?" she asked.

"Beatrice Esparza," Lars confirmed. "Augmentin, five hundred milligrams, twice daily."

Doc whistled through his teeth. "That's a heavy dose. A kid her age and weight, I'd prescribe half that."

"What for?" Nicole asked.

"Could be she had a bad case of bronchitis. Maybe walking pneumonia. Urinary tract infection, a stubborn skin infection. Those are the most common uses for the drug. But five hundred milligrams?" His frown deepened as he considered it. "No."

Lars shook the bag, and they listened to the rattle of pills. "That's not penicillin."

"Can I take a look?" Doc asked.

Lars opened the baggie and removed the bottle. Gloved, he twisted open the cap and warned the doctor to look and not touch. MacAulay obliged.

"You're right. That's not Augmentin."

"But is it Rohypnol?" Nicole pressed.

"That or cold tabs," Lars returned. "You know where my money is." He replaced the bottle and zipped the bag and held it up for Nicole to take a good look, though she didn't need to. Lars was right. The pills and condom packet led them down an obvious path.

Date-rapers were smooth and deceptive. They were violent offenders who spun lies that looked like gold.

Lars peered over her shoulder, into the darkness beyond the halogen lamps.

"Two perps. We need to know if they worked together," she said. "Right now it's just best guess they didn't."

"We need motive for the soft-soled guy. He was after something."

"It bothers me," Nicole said. "The two perps. It makes this more than a date rape gone wrong."

"Something else is at play," Lars agreed.

"And the roofie," Nicole said. "It has more than one use." Of course it did. The drug wasn't manufactured to facilitate sex crimes. Though illegal in the United States, it was widely used in Mexico and Europe to treat anxiety and insomnia. "It makes a victim agreeable. It wipes out memory. But sex isn't always the prize."

"The condom makes it the go-to."

She agreed, but there were too many players on the board. And the UGG boot—more women wore those than men.

"We're missing something." Nicole said. "Find it." She turned to MacAulay. "Bag the body. A thorough exam," she reminded him. "Make sure you look for bruising around the thighs and hips, inside her mouth."

"I know how to confirm rape," he said, but his voice was tight, and when Nicole looked into his face she found what he never tried to hide: his humanity.

"But you don't know how to think like a cop—or even an ME," Nicole pointed out. Brutal, and she was sorry for it, but sorrier that it was necessary. "Someone killed this girl. It's our job to speak for her now."

"Agreed," he said. "I want him caught as much as you do."

Nicole held his gaze and took a breath. Then she nodded, because she knew his words were true. MacAulay cared. "Was she wearing underwear?"

Because sometimes, especially in cases of date rape, the victim's clothing was restored after the crime was committed, and the underwear almost always forgotten.

He bent and peeled back the waistband of Beatrice Esparza's jeans, exposing a strip of pink cotton.

"Sheriff?"

A deputy approached, wrapped head to toe in Gore-Tex and down. He held up a sealed evidence bag. The gloves. They were insulated, lined with fleece, and looked new.

"Maybe," Doc said. He took the bag and flattened it between his hands. MacAulay was a big man with hands the size of oven mitts. By comparison, the gloves were ridiculously small. "The hands that fit these gloves could also fit the bruise markings on Beatrice's neck."

"Who are we looking for, MacAulay? A kid or an adult, small or medium?"

He looked beyond her, his eyes focused as he thought. "I'll know better after I've measured the markings and completed some comparisons. But without the forensic backup?"

"For now," she assured him.

"Aged fourteen to seventy. Small to medium stature. During strangulation, it's the pads of the fingers that dig in, leave their mark." He nodded toward the body. "These hands were thin but average in length. The killer was taller than the vic by maybe seven or eight inches. I can tell that by the angle of the bruises. What does all this mean? Small to average size for a man, taller for a woman." He hesitated. "If it was a juvenile?" he posed. "Tall and thin. But this is all guesswork."

"That's good," Lars said, and the surprise was evident in his tone. MacAulay wasn't known for extrapolating, and they were rarely able to get him to manipulate facts for direction. Nicole chewed on it for a moment as she began to profile the perp.

"The impressions in the snow—are the castings finished?" she asked.

She loved impression analysis. One hundred percent factual. Castings were tangible evidence that the DA often lined up on a table in front of a jury, next to each the shoe that matched the print. It was a solid link between perpetrator and crime. It was like building a stone wall in an open field. Obvious. Small but unmistakable, even in satellite photos.

Lars nodded. "Until we hear from Arty, I'd say our killer is somewhere between a hundred fifteen and a hundred and fifty pounds. The other guy, the soft-soled boots, he weighs in between one twenty and one hundred, sixty-five pounds."

Jordan, at eleven years old, weighed a hundred pounds soaking wet. But he was small. Nicole wanted a probable age range. She was building a profile of their most likely suspect. Rarely was murder committed by a person under fourteen years of age.

"How much does the average fifteen-year-old boy weigh, Doc?"

MacAulay shrugged. "Current guidelines, about one hundred twenty-six pounds. That gives us a range of one nineteen to one hundred thirty-two pounds."

He pulled up his hood and stepped closer to the body. He raised an arm and waved the attendants over. Nicole noticed that his limbs had stiffened and knew the cold wasn't to blame for it. MacAulay took death personally, and it was even more offensive when it was murder. Talk of kids harming kids wasn't just disturbing for the doctor. It was unnatural.

Nicole was stuck with a temperamental family doc for an ME, and at this point she doubted that she would change that.

"He's a healer," Lars said, and Nicole noticed that some of the past complaint was absent from his tone.

"Lucky for us." Nicole watched MacAulay hunker down next to the body and slide his hands under her shoulders. The girl's head settled into the cradle of his arms. He nodded his readiness, and the forensic tech lifted her feet. Together they tucked Beatrice Esparza into a body bag.

3

The resorts were northwest of town, many of them in the foothills of Glacier National Park. Part of the allure of Montana, especially this far north, was its rugged, secluded landscape, and Big Business knew this. The consortiums that came in and bought large tracks of land left as many trees standing as they could. The Huntington Spa was set back from the road and was perched on a small rise nestled between mature aspen and evergreen. On its list of amenities were snowshoeing, tobogganing, and tubing, and the place was classy enough not to charge an additional fee for the fun.

Nicole turned into the sweeping driveway and followed the blacktop to the front doors. The place was big, accommodating a maximum of 433 guests. A wall of paned glass let the ambient glow from the lobby seep into the parking lot. Christmas lights were strung from the eaves, red and green, yellow and blue, twinkling to the tune "Silver Bells." A twenty-foot noble fir stood in the center of the lobby, lighted and tinseled. Beneath it were an assortment of boxes wrapped in bright paper. She parked and climbed out of the department Yukon, then looked back the way she'd come. Lake Maria, the site of their crime scene, was less than three miles southeast. How had their vic gotten there? Despite her time in the elements, Beatrice Esparza hadn't looked chapped by the wind, and she'd died before frostbite could set in. There'd been no gray patches of skin nor missing fingers or toes, which were a common find in people exposed to the cold.

And somewhere along the way she'd taken off her coat, hat, scarf, and gloves. Had she bolted from a car, stopped along the Lake Road, suddenly fearful for her life? Or from a nearby home, chased by malignant intent?

They knew what their killer had wanted, but what about the soft-soled pursuer?

Nicole walked through the glass doors and stood with her hands on her hips as the warm air pressed against her skin. She turned and looked through the windows toward the horizon. Nothing yet. Sunrise was still a few hours away, but when it touched the sky and warmed the air, snow would fall from the banked clouds.

Her team was scrambling over the ice, preserving evidence. Still, much would be lost, destroyed by the weather. And there was nothing they could do about that. She had depleted her department of manpower and borrowed from MHP. Even Border Patrol had sent over dogs. She looked at her watch. They'd have arrived by now. A handful of German shepherds and their handlers prancing through the snowy woods. They would scent off the gloves easily. Where would it lead them?

The rapist-turned-murderer and the watcher.

Who was Beatrice Esparza? Why had she caught the attention of two predators?

Nicole approached reception and smiled at Daisy Le Duce. The woman had worked at the Huntington as long as Nicole had been in Toole County, but she was also the matron of the arts for the Summer Sunlit Festival and volunteered one evening each month at the lockup. She read Bible verses or recipes from the *Betty Crocker All-American Cookbook*—the only reading material currently allowed at the jail.

"The Esparza family," Nicole said. "What room are they in, Daisy?"

The older woman was slow to move. The papery skin around her eyes crinkled and she leaned against the counter, closer to Nicole's words. "She never came back, did she?" Daisy asked.

"Who?"

"The girl. Beatrice."

Nicole removed her gloves and tucked them into her coat pockets. Then she leaned against the counter and studied Daisy's open face. She was solid. She fussed some but stepped up more. "You saw her leave?"

"Yes. And I haven't seen her since."

"When was that?"

"Yesterday, around four, I think. When the family left for Christmas dinner."

Twelve hours had passed. "And she didn't return with the family?"

"No. I asked Dr. Esparza about her. Beatrice was a talker. Real friendly. She would have stopped by to say good-night."

"But not yesterday?"

"No."

"And you've been on shift?"

She nodded. "A double or swing every day this week and next—for the families, you know."

Daisy's husband had passed away two years ago and her children lived out of state. She visited them every spring, but they seldom came north to see their mother. Daisy filled in so others could spend time with their families over the holidays.

"Dr. Esparza? That's Beatrice's father?"

"Yes."

"What did he say when you questioned him?"

"He said that Beatrice was tired," Daisy informed her. "That she'd been on the slopes, in the hot tub, that the whole family had gotten up early to open presents, so a long day."

Plausible. But it was 4:00 AM. The parents had to know their child was missing, and yet they hadn't called the police. That was like waving a red flag in front of a bull.

"When did the Esparzas check in?"

"December twenty-first. They're staying through the New Year."

Nicole nodded. "Call their room."

Daisy dialed and handed the phone to Nicole. It rang only twice before it was picked up, and the male voice on the other end was crisp, clear, and bore no evidence of sleep.

"Dr. Esparza?"

A long pause, and then the single word—"Yes"—wavered in the thick, slightly accented voice.

"My name is Nicole Cobain, sheriff of Toole County." She waited. She let the moment draw out a full thirty seconds without a response and felt the tension gather on the other end of the line. She heard the exhale of breath, a steady, almost measured movement. She heard a voice behind him, in the room—muffled, rapid speech. "Sir?" she prompted.

"Yes, Sheriff?"

He put weight on her title, spoke louder than he had before. The changes weren't subtle. He was sending someone in the room a message: police.

This wasn't a first-time experience for Nicole. A call from the police made a person edgy. In the early-morning hours it intensified fear, narrowed purpose. Something was wrong, and it would be life changing.

"I'm on my way up, sir," Nicole informed him. "Could you wake your wife, please?"

"She is awake," he assured her.

Nicole took the elevator to the third floor and, following Daisy's directions, turned right into a corridor that was more window than plaster. Outside, scattered light poles pressed back the shadows of evergreen trees. The courtyard had been shoveled, and the stone tables and benches were ready for seating around fire pits that were ignited at dawn and extinguished at 10:00 PM. Inside, the walls were covered in local art. Mostly landscapes, but there were a few canvas portraits. Nicole recognized Standing Bull and Asiniiwin, the Chippewa leader who had managed, through much strife, to keep peace during the Land Act years. Artifacts from the cowboy life were mounted on the walls—a frayed and obviously used lasso; a collection of spurs dating back, according to one placket, 118 years; and a series of shots of the once-famous Jim Shoulders, the sixteen-time pro-rodeo world champion, in full motion atop a Brahman bull.

The Wild West was a best seller.

She found the room and knocked on the door. She let a moment pass and then identified herself through the solid wood, keeping her tone even. She was aware of three things: their daughter was dead; if Beatrice Esparza had gone missing, the family had neglected to alert police; and Dr. Esparza was a careful man.

He answered the door wearing flannel pajama bottoms and a hooded sweat shirt. He stood an inch or two shorter than Nicole and was slim and graying. A small dagger of hair grew under his bottom lip.

"Come in." He stepped back and allowed Nicole into the suite.

Mrs. Esparza sat on the couch, perched on the very edge of it, with her hands clasped between her knees. She was wrapped in a fleece robe but hadn't removed her makeup. Their son, whom Dr. Esparza introduced as Joaquin, slouched in the doorway of one of the bedrooms. His long hair was pulled back in a ponytail.

None of them looked like they had slept.

The tension in the room vibrated with a frequency Nicole wasn't able to tap into. It was more than the arrival of bad news. This family had been awake and alert long before Nicole arrived. If the exhaustion around their eyes and the tightness of their shoulders and limbs were anything to go by, they'd been waiting for Nicole about as long as they'd been waiting for Beatrice.

"You have a daughter," Nicole began.

"Yes, Beatrice," the mother said. She leaned forward, and Nicole recognized the look of hope in the woman's eyes, the defeat in her flat mouth. And Nicole felt a tremor in her own limbs, an unsteady connection to this woman, this mother, who was not unlike Nicole herself, whose worst nightmare would be the loss of her son. Her stomach churned with the news she would impart. There were no soft words, there would be no promises. Simply an end.

"I'm sorry, Mrs. Esparza," Nicole began.

"Have you found her?" the mother persisted.

"You knew she was missing?" Nicole countered. "But you didn't call the police."

"We weren't sure," Dr. Esparza stepped into the conversation. "She has friends here already. They could be talking and she lost track of time."

"We told her be back at two. She's not so late that we should call the police."

They were grasping at hope. Did they already sense how slippery it was? How fragile?

"I wish I had better news," Nicole said. She stood in the center of the room, turned so that the mother was her focal point but also so that she could keep both male Esparzas in her scope. Her words caused a ripple through the family. Shoulders jerked; facial tics were triggered. The tension inside Mrs. Esparza reached a breaking point and was released in a sharp humming from her lips. "We found Beatrice early this morning, out on Lake Maria. She's dead."

Joaquin straightened in the doorway then, his arms dropping to his sides. "You're wrong," he said.

A whistling noise rose from the throat of Mrs. Esparza, almost as if her airway had narrowed.

Dr. Esparza wavered on his feet. His hands were stuffed into the pocket of his hoodie and his elbows flapped once, twice.

"I'm sorry for your loss," Nicole said. She made her breaths long and deep and waited, mired in their pain. Steady. Ready to offer what she could but unable to ignore a voice in the back of her brain. Some things weren't adding up. The tension in the room when she'd entered, the division she sensed between the family members. The body of a young girl on a frozen lake.

Nicole thought of Jordan at home, sleeping peacefully, and wanted to be there, with her son, holding him, though he was much too old for that and seldom allowed it now.

"We need a positive identification," Nicole said, and pulled the snow bunny ID pass, still in its evidence bag, out of her coat pocket. She held it up, and the father closed the space between them. He touched his fingers to the plastic, and Nicole noticed their fine tremor. He stroked his daughter's face and confirmed, "Yes, my daughter. My beautiful Beatrice."

Mrs. Esparza began keening then, and her husband crossed the room and sat down beside her. Joaquin kept his vigilance in the doorway. There was more in his face than shock; there was surprise. He had believed he'd hear something else. His parents had hoped for something different, but the teen had actually expected it.

Later that day, Esparza would have to come to the hospital for an official ID. Nicole explained this to him.

"Of course," he agreed immediately, but his voice was hollow, the words adrift. He held his wife's hand, and his gaze was fixed on their woven fingers.

Nicole stepped farther into the room, hoping to draw his attention.

"When was the last time you saw your daughter, sir?" Nicole directed her question to the father but watched Joaquin. The shock in the young man's face eased and the surprise morphed into something else. Grief, certainly, but anger too.

"Dr. Esparza?" Nicole prompted.

"Last night. We had dinner together and returned to the room," he said.

"Eight twenty." The words were whispered, patchy. Mrs. Esparza lifted her eyes from the study of her hands and hooked Nicole's gaze. "We left the room at eight twenty, my husband and I."

20

"We skied the moonlight run," Dr. Esparza clarified.

"Yesterday we stayed in with the girls—our little ones. They have colds."

"We have two young daughters," the doctor said. "Not even teenagers yet."

"They are eight and ten," the mother said.

Color was slowly returning to their faces and strength to their words.

"And you, Joaquin? When was the last time you saw your sister?"

Nicole stepped toward him. The young man was lanky, had more height than his father but the same slim build. But where his sister had had rounded cheeks and curves, he was broad angles and plains. And no small amount of defiance. His arms were crossed again and he shrugged before answering.

"Last night. We ordered cable." His gaze adjusted until he was staring at the blank face of the flat-screen TV. "I brewed hot chocolate in the coffeepot."

"What was the movie?"

"*Fast and Furious* six."

"Did Beatrice watch with you?"

"Some. She only likes reality shows."

"What time did she leave the room?"

"I didn't see her leave."

"The movie was that good?"

"I went to bed," Joaquin said. "I was tired."

"What time?"

He eased his shoulder against the jamb and didn't pretend to give her question thought. "Nine thirty."

She called his bluff. "It doesn't look like you ever made it to bed." The pajamas, for all his vinegar, could simply be a costume call.

Nicole turned to the parents. "What time did you get back to the room?"

"After eleven," the father said.

"It was midnight," the mother corrected.

"Exactly?"

"I heard the bells chime in the lobby. I think there's a clock there. It chimed twelve times as we were waiting for the elevator."

Dr. Esparza spread his hands. "So it was midnight."

"Where do you live?"

"Live?" Dr. Esparza repeated, struggling with the change in questioning.

"Yes. You're here on vacation, right?"

"Oh, yes." He shook his head—an attempt to clear his mind. "San Diego."

"You don't get a lot of skiing in there," she commented. "Are you a medical doctor, sir?"

"Yes. Oncology," he offered.

Nicole nodded. "Is the purpose of this trip solely vacation?"

"We ski every Christmas holiday," the mother said. "Last year it was Telluride."

"The year before, Stowe," Dr. Esparza continued. "Every year we find the snow. For Christmas."

"Do you work, Mrs. Esparza? Outside the home?"

"No, not anymore."

"She was a nurse," Dr. Esparza said.

"For a few short years."

"How old are you, Joaquin?"

"Seventeen."

"And Beatrice?"

"Fourteen," the mother said. "June fourth, two thousand five. Her birthday. Just one day before mine."

Nicole pulled a small notebook out of her coat pocket. She'd make a note of the important details of their conversation when she got back to the Yukon. When she interviewed people, especially the first pass, she liked to watch their faces, read their body language, which often told her more than words or tone.

"We'll need some information," she told them. "Your full names—all of you, Beatrice included—ages, address, phone numbers." She handed the notebook to the doctor and then gave her full attention to Joaquin.

"Your sister left to meet with friends?"

He shrugged, as much as he could and still maintain his sloucher pose against the doorjamb. "I don't know. Probably."

"But she has some here? New acquaintances?"

"We've met a few people on the slopes. We've been invited to parties and stuff."

"Could Beatrice have gone to a party last night?"

His gaze remained steady. "Maybe, but she didn't tell me that."

"Would she have told you?"

He seemed to think about that. "Yes."

"Sheriff?" Dr. Esparza stood. His wife sat in his shadow, teetering on the edge of the couch. He extended his hand and offered her the notebook. It was open, and Nicole could see that he had filled the page with a thin, scratchy print she would have difficulty reading.

Nicole left Joaquin at the door and pocketed her notebook, but she had a few more questions for the Esparzas.

"Was Beatrice sick?"

"You mean like a cold? The flu?" Dr. Esparza asked.

"I mean like bronchitis or pneumonia."

"No," the mother answered. "Not even the sniffles."

"But your younger girls have colds?"

Dr. Esparza stepped forward. "Yes, we told you that. And Beatrice was rarely sick. She took care of herself. She ate the right foods, took vitamins. She trained. Exercised regularly. She expected more from her body than illness."

"She's a top runner," Mrs. Esparza added, and she smiled brightly though her tears were still falling. "Always first place."

High expectations, and Nicole wondered, how wide a margin had they given their daughter for failure? For learning? For being a teenage girl craving exploration and independence?

"Then why was she prescribed Augmentin?" Nicole asked.

Dr. Esparza shook his head. "You're wrong. Beatrice had no need for the medication, and had she, it never would have been Augmentin."

"Beatrice is allergic to anything in the penicillin family," the mother explained.

Nicole chewed on that, then pulled her smartphone from her parka pocket. She asked the Esparzas for a moment's patience and pressed speed dial for Lars.

"Yeah, Chief?" Lars's voice was sharp, slightly breathless. He was still in the field, knee-deep in yesterday's snowfall and rummaging for any beacon of evidence.

23

"You close to the evidence bin?"

"I'm sitting on it."

He'd pulled chain-of-evidence duty.

"Good. I want you to take a picture of the pill bottle—get Beatrice's name, doctor's name, drug, and dosage—and send it to me."

"Doing it, but do you want to tell me why?"

"Beatrice didn't get sick," Nicole informed him. She sensed that the Esparzas weren't raising merely a child in Beatrice. The girl had been in training, possibly from conception. Cultivated—mind, body, spirit—for high performance. The doctor's tone had said as much. And that bothered Nicole. "And she was allergic to Augmentin."

There was a pause on the other end, and then Lars said, "No shit?"

"No." Cell to ear, she glanced at the Esparzas. Joaquin leaned. Mrs. Esparza rocked. The doctor stood, hands in pockets, elbows twitching, eyes locked on Nicole.

"Done," Lars announced, and a moment later a ding sounded from her cell. She ended the call.

"We found a pill bottle," Nicole explained. She walked deeper into the room until she met the windows, the drawn curtains, and turned. It put her closer to Joaquin, to Mrs. Esparza, and left the doctor outside the tight circle Nicole had created. "The prescription is written out for Beatrice. Five hundred milligrams of Augmentin, two times daily."

"One thousand milligrams daily?" Dr. Esparza stopped just short of a scoff.

Mrs. Esparza shook her head. "That's too much. A girl her size, half that would do."

"But she's allergic to Augmentin," Nicole pointed out.

"If she wasn't allergic," the mother said. "If she were prescribed that, as you say."

"What happened to Beatrice if she took Augmentin? What symptoms?"

"A rash. It's called a body flush, because on Beatrice it erupted on her torso, traveled up her throat and into her underarms," Mrs. Esparza explained. "It's itchy and uncomfortable, and Beatrice would never take it. She knew better."

"And she was never sick anyway." Nicole continued to probe.

"She wasn't." Joaquin spoke, and his voice fell on the room like a solid chunk of cement. Strong, heavy, unyielding.

Nicole chose to ignore him for now and continued with the doctor.

She opened the attachment Lars had sent her. The photo was blurry, but the type on the prescription label was readable. "You want to guess the name of the prescribing physician?"

"Not my husband," Mrs. Esparza said. "No, never. That is against ethics. He wouldn't do that."

"He wouldn't make so big a mistake, Mrs. Esparza?" Nicole led. "He wouldn't prescribe his daughter a drug he knew she was allergic to? Or a dosage that was too much? Or he wouldn't risk his career by prescribing for family?"

"I would not," the doctor interrupted. "And I did not." He paced to the edge of their circle. "You're mistaken, Sheriff."

Nicole held his gaze as she lifted the cell phone. His eyelashes flickered. Creases fanned out from the corners of his eyes. Then he disconnected and focused on the incriminating photo.

4

Dr. Esparza was careful. He was methodical. He was a man of science, a surgeon with a reservoir of strength that steadied him when he found himself in treacherous territory. Nicole recognized that in him because she relied on it herself. But before he could tap into it, his bottom lip trembled and his knees knocked as shock flew through his veins.

"Impossible," he murmured.

But Nicole knew all things were possible. And she knew his initial reaction could be as easily attributed to being caught as it could to the very existence of the pill bottle.

"Evidence doesn't lie." But that wasn't true. Nicole had often seen evidence manipulated, solid proof reduced to hearsay.

"I didn't prescribe that," he said.

"Your name is on the bottle."

He nodded. "So it is."

His tone had a finality about it, so Nicole pressed, "No claims of a stolen prescription pad, Doctor?"

"Most prescriptions are submitted electronically these days."

"No signature required?"

"Each order is uniquely stamped."

"Who has access to your stamp?"

"Just a handful of people."

"You don't sound concerned."

"I treat cancer patients, Sheriff. I have no reason to prescribe Augmentin to anyone. Neither do any of my staff."

"And yet here it is."

"Here it is," he agreed.

A dead end. Nicole changed direction.

"Is it possible Beatrice ran away?" Nicole offered a way out for the family, but they didn't take it.

"No," Dr. Esparza insisted. "Where would she run to?"

Not *why*. No protests about a loving home and all that money could buy. Nothing about the vic having everything she could want and need.

"When did you realize your daughter was missing, Dr. Esparza?"

"We didn't," he said.

"We didn't know," the mother agreed, "until you called."

"You didn't check on the kids when you returned from the slopes last night?"

"They're light sleepers," the mother said. "We didn't want to wake them."

Nicole let her doubt show through her unwavering stare. The mother's lips trembled. Dr. Esparza patted her hand and remained firm. He made no move to further support their claim and held Nicole's gaze with his own.

Cold or confident? she wondered.

"The receptionist says Beatrice hasn't been around since about four yesterday."

"She's wrong," the doctor insisted. "I told her that."

"Did your daughter leave the resort willingly, Dr. Esparza?"

"Yes," Mrs. Esparza said. "She took her purse."

"And her coat?" Nicole asked. "Is Beatrice's coat missing?"

The woman pushed to her feet. Her hands, no longer pinned between her knees, fluttered in the air in front of her. "The closet," she said, and moved toward a door near the front of the suite. "She was a responsible girl, you know? An A-plus girl, honor roll and track. My daughter loved to run. She was like wind. Fast. This was her first year on the cross-country team, and she has many ribbons. That's good for her first year, yes?" She opened the closet door. Nicole was standing behind her now and peered over the mother's shoulder. Three thick parkas hung from the pole: black, cobalt blue, red with a fur-lined hood. "No," Mrs. Esparza said. "It's gone."

She turned to Nicole, her eyes wet and pleading. "Her coat is gone."

"What color is it?"

"Purple. Her favorite color. Her gloves and scarf too. Everything purple. The school color, you know?"

Beatrice had been wearing a purple cashmere sweater, Nicole remembered. And purple knee-high socks.

Nicole looked at Joaquin. "Did you and Beatrice attend the same school?"

"No."

"Beatrice attended private school," the father said.

"Joaquin did too," Mrs. Esparza offered. "But—"

"It was not a good fit," Dr. Esparza finished.

Nicole ignored the parents in favor of Joaquin and his angst, which promised a better chance at truth.

"Public school?" she asked.

"Yes."

"Voluntarily? Or were you asked to leave?"

"Why does this matter?" Dr. Esparza cut in.

"Joaquin?" Nicole pressed.

"I was kicked out." For a moment he looked apologetic as he glanced at his parents. "It wasn't their fault."

"Why?"

Dr. Esparza stepped forward, blocking Nicole's view of his slouching son. "My son is not in question here."

"Everyone is in question," Nicole corrected him. "Your daughter is dead, sir, and we have a lot of questions about that. You should too." She stepped closer. "In fact, it's a little concerning that you don't."

She stepped around the doctor and caught Joaquin's gaze. "Why?" she asked again.

"It wasn't one thing," he began.

"It never is," she agreed.

"My father's right. Private school wasn't a good fit for me. Most of the kids there are—"

He stumbled for the right words, so Nicole began a list of adjectives for him, "White, privileged—although this would describe you too—narrow-minded . . ."

"White," Joaquin agreed. "And spoiled."

"So this made you a loner?"

Joaquin nodded. "I stopped following their rules. Got in a few fights."

"My son was caught with marijuana," the mother revealed.

Joaquin shrugged. "I was experimenting."

"Did Beatrice experiment too?"

But Joaquin was shaking his head. "Never. She was all about being healthy. Training. Winning. She's been running a long time. If middle school had a track team, she would have been on it."

"She'd have been their star," Dr. Esparza said, but Nicole ignored him in pursuit of Joaquin.

"And she never tried marijuana or any other drugs?"

"I'm telling you, she was always blending up vegetable and fruit smoothies, preaching about runner's high, and writing every little thing down in her diary."

Nicole turned to the mother. "Beatrice kept a diary?"

"Yes. But it was only for sport. Not about her feelings but about how well she did each day."

"I'd like to borrow it," Nicole said.

The mother's eyes flared, and she sought her husband.

"You want to know how fast she ran the mile?" he challenged. "Or how many days a week she did sprints?"

"I want to know everything there is to know about your daughter," Nicole confirmed. "The better I know her, the easier it will be to find justice."

"Justice?" His tone was full of doubt, shredded by grief.

"Yes." Nicole felt her face stiffen. "I want to find the person who murdered your daughter, Dr. Esparza. Don't you?"

He held her gaze, and soon his features began to relax. The corners of his eyes and mouth softened. He nodded. "We would like that too."

He looked over her shoulder to Joaquin. "See if you can find it."

Joaquin left his position at the door and walked through the living room to a cozy set of chairs and side tables. Nicole could see a stack of magazines and a guidebook. Joaquin disturbed the pile, surfacing with a slim volume, the leather cover cracked.

"It's all numbers and notes," he told her as he handed the journal to Nicole. "Notes about her performance," he clarified. "Nothing personal."

Nicole accepted the diary and thought about Joaquin's words. *Nothing personal . . .* She doubted that.

She turned to leave, still thinking about them. Murder was always personal. The family was hiding something. It was the natural inclination of the human spirit. But in this case, there was more. She felt it in their hesitations, in the anger emanating from Joaquin; in the faltering strength of the mother and in the doctor's resolve.

She felt footsteps following her and was soon stopped by the doctor's words.

"Sheriff?" He waited for her to turn, until he had her full attention. "We do have questions. And heartache. And fear. We have emotions we are only beginning to get to know. We are devastated."

The doctor's voice was raspy, his words tumbled and slurred into one another. Loss sometimes took hold of a person slowly. It was an insistent, stubborn pressure. It throbbed in the temples, clipped the lungs, escaped in words meant to cut. Sometimes it was immediate. Nicole had had surviving family collapse at her feet. Most times people fell in between, surfacing long enough to gasp and breathe a word of denial. Nicole acknowledged the signs in all three Esparzas and nodded.

"You said murdered, but you didn't say how," the doctor began, then paused to clear emotion from his throat. "Sheriff?"

She noted his pale face, the streak of a single tear, but told him anyway. "Asphyxiation."

His lips quivered, but Nicole pushed forward.

"Don't leave town, Dr. Esparza. None of you are to leave town."

5

Benjamin woke before dawn. He'd kept the curtains open the night before because he liked looking at the constellations before he fell asleep. Every time he found the archer, he felt the tendons in his neck and shoulders flex. His heartbeat quickened. His birthday—November 29th—made him a Sagittarius. He was by birthright a hunter. And he loved picturing himself etched out in the stars, his mighty arm drawn back, firing a flaming arrow from a golden bow. He was that big, that strong, that bold.

He understood that a clear night sky in the Montana winter was a rare sighting, but he'd hoped. The archer was his North Star. It inspired him, gave him direction. So that morning he woke not certain what he should do. About Esparza, sure; he had a plan. He'd discussed it with the boss and they were of like minds. But about Jordan—he hadn't worked it out yet.

Yesterday he had sauntered into Nicole's backyard, a new man. He wanted her to see that. He wanted her to fear it.

But he didn't want to see Jordan. That was one big fail. Benjamin had never been meant to be a father.

It had always been about Nicole. First, controlling her. He'd wanted a hammer he could pull out of his toolbox whenever he needed it. But she hadn't cooperated. Now he wanted her to see him and lose her lunch. He laughed at that image. She was cold and scheming and he doubted she'd ever felt fear deeply enough that her stomach heaved with it. She'd never hidden because of it. She'd never run. Even her great exodus from Denver to this bottom-of-the-butt hole had been calculated. And that was totally Nicole.

She threatened. She planned. She executed. She'd cut him off at the knees and devoured the carnage. Benjamin wasn't a vindictive man, but he

31

did require payment in kind. And what better way to reach Nicole than through their son?

She didn't know that he had new clientele. People in high places who relied on him, for product and discretion. In his current circle, favors were distributed like candy at a parade.

It was time to announce his arrival. To take out the trumpets and make it known. Benjamin Kris was in town, and he was a new man.

Beside him, Charlene's breath moved smoothly in and out of her lungs. It didn't rattle in her chest. It didn't guzzle in her nose. She was a quiet sleeper. He appreciated that. He lifted the blanket, slid out of bed, and tucked it back around her shoulders. He grabbed his smartphone and padded across the thick carpeting and out onto the terrace, barefoot and bare chested. Snow flurries melted against his skin, and the cold shot up from the soles of his feet, pinged the joints at his knees and hips, and lodged unnoticed in his heart.

His skin puckered, but he didn't shudder. He'd often thought about joining those crazies for the polar bear plunge, but New York was a cesspool and he tried not to travel east of the Appalachians.

He opened a file on his phone and clicked through a series of photos. Charlene thought that Christmas photo when Jordan was three years old was the most recent they had of his son. But she was wrong. Nicole hadn't cared enough to send any, but he had hired a private investigator to do the job for him. He had photos of Nicole dating back to the year she'd left Denver. Recently he'd had photos taken of Jordan as well. The boy had Benjamin's build, thin but with potential. The awkward shoulders that might fill out. The small feet that never would.

Nicole had bought his wrong-place-wrong-time story, and he had seduced her. If nothing else, he was damn charming. An important quality for a man who made his living as a salesman.

"Benjamin?"

He turned. Charlene stood in the doorway, a thin silk robe tied loosely around her waist. She held a gun in her hand. A Sig Sauer 9mm. A cop's pistol and chosen for that very purpose. Charlene loved irony.

"You're going to get pneumonia out here," she said.

Her tone wasn't chiding or corrective. Charlene could be concerned without criticizing. He'd lucked out there. Most women were born to mother and smother. Not Charlene. She was mommy material, but she had her own needs too, and those kept her from dwelling on the comfort of others.

"You can put the gun away," he said. "There's nothing out here."

"I like it, though, you know?" She raised her hand and pressed the magazine against her cheek. "Cold. I like that. Death is cold, and its means should be too."

He smiled. He loved when she spoke about life and death. She had a perspective that made sense. "You didn't need it this time."

She hesitated before she agreed. "No, I didn't."

He walked toward her and took her free hand in his. Even barefoot she was taller, leaner, stronger than him. Another thing he loved about Charlene. She was no pushover. And still she let him be the boss. She preferred it, looked to him for that kind of guidance. "You're just as good up close. It was better that way."

Less trace evidence when it was done right.

"I've done it before, but I don't like it. Life pulsing under my fingertips. Warm breath. Tears. I don't like any of that. I prefer cold steel." She rubbed the pistol against her skin, and he knew she really felt it was an extension of herself.

"It would have been better if you hadn't let her run," Benjamin said. "Work and play don't mix, Charlene."

She nodded. "You're right. Of course."

He took the gun out of her hand and pushed it into the waistband of his pajama bottoms. The first touch burned, the steel was so cold. Kiss of death. It should be exactly like that. His hand tightened on hers, and he pulled her through the door and into their bedroom. Sometimes Charlene liked to be reminded of that. How close the two existed. How the difference between life and death was a dotted line at best.

6

The towers stood 328 feet tall, each with three blades that tilted slowly, creating a whooshing sound as they picked up and recycled the air. There were several wind farms in Toole County now, and Nicole had grown used to them. It seemed that every time she descended a mountain pass, it was into a stretch of valley populated by the turbines. She didn't like them. There had been too many accidents in the few years since they went up, and jurisdiction had recently shifted from the county to the state so that even Nicole had trouble figuring out who was responsible for regulating their safety.

That morning, with the sun just rising and the shadows of the turbines elongating, an unnatural hush fell over the hills. Nicole knew that silence was deceptive.

She had stayed with the Esparza family for more than an hour and during that time had received few straight answers about the night before. Perhaps nothing accurate about their stay in Montana. When a simple yes or no to a direct question was called for, Nicole had gotten evasion: *Did you watch TV with your sister? She only likes reality shows . . . Does Beatrice have friends here? We've met a few people on the slopes . . . Did Beatrice go to a party? Maybe, but she didn't tell me that . . .*

Until she'd asked if Beatrice had left the room willingly. Then Joaquin's reply had been explosive.

She'd left. She wasn't taken. She wasn't coerced. And it angered Joaquin. But that was the perspective of a seventeen-year-old boy, and the act was tangled in the barbed wire of pubescent emotion. Was it truth? Or was it as skewed as the other answers Nicole had received?

She needed to decide a point of entry into the investigation. Murder was the certainty, but how had Beatrice arrived at that moment?

Rendezvous or runaway? Or neither?

The mother's sharp keening had reached deeply into Nicole's heart and, like fingers stirring a pool of water, left turbulence where before there had been peace. She wanted to see Jordan. To wake him, put his breakfast on the table. Motherly things. Normal things. Because despite what MacAulay had said, normal did exist. For her it did, because she had created it. She relied on it. When life got crazy, she bumped along its shores seeking anchor.

She turned the Yukon south, the tires singing on the wet pavement as she drove toward the town proper of Blue Mesa—a main street, stubbornly called Merry Weather Boulevard, and two crossroads. A diner, an art gallery, several outdoor adventure shops, and a grocery store. The station was isolated from commercial business and took up half the block on the east end. Gas stations and mini-marts, fast-food pit stops and a coin-operated car wash were perched atop freeway exits but still close enough to Blue Mesa to be a convenience. Open space, rolling hills, quiet homes—modern and rustic—and rugged mountain peaks were like a membrane that surrounded their little piece of the pie and isolated them from a bigger, badder world. Usually. The familiar sights made for an easy ride that let her think.

She began a mental catalog of all she knew so far about Beatrice Esparza. The girl had been in the ninth grade, had earned high academic marks and enjoyed cross-country running—she'd won several first- and second-place finishes, her mother had boasted through her tears. She'd had a social group, was extroverted and made friends easily.

Beatrice Esparza was no stranger to responsibility. Grades were earned and honor roll was not easily attained. Placing in a sporting event took discipline and training. Would Beatrice sneak away, into the cold and dark, in a strange place? Teenage hormones aside, Nicole was leaning toward no.

They'd eaten Christmas dinner at five o'clock—the steak house on Queens Road—and returned to the resort after that. That was the story Dr. Esparza had given her. The waiter would probably remember the family as a whole—but individually? Could a witness confirm Beatrice's presence? It was worth sending a deputy out to check.

The victim and the brother, Joaquin, had stayed up and watched—or not watched—a movie on cable after the two little girls went to sleep.

They'd used the microwave for popcorn and brewed hot chocolate using the coffeemaker. Joaquin had turned in before Beatrice. The parents had taken the moonlight run at the resort and returned to their room at midnight. They didn't check on the kids—the girls were light sleepers and the parents didn't want to disturb them.

Or Beatrice had gone to a party, leaving before or after her parents. Nicole had taken another shot at that line of questioning but with no progress. Joaquin had been unrelenting in his pose, slouching, arms crossed, mouth closed, and Dr. and Mrs. Esparza had insisted that they knew of no party plans.

There were two certainties—the victim had left the room, and she had been murdered. Could it be as Daisy believed—Beatrice Esparza had never returned to the resort after Christmas dinner?

Nicole had felt what she called her inner tuning fork vibrate several times during the interview. Parents checked on their kids. Especially if they'd been out. Maybe not every mom and dad and not every time, but strange place, late hour? In that set of circumstances, Nicole was willing to bet an all-or-nothing on the parental check-in. She knew she would be back, she would question the parents further, and she knew from the way the information had been delivered—hesitantly, vaguely, and without commitment—that she would get different answers.

She wanted a look in the mother's closet. Did she own a pair of UGGs? Did Dr. Esparza?

She would question Joaquin and the doctor on their shoe size and examine every pair for tread. She hadn't brought it up in the room—she didn't want to alert them to specific evidence when they had an opportunity to dispose of it—but both Esparzas seemed to have smaller feet. Hands too. And she doubted that either Esparza—father or son—weighed in at 150 pounds.

They were both suspects.

No, they didn't fit the date-rape angle, but Nicole knew better than to forge ahead with only one possible motive in mind. And the additional set of footprints in pursuit of their victim complicated things. The watcher. Certainly a different motive there, but what was it?

Of the two, Joaquin and his father, who was the most likely? Both had been evasive, but the doctor had been firm with his answers and even challenging. Joaquin had been a typical teen, angry, grieving, grudgingly giving answers that he doubted would help.

The call, her initial point of contact with the family, bothered her. The father was a doctor, accustomed to late-night disturbances. But the man was on vacation, and the police were calling. At some point in that brief conversation, that had to have sunk in. Yet there had been no alarm. He'd been cautious, as though poised at the precipice between disaster and redemption. Life and death. Hope and despair. If he hadn't been expecting her, her voice at the end of the line was still a relief.

The family had known Beatrice was missing—Nicole believed that— but for how long?

Nicole turned east, away from Glacier National Park and directly into the rising sun. The glare off the snow was blinding, and she slowed the vehicle. She passed a small gift shop, its turnout parking lot empty and its windows boarded against strong winds and sleet.

She felt that irritating rub, like a finger scratching beneath the surface of her skin. She knew from experience that it was revelation. There was something else not quite right about her conversation with the Esparza family. Something out of place, missing or imposed on a scene that didn't fit. And she was close to knowing what it was.

*   *   *

She turned off the county road and felt the world grow smaller as the trees thickened and darkened the gray sky. The homes here were built on acre plots and separated by fence lines that marked boundaries and contained livestock. Her neighbors kept horses and even a steer or two, raised to feed the family. When Jordan was seven he'd talked Nicole into a dog, but she had refused every other request for pets. She wasn't good with animals. They required time, of which she had little, and maintenance. But the dog, a Saint Bernard–husky mix, served two purposes. He was a natural protector as well as a friend. Trips to the vet and chew bones for tartar—she could do that. Training, exercise, companionship—Jordan took care of all that.

Set back from the road and tucked between two hillocks in the rolling valley, her home came into view. It had a calming effect on Nicole. Tranquility. The house had been built in 1961, a ranch with three bedrooms and a detached garage. It was big enough that the cleaning was more than Nicole wanted to deal with, and she hired a woman who came in once a week and took care of the bathrooms, floors, and windows.

MacAulay's comment earlier was still lurking in her mind. She wasn't opposed to help. She utilized her officers, had support at home. MacAulay knew that, so his observation had been personal. Possibly a complaint and definitely an encroachment—she was determined to keep work and relationship in their own tidy places.

She turned onto the gravel drive way and focused forward.

She and Jordan had decided on a small, natural scene to display their Christmas spirit this year and had strung lights on two trees and put up a scattering of lighted deer, some of which moved. Colorful lights on the trees; the deer in white lights. And above it all, the Star of Bethlehem. It had a diameter of five feet and bulbs a brilliant shade of yellow.

Nicole had been raised on Sunday morning church and afternoon pot-lucks and didn't have to reach deep for faith or conviction. She wanted to raise Jordan the same way, but she'd lost count of how many weeks had passed since their last appearance in church.

Her tires spinning on the gravel drive woke Mrs. Neal. She was waiting for Nicole at the front door, wrapped in her fleece robe, her short gray hair alternately spiked and flattened from her pillow.

"Anyone we know?" she asked, closing the door after Nicole.

"A tourist, but a child," Nicole said, and watched Mrs. Neal's eyes water. That quality of genuine empathy was why she'd hired the older woman. Her son was sensitive, soft in the heart and easily led by compassion, sometimes into harm's way. Mrs. Neal nurtured, never criticized, and maybe she hovered just a little. "I want to look in on him," Nicole said, walking down the darkened hall to the back of the house.

"Of course you do."

Jordan's bedroom was currently the victim of an intergalactic attack: Star Wars mural, shelves with action figures, Styrofoam planets suspended from the ceiling. The curtains were Wookiee and C-3PO, the comforter set Luke and Darth Vader. Her son was small for eleven and slow to develop in height and breadth. Nicole stood at five feet nine inches and was a constant reminder that once Jordan hit puberty, anything was possible. She watched the blankets lift with his breath. Her gaze caught on his blond head as he turned onto his back, his eyes wide open.

"That bad?" His voice was scratchy, thick, rising through layers of sleep.

"You're supposed to be deep in dreamland."

"I always wake up when you check on me."

"Squeaky shoes," she said.

"No. You don't even have to touch me and I feel it sometimes."

"Strong love," she sang it to him, changing the words but not the melody of the Marley tune.

He rolled his eyes and pushed to his elbows. Then his soft cheeks pulled in a frown.

"Someone died."

"Yes. A girl. A little older than you," she disclosed, because he'd know about it before he sat down to breakfast. Small towns were like that.

"I'm sorry."

"Me too." She leaned against the door and thought about ruffling his hair, kissing his cool skin. But he was almost twelve. Too old for that, he'd told her a few times. Only with Jordan did emotional separation feel like the tearing of skin.

"It's okay," he said, and sat up. "So long as you know you need it more than I do."

He smiled, and the light from the living room reached just far enough to make his eyes shine. He waved her over.

Nicole sat on the edge of his bed and snuggled him close. "Be safe today," she said. He had a Scout meeting and after that a Lego build-off planned with friends.

"Always."

"I mean—"

"Don't fall for the usual tricks?"

She nodded, her chin rubbing against his silky hair.

*　*　*

Lars stood knee-deep in drift. Flurries swirled around him, lowering visibility, but Nicole was able to find half a dozen of her men and women scattered across the lake, following the perimeter of the woods, weaving between the trees. Lars raked through a three-by-three-foot patch of snow and then moved on. Grid search. The girl's coat, scarf, mittens were still missing.

She checked her watch: 7:20. The flurries had started eight minutes before, were thick and warm when they burst on her cheeks. They were seven hours into their crime scene. The body had been discovered just after midnight by a local couple as they traveled home from a party. They'd brought their snowmobile close enough that it might have compromised evidence, and the woman, an ER nurse, had approached the victim and felt for signs of life. They had waited with the body, had been questioned, but they'd neither seen nor heard anything beyond the norm. But the couple helped establish time of death, and MacAulay was still working on that too.

"MacAulay narrowed the window. He says the girl died between ten and twelve."

Lars looked up from his sweep of the area. "He's been attending more of those Quantico classes."

The department had sent the ME to several conferences over the past two years.

"A two-hour spread." Lars was hopeful.

"The changing temperature. Exposure. Time of discovery. They're all variables." She used the doctor's reasoning, which she knew to be sound. Lars did too. They just wanted it to be different. They wanted TOD to the minute but were lucky to get it to the hour.

Nicole hadn't stayed to make Jordan's breakfast but had pulled the covers up over his thin shoulders and watched him settle back into the pillows. She hadn't taken the time to brew a cup of coffee. She was regretting that now. The cold was numbing her fingertips.

"The vic has an older brother," Nicole said. "He knows more than he's saying." The whole family did.

"So we talk to him some more."

She nodded. "As soon as we're finished here."

"You get anything useful?"

She shrugged. "The brother thinks the vic went to a party."

"Good."

It was a place to start, and in many cases the epicenter of trouble.

Nicole gave him the details of her interview but hesitated before sharing her impressions—she was still forming them herself.

"What?" His eyes narrowed, his face ruddy with cold. He planted the rake and leaned on the handle. And waited.

"They knew I was coming. Or that someone was."

"Why do you think so?"

She explained the phone conversation, the breathless relief, and then the brother's surprise when Nicole delivered the news.

"She wasn't supposed to die," Lars said.

"Exactly. They knew Beatrice was gone and didn't call us. They knew she was in danger but expected a better outcome."

"There are only a few reasons for that. One, if she did run away, it could be an embarrassment. If she left to meet up with a boy, equally embarrassing."

"And if she was kidnapped?" Nicole knew this was a stretch. They had absolutely no reason to go there except for the feel Nicole had gotten off the family. The poised tension. A breath held too long. She'd stood in a vacuum of expectation.

Lars thought about that, stomping feeling back into his feet and shifting so that snow gathered in the wells made by his boots. "Why not tell us now that they know their daughter is dead?"

"They would have," Nicole agreed.

"So how are we going to go about this?"

Rendezvous or runaway? "Something wasn't right," Nicole said. "I could feel it. It's more than runaway, less than a kidnapping, something in between that paralyzed the family but kept their hope alive."

"Something inside the family, then?"

Nicole nodded. "I worked a case once where the uncle was the perp. A kidnapping, crimes-against-a-child thing. This case has that kind of feel."

"A reasonable expectation of return."

"The brother thought so. The father was cautious expectation."

"And the mother?"

Nicole thought about Mrs. Esparza and the way she'd stood by her husband at one turn and the next groped futilely for her daughter. "Desperate."

"Sheriff?"

Nicole and Lars both turned as a deputy clambered toward them through the snow. The flurries had thickened and with them the fog had rolled in, creating an almost opaque cast over the scene. Still, she was immediately able to identify the object dangling from the officer's hand: the victim's purse. Purple leather, braided shoulder strap, the gold plate upon which she would find Beatrice's name engraved, all exactly as the mother had described.

"Good work." She accepted the bag and turned it, finding first the victim's name in fine calligraphy and then the slot for her cell phone. The curved edge of an iPhone was visible above the pocket. Nicole took it out and held it in her gloved hand. Pressing the buttons would be a challenge, wrapped as her fingers were in Gore-Tex and thick lining.

She handed the purse back to the deputy. "Bag this and get it back to me." Then she turned to Lars. "I don't know a teenage girl who'd willingly turn her phone off." But this unit had been shut down, the buttons unresponsive and the screen black.

"Maybe the battery ran out," Lars suggested. "Or froze."

Nicole took a plastic evidence sleeve from Lars and dropped the phone inside, then turned it over so that she was staring at its blank screen. She used her teeth to pull off her glove and blinked away a rush of flurries as the wind shifted. "It'd be gold if it turned on."

She pressed the power button, and blue light flickered in response. The screen came to life with an animation of a flower opening, its fuchsia throat a vivid contrast against the white petals, and Nicole couldn't help comparing that to the markings on Beatrice's neck. Or keep herself from remembering that the young lady had been on the verge of blooming into womanhood.

Nicole didn't tear up at crime scenes. She hadn't puked at the sight of murder in at least a decade, no matter how grisly. But she was moved by the sudden loss of life here, when the girl had been so close to realizing her potential.

"Password-protected?" Lars asked.

She slid her finger over the screen, and the flower disappeared. In its place was a photo of the vic and an older man, Caucasian and graying at the temples.

She shook her head. "So far, no."

The man wore a tailored jacket, shirt open at the collar, and he was smiling. He had his arm wrapped lightly around the girl's waist. Beatrice looked into the camera, bold, smiling, happy.

Lars moved so that he was looking over her shoulder. "An uncle?"

"Maybe." There was no familial resemblance, but Nicole didn't have long to study the photo before it changed to another. This one of a girl younger than their vic, blonde hair and blue eyes, who looked up at the camera from an awkward angle. She was smiling, braces and dimples. And she was in a wheelchair.

"Who's that?" Lars wondered.

"Friend?"

Someone important enough that their vic had placed her photo on the rotation app that drove the slide show. Next up were two little girls, dark hair and eyes, pink parkas and rosy cheeks.

"Her sisters," Nicole said. She could see their vic in each of the faces. "Let's see what else we can find."

She rubbed her fingertips together, ignoring the sting and the falling snow. She paged through a few screens, over the protective evidence film, and brought up the girl's call log.

"A lot of calls from the same three numbers, all California area code, I think."

"Parents, brother."

"Yeah. Last call in came at four twelve this morning."

"What time did you get to the Huntington?"

"I knocked on their door at four fourteen." She looked up and caught Lars's gaze. "Give time for me to get directions to the room and get up three flights—they called her when I was talking to Dr. Esparza or as soon as we hung up."

"Hope has teeth."

She scrolled through the log. "Last outgoing call was Christmas Day, early evening." She brought the phone closer to her face and peered through the snowflakes, which had grown denser. "Six twenty-two. It lasted three minutes six seconds."

"Where to?"

"One of the family lines," she guessed. She had glanced at the numbers the doctor had written in her notebook but would cross-reference them when she got back to the station.

"Look at the texts," Lars prompted.

Nicole had to wipe moisture off the protective plastic, and she cupped her hand more firmly around the phone. "There are four threads."

The wind whipped the treetops close by and screamed as it tore over the lake. Nicole looked up as the deputy materialized out of the gloom, holding the victim's purse, which was now wrapped in an evidence bag.

"You going to take it in?" Lars asked, nodding at the cell phone. He took the purse and handed it to her.

"Yeah. It looks like she has a digital diary on here. And a lot of photos." A gold mine. She looked up and caught his gaze. "I'm going to take a look before I pass it to forensics," she decided. "And when I'm done, we'll head over to the Huntington together."

"We going with family involvement?"

Nicole nodded. "We're going in with three possibilities. Leaving, I hope, with one direction in mind."

"And which would that be?"

She'd already told Lars that Esparza had denied prescribing the Augmentin. "You know what really bothers me about that?" she said. "He dismissed it. He was cocky about it, until he took a look at the photo and saw his name on the bottle label. He was surprised." The tremor that ran through the doctor's body had been brief but betraying: Esparza had felt fear. "But then nothing. Like he shut himself off."

"He's got to know we can pull the records."

"With a court order that will take time to get. To open a confidential record already available to a handful of people."

"All working in the doctor's office?"

"Yep."

"Reasonable doubt," Lars agreed. "But was he thinking about that?"

Nicole shrugged. That would mean that the doctor was calculating, and he hadn't seemed cold as much as caught. But at what? "We'll pull the record, of course. But I'm not thinking Esparza for the pill bottle."

There was a great pressure building inside the doctor, his wife, Joaquin. They were holding back, and whatever they weren't saying was pushing against that restraint. It threatened to fracture the mother's composure. She was equal parts desperate and reaching, scared and powerless. The doctor was all about self-control, but he was slipping, his gestures

44

beginning to reveal what his words would not. But the secret seethed inside Joaquin, and that made him the most likely to explode.

"I'm thinking the mother." She had a medical background. She would know how to fill out a prescription, and she had access to the doctor's electronic stamp. She didn't fit the physical profile of their suspect—not as her husband and son did—but she was their way in. "She gave the Augmentin to Beatrice."

"Why?"

"Because her daughter was sick." It was simple, but it made sense. "You mentioned once that Amber was taking a medication that had some pretty big side effects." Lars's oldest daughter had survived leukemia, but it had been an arduous fight, and medication had been just one of the struggles. "But you kept her on it, right?"

"The benefits outweighed the drawbacks. But when you're fighting a deadly disease, you pick your battles."

"So maybe that's what happened here. Maybe Augmentin was the most effective medication for the vic's need."

7

Two of the text threads on Beatrice's phone were truncated and populated with the lingo of teens and tweens. Nicole recognized most of it because her son used it when he texted her. One of the threads was a conversation between the vic and her brother Joaquin, some sharp words, some soft, much of it about their father. The other thread held the cloying language of pubescent love. There were bold statements of emotions from a boy named Kenny and bitter words of disappointment when they weren't returned by Beatrice.

I want you, Bea. As my girl. I want you in every way, to be mine . . .

We're friends, Kenny. Friends only . . .

The thread deteriorated with: *That's bullshit . . . we were never friends . . . For me, it's all or nothing . . .*

And ended with a plea from the vic: *Friends, please.*

If they were looking at date rape turned murder, Kenny made the top of their list as a person of interest.

Rather than a profile picture for Kenny, Beatrice had inserted an internet image of a sword stuck in stone. Nicole stopped and pondered a moment. Her mythology was weak, but she had an eleven-year-old son who enjoyed the King Arthur and the Round Table tales. And she wanted to hear his voice anyway.

"Hey, Mom." Even bored, he lifted her mood.

"How's it going with Mrs. Neal?"

"We're making caramel corn," he reported, and his tone made it clear that it was as much fun as watching grass grow.

Last week it had been Christmas cookies. Snowmen and Santas. "In a few weeks it'll be chocolate cherry fudge." In honor of Valentine's Day.

Jordan loved the stuff. "I have a question. King Arthur and his sword." She laid it out for him.

"Excalibur," Jordan said.

"Which is what exactly?"

"The name of his sword. Really, Mom, you should at least know that."

"Of course I should," she agreed. "So, didn't he have to pull it out of a stone?"

"Yeah, why?"

"Related to a case," she returned. "Why did he have to pull it out of a stone? There's some significance there, right?"

"Only a ton."

"Enlighten me, and I'll tell you all about it when I can."

There was only a slight pause, and then Jordan said, "Only the true king could pull the sword from the stone. It was a test. A lot of people tried, but only Arthur succeeded, and that's how he became king."

"And that's it?"

"Are you kidding? That sword is, like, the most important part of the Arthurian tales. It gives Arthur power and position. It's capable of magic."

"What kind of magic?"

"Well, it protected Arthur, until Morgan le Fay stole it."

"And then what happened?"

"Arthur died." She could hear the shrug in Jordan's voice. "That's the short version."

"What happened to the sword?"

"It was thrown back into the lake."

"Really?"

"Always," he confirmed. "Doesn't matter who's telling the story, the sword of a knight is always thrown back into the lake. Why? Did you find a sword?"

"No." But it was interesting, the lake connection. She doubted that Beatrice had been out there looking for a mythical sword. Still, it teased Nicole's mind with the possibility of connection.

"If you think of anything else I should know about it, call."

"'Kay. Are you coming home soon?"

"Not until late. I'll call before you go to bed." It was the best she could do. There were many tasks to be done before she could think about food or sleep. "Mrs. Neal is making beef stroganoff for dinner."

"I know. And then it's checkers or backgammon."

Nicole's smile grew at his quiet disgust. "Visiting hours at the nursing home?" Although Mrs. Neal was a square fifty years old.

"I like her."

"I know you do."

"I don't like board games."

"She's trying."

"Yeah."

And he'd put up with it because he really did like Mrs. Neal, and he couldn't bring himself to swat a fly.

"She's a comfort to me," Nicole admitted.

"I know."

"Thanks."

"For putting up with a grandma?"

"For treating her like one."

Nicole disconnected and returned to the text messages on Beatrice's phone. She did a quick internet search. Beatrice had given Kenny the icon of a sword from one of the best-known romances in literature and film. Excalibur was symbolic of many things: strength and weakness, life and death. The list was exhaustive. So Nicole moved on to extrapolation. Had Beatrice seen herself as a Morgan le Fay—a young woman of mystery, capable of shape-shifting and even manipulation? In many tales, le Fay was portrayed as a heroine, in others as a woman who used her beauty and sexual allure to defeat her foes. Which of those qualities had Beatrice seen in herself? What was she to Kenny: ally or adversary?

And who was Kenny? A classmate? A friend from home? There had been passion in his words, a shared affection in the thread, and Nicole felt comfortable ruling him out as a new acquaintance. And yet the last series of messages referred to a meet on the Diamond Run on December 22nd. A done deal, because Kenny had "enjoyed the ride" with her.

Kenny was here, in Montana, but who was he? That and the shoe size would drive her visit with the Esparzas this afternoon.

Beatrice had kept up a running conversation with her brother. The first message was dated December 16th:

We're not going. Dad keeps driving.

No response from Joaquin. A few minutes later, Beatrice tried again:

Like we're on one of those racetracks. Round and round. He won't stop.

Silence. Then two minutes later:

Mom isn't picking up her phone. Beatrice punctuated it with a sad-faced, crying emoji.

Joaquin didn't respond. The vic had waited six minutes before another attempt:

I want to come home.

What's your contribution? he'd written back, and the words stirred something elemental in Nicole. They weren't a threat but felt like one. She could hear the challenge, or the sarcasm, in his tone. That was one of the problems when conversations were conducted electronically—tone was always an assumption.

Too much. Too soon.

Lab rats have no say, Joaquin wrote.

The vic's response was another emoji, this time the classic heart breaking in two.

The thread grew cold, and then on Christmas morning, Joaquin wrote her: *You want to do this?*

Dad's counting on me.

Joaquin didn't respond.

Then at 10:20 Christmas night, Beatrice wrote her final text. An appeal to her brother. *SOS.*

When they should have been watching the movie and drinking hot chocolate brewed in the coffeepot.

The timing was good. It fell within MacAulay's time-of-death window.

Had Joaquin ignored his sister's plea for help? Or had he acted on it? Nicole thought about the condition in which she'd found the family just six hours after Beatrice's final attempt at contact. All of them had been wide-eyed, tense, expecting the worst. Except Joaquin. He had seemed to know the situation was bad but believed all was not lost.

The two remaining threads were messages from Beatrice's parents.

The mother had written many unanswered messages dating back to December 20th and ending Christmas afternoon. Most were along the lines of family plans: *We're leaving for dinner at . . .* or *Your sisters would like to ski with you . . .* Others were corrective. Eerily, the first and last messages were the same: *Good girls don't do this.*

But what had the vic been doing that upset her mother? It wasn't stated, but known. Mother and daughter had their opinions on it, equally strong.

The father had sent one message to his daughter, early evening Christmas Day: *Cooperate.* A single word that managed to stir the hairs on Nicole's nape. Cooperate. With whom? Esparza? Why would he need her cooperation? With the people holding her captive? Either was equally possible. As were a number of other less-than-nefarious possibilities. But she would be a fool to ignore the obvious.

She sent a text to Lars. They were going back to the Huntington Spa, and they weren't leaving without answers. Then she returned to her exploration of Beatrice's cell phone, hoping to find further implication. The most promising app was a digital diary, but it was locked. Nicole sent an email to forensics, indicating that they should attend to this first.

Nicole put the cell phone aside and picked up the slim diary. The one the vic had used solely for sport. She fanned through it and realized there were as many words as there were numbers. She opened to the first page. It was an accounting of that day's performance on the track, followed by Beatrice's commentary arranged in two columns. Under the title *Negatives* she'd written *sluggish, bloated, swollen ankles/wrists.* Positives included one-tenth of a second cut from her sprint time. That was May 8th.

On May 9th she'd recorded her mile time—four minutes thirty-two seconds. In italics was the word *slow.* And she'd noted, *Coach asked about my time. What could I say? Tired, I guess. Maybe more sprints would help. Tomorrow.*

The doctor was right. Beatrice had expected better from her body. It seemed to Nicole that the girl had set goals that were nearly impossible to attain. She'd run a mile at four and a half minutes. Nicole had never broken five. And yet the vic hadn't been happy.

She turned to the next page. Same setup. Beatrice was organized. Every page began with the date, the type of run, followed by the time it had taken to complete it and reflections on her performance. A pattern began to emerge. Two days a week the vic completed sprints and fartleks at the high school track. Sometimes she wrote down comments her coach had made to her—most of them balanced on the tail of reasonable. Two days a week Beatrice ran a fast mile on the track and indicated her time. On

Wednesdays she ran a 5K to build her endurance. This was also the vic's cross-country event.

At first, Nicole noticed small achievements. In late May Beatrice had run a four-twenty-eight mile and noted next to it that there was only one other girl her age in county competition who could best that time. On July 4th, Beatrice trimmed her mile to four minutes twenty-two-point-zero-three seconds. But on July 20th there was a sudden drop in her performance and her mile clocked at four minutes fifty-five seconds. An exclamation mark was noted beside the time, the ink dark and smeared, the paper carved by the many repetitions of the pen point over it. Beatrice had been upset. Clearly. And below the time she had scrolled *Nueva Vida*. That same week, Nicole found, Beatrice's longer run—three-point-one miles on the cross-country field—took significantly longer to complete. Her coach was concerned. So were her teammates. The vic had written in the margins, *Coach wants to speak with me and my parents. He wants to know what's going on. If something's wrong. What happened to my edge? Lauren is catching up to my time.*

Nicole paged through the next week and then the next, noting the continued and not-so-subtle decline in Beatrice's performance. The last week of August showed a turnaround. Not just a stability of numbers, but a climb in the right direction. Nicole continued to turn pages and found that by September 9th, Beatrice was back to the numbers she'd put up in early July, and then she exceeded them. Her mile time improved to four minutes seventeen seconds. Nicole turned two pages forward, to the vic's next mile run, to find that Beatrice had shattered her own personal best by clocking a four minute eleven-point-seven mile. At that level, shaving six seconds off a PB in just days was not possible, was it? And yet, Beatrice had indicated it was. Three more pages in and Nicole realized the mile times cantered at a crazy four minutes and one one-hundredth of a second. They teetered there for twelve days and then there was another sudden decline: four minutes thirty-one seconds. *Dad told coach running isn't everything. His daughter should be well-rounded. And he asked me to drop from the team. There will be time for sports later, Beatrice. Next year. But I won't. I'm not a quitter.*

A father with great expectations—why would he ask Beatrice to sacrifice certain glory on the track and the real possibility of a full scholarship to a top college? What was there to be gained from that? No good reason surfaced, so Nicole left that thought alone for a while and went back to the diary. She counted backward. Each slide in performance hit after three weeks of excellence.

What had happened every three weeks to cause the dip in performance? What had caused her to wallow in that trough for—Nicole paged backward to get an accurate read—four to five weeks, followed by a remarkable improvement in time?

She pulled out her cell and sent off a text to MacAulay. *Steroids?* She didn't expect a quick reply. MacAulay sometimes forgot he had a cell phone, and he complained his fingers were too large to use the keyboard. Nicole had given him a stylus—actually three or four, so he'd always have one handy—and this had resulted in same-day returns. Rarely within minutes, but this time MacAulay surprised her.

No trace in prelim.

8

The snow came down in sheets so that objects were reduced to color and shape without any clear identity. Visibility was about three feet. By the time Nicole left the station, two hours after leaving the crime scene with the victim's cell phone and purse, the Yukon was snowed in. She opened the back hatch, rummaged through the cargo area for the small miner's shovel, and dug out her tires, then used a scraper to push the snow off the roof and hood of the SUV. She cleared the windshield and slid behind the wheel. The windows were streaked with ice and gave the outside world an underwater look. Across the street, storefronts twinkled with holiday lights. She put the SUV in gear and rolled out of the lot.

She was meeting Lars at the Huntington Spa. She had called ahead and told Dr. Esparza to have his wife and son with him when she arrived. He hadn't asked any questions, but agreed as though he'd expected her call. Again, Nicole had the feeling the family was waiting for her.

She didn't like when those being investigated were one step ahead of her. This afternoon she would change that.

Nicole slowed as she passed the turnout for Lake Maria. The trees were shrouded in white powder and the iced lake lost under the steady fall of snow. Their crime scene was completely wiped out. What had been gathered was all they would have to work with. She had given the call ten minutes before—pull back. When she and Lars returned to the station, they would sift through evidence and follow the leads it provided. It was nearing ten thirty, and they'd had the crime scene for a total of ten hours. They needed more; she'd worked with less.

Nicole parked the SUV under the peaked roof in front of the resort lobby. She cut the engine and pushed the vehicle door open against a swift wind. She could see Lars standing under the grand chandelier, working his phone. His face was still rosy from the hours he'd spent raking through drift. They hadn't recovered the girl's outerwear. In fact, there were no further big finds at all. The dogs had tracked the scent off the gloves. It had taken them through the trees, to the Lake Road, then faded to confusion. The dogs had circled, stopped, and stood their ground.

Sometimes the snow, the below-freezing temperatures, tampered with the dogs' sense of smell and direction. Other times the scent was lost because a car or snowmobile had been used to leave the scene. There was no physical evidence to suggest that either was the case.

She stepped into the lobby, and Lars turned when the cool wind hit him.

"You think any more about motive?" she asked.

She'd briefed him on the text messages and hoped he'd spent some time thinking about them, that he'd come up with some of the same questions and conclusions she had.

"*Cooperate*," he said. "That has some pretty sinister implications. Makes me think right away a kidnapping. But you're right, there's something more here. Something within the family dynamics. And whatever it is, it's keeping Joaquin in check, and either Esparza or the wife too, depending on who's holding the cards."

All things Nicole had already thought of herself. "Of the three, where's your money?"

He shook his head. "You think Joaquin is the weak link, that his anger will make him talk. Maybe. But Mrs. Esparza is just as likely to lead us to the killer."

"She's keeping secrets," Nicole said. They all were. So why did it bother her more that the mother wasn't telling all, doing all for justice? "But she's not our prime suspect."

"Physical evidence doesn't lie," he agreed.

The woman wasn't tall enough to wrap her hands around her daughter's throat from the angle carefully measured by MacAulay, not unless she'd stood on an object seven to ten inches in height. Not plausible. Her shoe size was too small for the hiking boots, her legs too short to fit the strides measured on the slopes.

"My guess, she's covering for Joaquin or her husband. But for what? Neither fits with the date-rape angle."

No. That was Kenny, the sword in the stone, elusive but almost certainly the killer. They needed to find him.

"The mother knows something," Nicole asserted, because she just couldn't let it go. Alma Esparza rubbed her the wrong way. "She wasn't surprised to see me. And the soft soles, they could belong to her."

"Size seven or eight," Lars said. "That's the best we're going to get for the UGG."

The material of the sole and a slippery surface made the prints blurry, and casting them was a challenge. UGGs were a popular resort boot with women, and some men too. "Maybe we'll get lucky and she'll be wearing a pair."

"You don't think she'll open her closet for you?"

"She's picking up the pieces," Nicole said, because she could allow the woman that. She'd been genuinely distraught that morning. "But she's not above cutting corners to make them fit."

She thought on that a moment longer, until Lars interrupted her with more facts.

"I looked up that mile time," he continued. "The vic's rate of improvement is unheard of. Anything under a sub-five-minute mile makes her an elite athlete. They shave time by the hundredth of a second."

She'd thought so. "She wasn't making up those times." There was no reason to. The diary was the vic's personal record of her performance. She'd included the good, the bad, the ugly.

"No," Lars agreed. "So something else was at work."

"Not steroids. I asked MacAulay."

"But something," he repeated. "And maybe it's connected to that lab rat comment."

"Joaquin's text," Nicole said. "That's been on my mind too. Our vic was a lab rat, but for what?"

"First pass showed no evidence of chemicals?"

In prelim, bloodwork came back in minutes and would reveal the existence of a foreign substance if one was present, but deeper testing was required in order to put a name on it.

"The tests picked up something. MacAulay says he wouldn't be surprised if it turns out to be Rohypnol."

Lars nodded and moved on. "What do you make of Kenny?"

"He fits neatly into the date-rape angle."

"The sword-in-the-stone thing, the whole King Arthur connection, makes me think that the victim thought of herself as a heroine. Strong, smart, capable."

Nicole agreed. They knew a little more about Beatrice Esparza. Nicole was beginning to like the girl.

"Let's go see what the family's been up to," she said.

They fell into step. Lars, several years younger than Nicole but the bigger of the two the way a tree dwarfed a blade of grass, naturally took the lead in a barreling walk that stretched Nicole's long legs. He didn't assume a commanding presence; it just was, and he never trod on her authority or challenged her decisions. He was the best backup Nicole could ask for—well, unless they were in a shootout, but something like that was rare. Nicole had discharged her weapon only twice in her fourteen years on the job and never since coming to Montana.

"So how do you want to do this?" he asked.

"Divide and conquer," she said. "You take the mom. She's more likely to respond, I think, to a strong male figure asking the questions." Nicole had appealed to her as a mother. Now they needed to dig into her role as a wife and a woman of means. Alma Esparza's loyalties were divided among her daughter, her husband, and herself. "I'll question the father. I'm going to keep it open. I don't think he'll say much. Not until we have something to press him with." She paused and worked the zipper on her parka. "I want to take Joaquin with us, back to the station. Away from the hotel and his parents."

"He's a minor."

"He doesn't think so."

They took the elevator up and walked past the familiar photos of Native American leaders and the heroes of the rodeo.

Lars knocked. He was an imposing Nordic figure with buzzed blond hair and shoulders that made a battering ram obsolete. Nicole stood one foot back and one to the right so that she'd have an unobstructed view of the room when the door was opened.

The doctor was surprised. He stared at Lars, and his eyes flared. The sheriff and undersheriff wore their department parkas, opened now that they were indoors, but no uniforms, and stocking caps that bore the emblem of the state law enforcement agency. They raised their badges in a synchronized movement that revealed side arms and cuffs. Lars said, "Police, Dr. Esparza."

"Yes." He nodded. His eyes hooked on Nicole's face. "We were expecting you."

"Why?" Nicole asked. She stepped into the room ahead of Lars and nodded at Joaquin, who was sitting on the couch dressed in denim and flannel. "Why were you expecting us, Doctor?"

"You told us you'd be back," the doctor returned. "And you called."

"But, you expected me last night too," Nicole said. "Isn't that true?"

His face softened. "Yes."

"Why?"

"It's not like Beatrice to run so late. To not answer her phone."

Mrs. Esparza stood. Nicole deliberately refrained from greeting her and spared her now only the briefest of glances.

"Detective Solberg will interview you, Mrs. Esparza. Here in the room." Nicole glanced at Joaquin. "Come with me," she said. "You too, Dr. Esparza."

"Where to?" the doctor demanded.

Joaquin stood and pushed his feet into a pair of heavy boots. Size tens? Probably. She glanced at Dr. Esparza's feet. Tennis shoes, name brand, and smaller than she'd expected to find. The whole Esparza family was small in stature, but Dr. Esparza seemed to have slim—even delicate—hands and feet.

"For now, we'll use the resort's conference room, but bring your coats," she advised. "And your identification."

"This isn't necessary," the doctor began. "You don't need to split us up like this."

Nicole held the doctor's gaze. "You're hiding something. All of you. And just so you know, this department considers lies of omission as damaging as bald-faced sinkers."

"We didn't lie to you."

"Put your coat on, Dad." Joaquin pushed the parka into his father's hands, then shrugged into his own. He walked across the room and opened the door.

"Joaquin," his mother implored. "Your father is right. We do not have to go anywhere with the police."

"Of course you do, Mrs. Esparza," Lars informed her. "Every one of you is guilty of obstructing justice."

At this point a bluff, but probably not by much. Nicole was beginning to suspect that the truth ran deep beneath their surface. They would have to pry it out of the parents, but maybe not Joaquin. The kid was waiting at the door.

"Your daughter is dead, and we're here to help. What aren't you telling us?" Lars continued to press.

Nicole watched Joaquin slip into the hall and nodded to the father. "Let's go."

She turned, fully expecting Dr. Esparza to follow.

"This isn't necessary," the doctor stated again. Control slipped from the man's demeanor. "I am the one to blame for Beatrice's death."

Nicole stopped; Lars stepped closer, blocking the door.

"No, Enrique. That's not true," Mrs. Esparza objected.

"It is." Dr. Esparza spread his hands in supplication. "I expected too much from her. Not in the way many fathers do. Wanting the best for our children, that is admirable. Allowing them to dance with danger, that is criminal."

He shrugged into his coat. "I will go with you, but not my wife. Not my son. They are not part of this."

"Did you kill your daughter, Dr. Esparza?" Nicole asked.

He paused. Nicole noticed a tic in the man's eyelid.

"Yes." His face was grim, his tone resolute. He hadn't made a confession but a decision.

"How?" she pressed.

"I strangled her, as you said."

He was deteriorating. His lips were trembling, his arms and legs shaking. He wavered on his feet. The man was near collapse, and Nicole hated the necessity of it, but she had to push him over the edge. They had to know if his confession was genuine or contrived; if truth was at its essence, or guilt.

"And did you do that with your bare hands?" Nicole asked. "With twine? With the start cord from a snowmobile?"

"Multiple choice, Sheriff?" he asked, his voice wafer-thin and about as substantial. "My hands, of course. Death, as love, is a very personal matter."

He held his hands up in front on him, turned over so that the pale skin of his wrists was exposed below the cuffs of his parka. His hands were small, the fingers thin and tapered. They were the hands of a surgeon, and possibly the hands of a murderer.

They had to take him in.

9

Nicole stepped off the elevator on the second floor and into a small lobby. She followed the signs to the business office and conference center but did not find Joaquin there. When she and Lars left the room, Dr. Esparza between them but not cuffed, Joaquin had been nowhere to be seen. She'd thought he'd gone ahead, found the conference room and waited, slouched in one of the padded chairs at the long table, but the room was so empty that her footsteps echoed on the travertine tiles.

She returned to the elevator and pressed the call button but didn't board. She'd caught movement out of the corner of her eye, a flash of cobalt blue that could have been Joaquin's parka, and she followed it around the curving corridor and into a sitting area.

Joaquin stood with his shoulder propped against a rustic beam, a panel of windows behind him showcasing the snowfall. His dark eyes were somber, but he met her gaze and held on.

"He confessed, didn't he?"

"Yes."

Joaquin nodded. "That was plan B," he said, and a smirk twisted his lips. "He got there pretty fast."

"What was plan A?"

"Denial. We're good at that. We've been living in it for years. Maybe forever."

"What have you been denying?"

He shrugged. "Lots of things. We pretend that we're as good as everybody else. Better, even. That's really big in my house. My parents still have the accents—Mexico City. Both of them, but if you ask them where they're from, they always say San Diego. We live in a big house with a view of the

ocean, drive new cars. My mother will only buy us clothes with a label on them, but it has to be the right label, and that's always changing. She wants—needs—to have everything right. Because she was poor, she says, and doesn't want to remember it. Same reason my dad drives the Lexus and chases snow in the winter. Because he can. Now."

He stopped and straightened. He shifted so that he was looking out the window. His eyes caught the swirling snow, and it held his attention.

Nicole followed him into the moment. He was gathering his thoughts. Steam. She saw sparks of his anger in the comments he'd made about his parents, but not as sharp as what she'd witnessed in the early hours of the morning. Loss could be a blunt object. It left a person dazed, and sometimes grateful for life and what they had left of it.

"What else, Joaquin?" Nicole asked. "What about Beatrice?"

"What did my father say?"

"That he killed her, but not much more than that."

"He loved her," Joaquin said. "He didn't kill her."

But Nicole knew that the dynamics in a family could be insidious. From their first conversation, she'd known that Joaquin had been branded as the black sheep and that Beatrice was emerging as the star. Children were often compared to one another, with one rising as a favorite. But the favored weren't always the safest. Fourteen years on the job had made that clear to Nicole.

"Sometimes we hurt the people we love. You're old enough to know that."

"Yeah." He nodded but lowered his forehead to the window. The snow was thick and frenzied. Flakes hit the glass and melted, leaving a thin film of moisture that quickly turned into ice and then slid down the pane and back into the cycle of precipitation. "Love isn't forever. It's not even all the time."

She stepped closer. Joaquin was taller by two inches but lighter, his slim build evident even in the parka. He still had time to grow into his body. To reach his potential, as Beatrice did not.

"What do you mean?"

"Parents don't love their kids every minute. We make that impossible." He turned to her and leaned back so that his head and shoulders were resting on the window pane. "I piss my dad off regularly."

"On purpose?"

"Yeah. But I make him proud on purpose too. It's all a choice, right?"

"What choices did Beatrice make?"

His head was tipped back, and the overhead lighting cast shadows on his sharp cheekbones and beneath his jaw. His eyelids lowered, and he stuffed his hands into the front pockets of his jeans. All signs that the defiance was returning. But he answered her.

"Bad ones."

"Why?"

"Not always." He shrugged. "She thought she was being good."

Good. Good girls don't do this . . .

"What does that mean, Joaquin?"

"You should ask my parents."

"I will. But right now I'm asking you."

"I don't know the whole story."

"Tell me what you do know."

"And you'll fill in the rest?" The smirk was back but pained. It softened his face rather than hardened it.

"I'll dig for the rest," she corrected. "That's what I do, Joaquin. I find the truth."

"Why?"

"So your sister can rest in peace. And so that you can too."

That made him tear up. He swallowed, and Nicole could almost hear him choke on his sadness.

"My father—" he began, his voice thick with emotion. "He's deep into something. It's not good. Medicine is supposed to be good, but not when it mixes with greed."

"Your father is greedy?"

"He wants to be someone, you know?"

"He's a doctor," Nicole pointed out.

Joaquin shook his head. "Not good enough. Not for him."

"So what did he do about that?"

"How good are you?" he wanted to know, and an intensity entered his eyes. More anger than revenge; more light than dark. Hope, maybe. "At finding the truth?"

"I won't disappoint you," she told him.

He considered her words and found promise in them.

"I think he sold his research," Joaquin disclosed.

"What kind of research?"

"I don't know. Something with cancer, for sure, because that's what he does. I just remember hearing him for years complain about being so close, if he could only get the hospital to pay for this or that, or get him some equipment he needed that would make a difference." He pushed away from the wall and stood over her, his hands now resting on his hips. "But that changed. Suddenly he was on cloud nine, you know? Walking around the house and saying things like 'I'm the man' and 'I finally did it. Me, a hungry little boy from south of the border.'"

"And you don't know what he did, Joaquin?"

He shook his head. "He called it Nueva Vida."

New life. Nueva Vida. Beatrice had scrawled the words in her diary, sometimes in sweeping letters, other times etched short and sharply into the paper.

"How was Beatrice involved in Nueva Vida?" What bad decision had the victim made that could have led to her death?

"She knew," he said simply.

"She knew what your father's breakthrough was?"

"Yeah. She knew, and she didn't like where he was taking it."

Had Beatrice done something to stop her father? Had she threatened to?

"How do you know she didn't like it?" she pressed.

"She said so. And they argued about it."

"Your father ever lose his cool?"

"Sure, but never with Bea. She was giving too much of herself already to 'the cause.'"

"How so?"

"I think she was the human sacrifice."

"'Lab rat,'" she quoted. "Your last text to your sister."

Regret rippled across his face. "Exactly."

"Why do you think so?"

But he shrugged and his lips pressed together in mutiny. Nicole waited. She eased back on her heels and watched him.

"I'm the help, Joaquin," she said.

"My father lied to you. The old Bea, she was strong and healthy. But that changed last summer. She got sick all the time. She looked like she was dying. Sometimes. Then suddenly she was better than ever." He shook his head, bewildered.

"And you think your father used Beatrice to test his breakthrough?"

"She would die for us," he said. "And maybe she did."

"Explain that."

"Whatever my dad was doing, it was too much. Bea said so. She told him she wasn't enough to make a difference. That it would take many more. They argued about that, a lot."

"Many more what?"

"She didn't say, and when I asked questions, Bea clammed up. But I think she was talking about test subjects. I think she was the only one, and Bea worried that wasn't enough."

"But she didn't quit?"

"No. My father said she was the traction they needed. She would get them the attention necessary. She was the catalyst for change. And Bea went with it."

"Maybe your father wouldn't let her quit."

But Joaquin was shaking his head. "Bea wouldn't give up. She was a people pleaser. She did it to help my father, but to save the world too, because she had that kind of heart. Open to everyone."

"Was your father's discovery big enough it would change the world?"

"I don't know. But my father is not altruistic."

"And Beatrice was?"

He nodded. "And naïve. That was the problem. They fought about that more than anything else. You want to know about Bea's bad decisions? Here's a big one, the worst it can get: she wanted to save the world, and she was willing to die to do it."

Nicole let that rest. She had other questions, other possibilities to explore.

"Would she defy your father, take his discovery to someone who cared?"

"No. She would never do that. She loved our father, our family. We always came first."

Strong words, but Nicole had seen family sell each other out for less. She changed direction.

"Who's Kenny?" she asked.

Joaquin's upper lip curled into a smile that was more cruelty than kindness.

"I told Bea she needed to scrape him off her shoe."

"You don't like him?"

"No one does."

"Except maybe Beatrice did," she pointed out.

"I told you, she liked everyone."

"But was he her boyfriend?"

"I hope not."

"But it's possible?"

"She wouldn't tell me if it was true. She knew how I felt about him."

"How do you know Kenny?"

"What do you know about the world of the wealthy?" Joaquin countered.

"From the inside? Nothing," she admitted. "So educate me."

"Protégé." He said the word like it was explanation enough, but continued when Nicole frowned. "Protect the legacy. That's number one. The spoken creed. You can't take it with you, and that really sucks. Worse, though, is if you can't trust it will survive future generations. So parents groom. And that's Kenny."

"The groomed?"

"Exactly."

"And you despise him for it?"

"That and other reasons."

"You're the son of a wealthy man," she pointed out.

"Yeah, but I'm the outcast. The black sheep." He laughed curtly, and it cut through the air like an explosion of glass. "Remember?" he prompted. "My father gave up on me."

"And focused instead on Beatrice." She let that sink in. "Did you hate her for it?"

He shook his head. "You don't get it. A protégé has to be ruthless."

"And that wasn't Beatrice?"

"She didn't have the right stuff either."

And Nicole wrestled with his earlier words, how Beatrice had been willing to die if it helped others.

"Because she would give it all away?"

"Exactly. My father hoped she would change."

"But you didn't think so?"

"I didn't see it."

"So who's Kenny?" she tried again.

"The son of one of my father's colleagues. One of the men from a Big Six pharm company. We saw a lot of them for a while. I guess that's what they do—throw our families together and pretend it's a good mix."

"What was wrong with Kenny? Other than the grooming?"

"Entitlement," Joaquin said. "He was so full of it, it floated in the air around him."

And a trait common in date rapists. Nicole felt her stomach tilt.

"And Beatrice felt the same way," Nicole said. "She didn't believe in privilege either."

"She was better at it," he said. "She could find something to like about everyone."

"What did she like about Kenny?"

"His father." The words were tangled in Joaquin's disdain. "Another 'big man.' Another rags-to-riches success story. Beatrice was impressed. She believed he wanted my father's cure available to everyone, not just the lucky few."

And that made Joaquin mad. She could hear it as his voice grew tight and his words sharp.

"The lucky few? You mean the rich," Nicole said.

"Yeah."

"And he could do it, because he was the CEO of a Big Six?"

"Could, but wouldn't. That world is all about money."

"Does he have a name? Kenny's father."

"Michael King."

"Did you see a lot of him?"

"No. My father and Beatrice did, though."

"Is that where your father and Beatrice were headed on December sixteenth?" she asked, and then prompted, "There's a text thread running between you and your sister that day. She was with your father, driving and getting nowhere—do you remember it?"

Joaquin nodded. "They were supposed to meet with King."

"But they never made it?"

"No."

"You didn't have a lot of sympathy."

Regret flickered again in his eyes.

"Crazy days," he said. "The pressure at home, it was intense. It was like living inside a balloon that grew bigger every day. It hurt my ears. My back was always up, waiting for the explosion, you know?"

"Someone was going to burst from it?"

He nodded. "I thought it would be me." He shook his head, mystified. "That day it looked like it would be my father. They drove for hours and got nowhere."

"When they got home, what did your father say about it?"

"Nothing. The usual. The big man was stepping up. All that bullshit. My mother said he was ready to make a decision. It was a very important time for him. But he was like, manic, always moving, talking. He never shut up, and none of it made any sense."

"Because you weren't in on the secret."

"Right."

"What did Beatrice say?"

"Nothing. She was mad at me. The 'lab rat' thing. I wish I hadn't said it, but I believed it."

"Did your mother ever try to stop what was happening?"

He shook his head. "She believes in him."

It was that simple. His words, his tone, his demeanor said as much.

"It didn't bother her that he was using Beatrice or that she was getting sick?"

"They both agreed that she was the one—you know, the other doctor in the family. Beatrice would keep us first class. Because money isn't everything. The one thing it can't buy is position."

And that should have been Joaquin's role.

"What about you, Joaquin? What will you do for the family?" *Contribution*. She remembered it from his text message. It was a weighted word, full of expectation.

"Early acceptance into college—that you can buy. My grades aren't good enough for a scholarship or even admission under normal circumstances. But my father's money and reputation have made it possible. And that really pisses him off. By my age he had his feet under him. He was already going places and under his own steam."

"You disappoint him," she said.

She expected the comment to draw sparks, but Joaquin became reflective.

"My mom believes I'll settle down. She says I have the fire, I just need to redirect it."

"And it didn't bother you, all the attention Beatrice received from your father?"

He met her gaze. "I loved her."

And in his own words, people who loved didn't murder.

"Why did your family come to Montana?"

"Vacation. At Christmas it's always about the snow, but my father invited some pharm guys. He said this was it. His round table."

That struck a chord with Nicole. "You mean like King Arthur?"

"Yeah. Bea was really into all that. Knights and the perfect quest. Fairy tales."

Beatrice had believed, and she had championed her father's cause.

"What did he expect to happen at the meeting?"

"He was going to let the dogs loose. That's what he called it, and it was pretty accurate. A lot of the pharm guys were foaming at the mouth. They didn't like my father's discovery. Or they didn't like what it would do to them. Except one or two, and they were the big guns. The ones who could afford to play the game."

To pay the price for Nueva Vida.

"When was that—the round table?"

"Christmas Day."

"And you saw Beatrice after that?"

He nodded, but he looked away from her, his eyes ricocheting around the room. "I told you I did."

"You also said you went to bed before her."

"And you don't believe that?"

"No. There's a lot about last night that isn't lining up. Maybe you did watch *Fast and Furious*, and maybe you did brew hot chocolate while sitting in front of the TV, but I think you did all that alone. Beatrice was long gone by then. And I think you have a very good reason for covering it up."

His face was set, but he swallowed and said, "What reason?"

"What size shoe do you wear, Joaquin?"

The question confused him, but he answered. "Ten."

"And your father?"

"I don't know. Smaller."

"Where did you go last night?" She wanted him to say he'd gone to Beatrice. That he had tried to find her. That he had answered her call for help. "That thread on your sister's cell phone—her last message was to you. She sent it last night. 'SOS.'"

She watched the enormity of it wash over him. His sister's last text. Hope dwindling, she'd reached out to him. It hit him hard, shock having a rippling effect, loosening the tension in his face. His shoulders and arms became liquid, his knees soft.

"I didn't go." His voice was thick with emotion. "I should have; I wanted to. I got dressed. I was putting on my boots when my mom saw me. I told her I was going to find Bea, and she . . . It was my mother. She went."

"Where?"

"To pick up Beatrice."

10

Mrs. Esparza wavered slightly. She stood framed in the doorway of their hotel suite, unable to step across the threshold. Nicole hadn't asked. She'd told the woman to grab her coat, her purse, anything she might need for the next few hours. They were going to the station where they would talk about the events of the night before. Mrs. Esparza refused.

"You're not cooperating?"

"I will talk to you here."

Lars had driven ahead with Dr. Esparza.

"Joaquin will stay with your children," Nicole told her. Joaquin remained a person of interest. Nicole was sure he had not told her all he knew, but he had given them a lead, and even a sacrifice—his mother. And she believed him. His regret had been tangible. "Not for the first time, I'm sure."

"I'm not leaving," she returned. "Unless you arrest me. If not, I'm staying where my family needs me."

Nicole relented. It was not the first time a suspect had refused to ride. She wanted to take Mrs. Esparza from a place of comfort and put her in foreign territory, where she was more likely to reveal information simply because an edge of desperation had been added to her existence. But Nicole thought she already had that here—Mrs. Esparza's fingers were pressed into the doorframe to hold her balance.

It would be easy to tip her over.

"You left here last night to pick up Beatrice."

"Yes," she admitted. "I thought so."

"Why the lie, Mrs. Esparza? Why say she was in the hotel room?"

"I did not want her to go," she said. "But her father said it was okay."

"But it wasn't?" Nicole prodded.

"No."

"So you went to pick her up. Why?"

"She sent Joaquin that 'SOS.' And then she called."

"From her cell phone?" There was no record of the call on the vic's log.

"No, from a different phone."

"Why?"

"She didn't say."

"And you didn't find that odd?"

"I didn't think about it. My daughter was calling and she was crying."

Nicole nodded. "What time was that?"

"I looked at the clock. It was ten twenty-eight."

"So no moonlight run for you, Mrs. Esparza?"

Her skin colored, but she maintained eye contact. "Sometimes I go. Maybe I take the lift just once. I am not like Enrique about the snow."

"Did Beatrice ask you to pick her up?"

"Yes. She was upset, and she wanted to come home." Mrs. Esparza's lips trembled. She closed her eyes tightly, and creases fanned out around them, carving deeply into her temples.

"Where was she?"

"At a party, somewhere on the Lake Road."

"She didn't know the address of where she was?"

"No."

"Was it a party, Mrs. Esparza, or a 'round table'?"

The woman's mouth parted, but it was a moment before she spoke. "You know about that."

"I know about a lot of things. Who did Beatrice go to meet?"

"I should know," she admitted. "But I don't."

"And Beatrice didn't tell you? She didn't mention any names?"

"No."

"And you didn't ask?"

"I put my coat on, got in the car, and drove."

"Why didn't Dr. Esparza accompany you?"

"Beatrice didn't want him to come. She was sobbing. But she repeated, several times, 'Don't send Dad.'"

Why? Nicole wondered. Because she knew her father wouldn't save her?

"Did they fight before she left?"

"They were always fighting. Then they'd make up and things were good for a while, but not for long. They both had ambition, but Beatrice felt he lacked compassion."

"And was she right about that, Mrs. Esparza?"

"My husband is a wonderful man in many ways. He says he has a great discovery, one that will change the world and the face of human suffering, and I believe him. But Beatrice is right too. We make allowances for the people we love, don't we, Sheriff? Enrique grew up poor, often missed meals and received little comfort as a child."

"Joaquin says you and your husband are from similar backgrounds."

"Women are born with the need to nurture, men with the need for achievement."

Nicole acknowledged to herself that there was some truth in that.

"So you got in the car and drove?" she probed.

"Beatrice said she was leaving the party, she said that she would start walking, that she would be on the Lake Road." Mrs. Esparza paused as emotion drew her voice taut. "But I didn't see her. The snowdrifts were tall and the wind was blowing, pulling powder across the blacktop. But I drove slow and there was no sign of my Beatrice."

"Were there other cars on the road?"

"I don't remember. It was dark, and I kept thinking I would see Beatrice just around the next bend in the road. My daughter was waiting, and I kept on driving."

"And you drove around the lake? All the way around the lake, looking?"

"Not once, but twice."

"Were you worried?"

"I was consumed with it. And dread. My heart was racing. I drove in a big circle, all the way around the lake and back again."

"And you called your husband?" Joaquin had said so.

"Many times."

"What did he say?"

"That she would come back when she was ready."

the burn from her anger. "I think so. She told your husband she was not enough."

But the woman was shaking her head. "Enrique, he had only to prove that his cure was viable; from there the real testing would come. And Beatrice was enough for that."

"Did your husband kill your daughter, Mrs. Esparza? When something terrible went wrong, was it Beatrice's refusal to be used further?"

Mrs. Esparza shook her head, tears clinging to her lashes, and said, "It could have been that, but Enrique did not kill our Beatrice."

The woman fell back against the doorframe, her hands pressed to her chest. She sobbed. Nicole stood silently and allowed her a few moments to grieve. There were still avenues to explore, questions that had to be asked. When Mrs. Esparza quieted, Nicole continued.

"Joaquin argued with your husband, didn't he?" She kept a measure of understanding in her tone. "He disobeyed, broke some rules?"

"He made bad decisions, and he was given consequences for them."

"What consequences?"

"Public school. Loss of his driving privileges."

"And loss of his position?"

She nodded. "As oldest, as the son, he should have been the one to follow Enrique into medicine."

"How did Joaquin feel about Beatrice taking over?"

"He pretended not to care, but he did."

"What happened when Beatrice challenged your husband's authority?"

"My husband has a softness for her."

"He didn't punish her?"

"Beatrice did that herself. When she was small, she'd send herself to her room." Mrs. Esparza smiled at the memory. "When she disappointed her father, for days afterward she was quiet, unapproachable."

"Did you know your husband was testing his discovery on your daughter?"

"No. That's impossible. Enrique's breakthrough is a cure. I know that much. But Beatrice is not sick, and so she couldn't be used for that kind of testing."

"Joaquin says she's been sick. A lot."

"But not cancer. Never that." Her tone was emphatic, and her fingers turned white where they pressed against the doorframe. "I thought there must be something, but never that."

"What then?"

But Alma Esparza had no answer. "Enrique denied and he assured, and then Beatrice got better. I was grateful for that."

"Where was the round table held?" Nicole tried again.

Alma Esparza shook her head. It was a short, decisive movement. "I was not told. And when I spoke to Beatrice that night, she was at a home on the Lake Road, a few miles from the town center. That was all she could tell me."

There had been a party, a gathering, a round table. And every Esparza had known about it but had kept their silence. She wondered who was at the controls—Dr. Esparza or his wife. And she thought about Alma Esparza out on the Lake Road, driving that endless loop, and knew the woman had lied. There were problems with her story.

"One more thing, Mrs. Esparza. You've been texting your daughter. 'Good girls don't do this,'" Nicole prompted. "What was Beatrice doing?"

"What all teenage girls do, Sheriff. She was testing her limits, and mine."

"Could you be more specific?"

"Sometimes she went off without telling me where she was going. Sometimes she stayed later than I told her she could."

That made sense. It fit with the tone and the wording of the text messages Nicole had found on the vic's phone. The mother's demands, and the girl's curt replies: *I'm growing up. And you have to let me.*

"Is she seeing a boy named Kenny?"

"She was too young for boys."

"She's fourteen," Nicole pointed out. "In high school."

"With a career laid out before her," Mrs. Esparza insisted. "I did not want her to have a boyfriend, and about that she had to listen."

Or hide the relationship, Nicole thought. "Where is Kenny?"

But Mrs. Esparza shook her head. "Somewhere on the mountain," she admitted. "Not at this hotel, I know that."

"We're having trouble locating him," Nicole said. They'd checked the Huntington and all the other resorts in the area, but the Kings weren't registered. "We want to talk to him, Mrs. Esparza."

"I don't know where they're staying," she said. "Do you think Kenny did this to my daughter? Did he kill her?"

"He's a person of interest," Nicole said. On a list that was getting longer rather than shorter. Top picks: Kenny King and Enrique Esparza. Runners-up: Joaquin and Mrs. Esparza. And Nicole never ignored the possibility of a wild card.

11

Nicole stepped outside into a cozy courtyard with bistro tables and BTU heaters. A fire burned in the ringed pit, the flames leaping above the iron grate. Several people clustered together, piercing marshmallows onto skewers and sipping mugs of hot cocoa. Lars had Enrique Esparza at the station, peeled out of his outerwear and waiting to be questioned, but Nicole wanted to speak to the hired help. Every year the Huntington hired college kids back for the summer or for the holidays. They were the most likely to have paid particular attention to Beatrice, and to have caught her eye in return.

"Hey, Sheriff."

The young man was taller than Nicole, but not by much. He was stocky and looked like a building block, size extra large. He stood apart from the small crowd, behind a beverage cart, and was topping off a latte with whipped cream.

"Hi, Andy. How's Boise State treating you?"

"It's good." He smiled, and his teeth took the light. "Changed my major, you know. Thinking public service is the way to go—benefits and a pension."

"Salary cuts and increased workload," Nicole added, but she smiled through it.

"Pros and cons," he agreed. Andy was solid, but a wanderer. He'd graduated high school three years before but had shifted through career choices so many times that he had to be a semester or two behind at college. "You out here investigating the murder?"

She nodded. "Did you know the victim?"

"Beatrice? Yeah, as much as you can get to know a kid on vacation."

"Tell me about her."

"Pretty and real nice. She talked a lot. Always said hello, coming and going." He paused and considered his words, then nodded. "Yeah, like I said, she was nice."

"What did she talk about?"

"Mostly she asked questions. She could do that, you know? Pull your life story out of you."

"Did she ever say anything about herself?"

He shrugged, and Nicole could see an unease creep in. He shuffled his feet and picked up a packet of hot cocoa. "The usual stuff. She was mad at her dad, and sometimes her brother too. She stayed close to her sisters and wanted to—you could tell that about her."

"What about her mom? She talk about her at all?"

Andy pushed back his wool cap, and tufts of his brown hair poked out around his ears.

"Just once. Her mom came out here looking for her. It was late and she wanted all the kids in, she explained. She was real nice about it, but when she left, Beatrice turned to me and said her mom was the great pretender. It was kinda weird coming in that context, but, you know, she was a teenager, and by definition a mystery, right?"

"Right." Jordan was still predictable. She hoped that didn't change. "Did you ask her about the comment?"

He nodded. "But she brushed it off. Said she and her mom were nothing alike. And I think Beatrice was a little mad about it, or disappointed, because for a minute there I thought she was going to cry." He shrugged. "But she moved past it pretty quick."

"What day was this?"

He thought about that. "She was here awhile by then—maybe the twenty-third?"

"You ever talk with Dr. Esparza?"

"Twice. He's one of those neither/nor kind of guys."

"Explain that."

"You know, he wasn't real friendly, but he wasn't a jerk either. He smiled but didn't linger. Said hello but not much else. That kind of guy."

"Do you know a kid named Kenny?"

"No."

"Was Beatrice friendly with anyone else here?"

"Everyone."

"But no one in particular?"

"Etienne, but he's not a kid. You gotta be at least eighteen to work here."

Nicole didn't know an Etienne. Blue Mesa was small enough that if she hadn't met a person, she'd at least heard about them. And, according to Andy's description, the young man was hard to miss at six feet two inches and two hundred fifty pounds. He usually worked equipment rental and handled the resort's plow steadily. He'd also, according to Andy, dropped out of a college in California after his first semester and drifted around. A loose anchor.

She found him in the garage, wiping down equipment. Andy hadn't been exaggerating about the size of the guy. He had shoulders like Atlas and hands the size of hams.

Her boots made small, whispery sounds on the cement floor, but even when she came to a stop not three feet behind the young man, she went unnoticed.

"Hello, Etienne."

He spun around, lost his footing, and fell back against a snowmobile.

Skittish. The young man was fearful or nervous, and both could be good or bad.

"I startled you. Sorry," she said. She pushed her department cap back on her head and gazed at him as he struggled to his feet. While he was big, he was not athletic. He was good for bulk, not finesse; for hauling, but he probably couldn't shoot a basket from midcourt—he didn't seem to have that kind of precision or coordination.

"Who are you?"

"Sheriff Cobain. I'm here to talk to you about Beatrice."

With Etienne at his full height and breadth, Nicole felt her own vulnerability. Beef and brawn, she reminded herself. Awkward swing, no connect. But she cautioned herself. He was twitching, bouncing on his toes, and a guy like Etienne would be at home in the WWE ring, slamming bodies to the mat.

"I don't want to talk about her." He had a small mouth in a very large head, and his lips were dry and peeling. Etienne wasn't used to winters this far north.

"I'm not asking, Etienne."

"Why?"

"You know she's dead?"

"I know you're saying that."

"But you don't believe it?"

"No. She couldn't be dead. Girls like her don't die."

If his reasoning was faulty, the wail in his heart seemed genuine.

"You liked her?"

He nodded. "She smiles a lot."

"You ever talk to her, Etienne?"

"All the time."

"You ever call her?"

"You mean like on the phone?" He shook his head. "No. She doesn't like phone calls and never answers them."

"She told you that?"

"Yes."

"Did that make you mad?"

"Why would it? She told me, 'Never call,' and I didn't."

"But you texted her?"

"Sometimes. She always answered."

"Have you tried to text her today?"

"No."

"What kind of messages did you send Beatrice?"

His ears were pink, his blond hair cropped close. "I wanted her to know I liked her."

"A lot?"

"Yeah."

"Did you know Beatrice was only fourteen years old?"

"She told me."

"So she's too young for you to date her."

His cheeks flooded with color. "We didn't date."

"But you wanted to."

"No. She needed a friend. She said so."

"So what did you do about that?"

"I brought her presents. I wasn't supposed to."

There was a simplicity about Etienne. His ability to understand seemed very black and white, and he muddled around inside those confines trying to make sense of Beatrice.

"What did she do with them?"

"She gave them back to me. Or her father did."

"Beatrice's father?"

"Yes. He said she had to stop collecting people. Do you know what that means?"

"He told you no more presents?"

"Yes, he said I was special and that Beatrice thought so too, but she couldn't talk to me anymore and I had to stop giving her presents."

"What did you give Beatrice?"

"Small things," he said. "A key chain. It was a dream catcher. She had big dreams. She said so. I thought she would like that."

"Anything else?"

"A magnet of Montana so she never forgets she was here. And a Ranger patch, because she's brave. And I gave her a picture of me, too, because she said I could be a foot soldier in King Arthur's army. I liked that."

"Do you know about King Arthur?"

"He loved Morgan."

"Like you loved Beatrice?"

But Etienne shook his head. "Morgan stole the sword, and that killed King Arthur. Beatrice wouldn't do that."

"When was the last time you saw Beatrice, Etienne?"

"Yesterday. Christmas. She looked like a princess. Her sisters too."

"They were going out to dinner?"

"Yes, with the family, and after that Beatrice was turning into the fairy godmother."

"The fairy godmother?"

"That's what she said." His smile was broad, and he had perfect teeth, straight and white.

"What was she really doing?"

"Hair and makeup."

"Christmas night?"

"Yes. She was getting all the girls ready for the party."

"Her sisters and some other girls too?"

"One other girl. Her name is Violet. That's a pretty name."

"Do you know where Violet lives?"

"She's just visiting, like Beatrice." He was shifting on his feet, and the soles of his boots scraped against the concrete. "Violet wants to make snow angels, and maybe one day she will."

"But she won't now?"

"Not today. Beatrice hopes someday."

"Why does Violet have to wait?"

Etienne frowned, clearly puzzled. "I don't know. I don't know Violet, but I know Beatrice, and she's going to make snow angels for Violet until Violet can do them for herself. She said so."

He picked his rag up off the floor and started on the Bobcat's rear fender.

"What else did Beatrice tell you?"

"Sometimes you have to give up everything. Sometimes that's what it takes to help people."

Etienne's voice sounded watery, and Nicole stepped closer. "Etienne? Are you okay?"

"I think that's sad. And I think Beatrice helped too much."

Nicole thought so too.

12

On the way back to town, Nicole made a left turn onto State Route 49 and skirted the lake for several miles, driving the same roads Beatrice's mother had claimed to have driven the night of the incident. The snow had stopped falling and the cloud cover was dense. Beyond the picnic areas and the scattered boat ramps, the lake stretched out like an oval platter, longer than it was wide. Called the Lake Road by citizens and visitors, it was the first road cleared after a snowfall and the only road other than Merry Weather that required a closure permit for celebrations or construction.

It was popular day and night, summer and winter, and so she knew that Mrs. Esparza had lied to her. In two hours of driving its winding ways, searching for her distraught daughter, she had to have passed a car or two. And probably a lot more than that. Tourists returning from the mountains, locals returning from work. It was common for the Lake Road to be a loose string of bobbing yellow headlights well into the evening. She would have remembered that.

Another problem with Mrs. Esparza's story: it was impossible to drive a complete circle around the lake. The road began and ended at a thick copse of trees, with more than a quarter mile of wild Montana separating the asphalt.

Nicole believed that Beatrice had called her mother and that Mrs. Esparza had left the resort afterward. But she didn't know where the woman had gone. She hadn't searched for Beatrice, not on the Lake Road. She had taken the rental out that night. Joaquin had said so and Daisy had confirmed it. He had shattered his mother's alibi—the moonlight run—and Mrs. Esparza had just as easily tossed it aside. But for what?

Facts about the case were slowly unraveling the family's stories, and neither Joaquin nor his mother seemed concerned about that. They were protecting something or someone. They'd lied to do it, covered for one another, and didn't care that Nicole knew it. And it all led back to the scene of the crime. She slowed the Yukon and gazed through the passenger window at the sheeted surface of the lake. It had a ghostly glow, reflecting what little sunlight burned through the cloud cover. Beatrice had run—a stumbling gait—over hillocks and drifts and onto the lake. Chased by an assailant who was both stronger and taller—the stride measurements showed this; the markings around her neck confirmed it. And that seemed to knock both Dr. and Mrs. Esparza out of the suspect pool. Neither was tall enough. They weren't the killers, but was one the watcher?

If Joaquin had killed his sister, would Mrs. Esparza protect him?

Had Joaquin answered his sister's SOS after all?

Could it have been Joaquin who had pulled out of the resort parking lot last night in the rented Tahoe? There was more than one way to enter or exit the building. There were, in fact, seven. Daisy might have seen Mrs. Esparza leave out the front door. She might have watched the Tahoe disappear down the winding driveway. But Daisy couldn't confirm Joaquin's whereabouts last night. The young man could have been crouched in the back seat, undetected.

But the roofie and the condom. The spilled evidence, the hasty attempt made to pick it up. That wasn't Joaquin.

He had spoken honestly about his family, about his own transgressions and his parents'. He'd given a candid perspective of Beatrice, and he had given Nicole a viable motive—Nueva Vida. A discovery that could change the world. That would shake up medicine and possibly extend human life expectancy.

There was a lot of money involved in that—to be gained and lost. And there was more. If Esparza was right: if he was the father of such a miracle, he would be exalted. Mrs. Esparza would have no worries about her station in life. It would definitely be a pinnacle existence.

Family or fortune? The field was opening, the suspects multiplying. Who among the Big Pharm companies would have the most to lose if Nueva Vida was a viable cure?

Nicole adjusted her speed. The road on the north side of the lake was always more treacherous in the winter. Though it was salted and sanded at regular intervals, ice still formed and increased the likelihood of a wipeout. The trees here were thicker, too, and crowded the shoreline. On the other side of the road, the geography was dramatically different—the earth sloped sharply downward, then leveled out, and it was here that yet another wind farm had been built. It was the biggest in Toole County and the most dangerous. Three deaths so far had occurred since its ceremonial opening four years before, each incident grisly and the result of weather and malfunctioning machinery. When the conditions were right, when the wind off the slopes met the currents of a storm front as it moved in, a vacuum was created that was strong enough to pull a man off his feet. It was now mandatory that anyone working the turbines did it by tether line.

She followed the curve of the road until she was parallel to the Huntington Spa. She had to guess, because the resort was not visible from that distance, not through the thickness of the trees. She knew that several paths led from the resort to the lake, most of them made by snowmobile and cross-country skiers. She watched for the trailheads, and when she found them flowing into the road, she slowed the Yukon more.

None of the drifts had been disturbed. No one had recently come down from the Huntington, crossed the street, and entered the lake area.

She leaned more heavily on the gas pedal.

In the dead of winter, trees along the shore often split from the sheer cold and fell onto the ice, only to be consumed by the lake at first thaw. The school hockey teams cordoned off a section, set up goals and bleachers and portable heaters, and played their games outdoors. Speed skaters were drawn to the open expanse of the lake, and a fishing hole had been drilled through the frozen surface near its eastern shore.

There was activity, but never at night.

She let the engine idle and stared at the lake. Their crime scene was out there, and beyond it the homes of the affluent as well as luxury rentals.

She called Lars.

"What's up?"

She told him about Beatrice's phone call and how both Joaquin and Mrs. Esparza had blown off the mother's alibi. She told him about Alma

Esparza leaving the resort to search for her daughter and the inconsistencies in her story.

"You think they could have been in on it together? Joaquin and his mother?"

"It doesn't feel right, but it's possible."

"But the roofie and the condom," he pointed out.

Yeah, that.

"We have two predators. Maybe more."

"Two sets of prints."

"And a lot more besides," she said. "Not in on the chase, but in and around the scene." The lake was a popular place. Plenty of old prints. Some fresher, but it was impossible to know when they had been made or by whom.

"And a growing list of motives," Lars said.

"Date rape, sibling rivalry, financial ruin—and we're not talking just one or two pharm companies."

"If the cure is a miracle."

Had their vic's death been a spectator sport?

"The brother fits the physical profile," Nicole said.

Even if she didn't like it. Instincts were sometimes skewed by emotion. So while Joaquin didn't feel right as the killer, Nicole knew she could be wrong.

She took another look at the lake. McMansions of natural wood and stone lined the shore not a mile from where she idled in the cruiser, and from somewhere among them Beatrice had run for her life, making it as far as the lake before she was stopped. "I like Alma Esparza for the watcher."

"Me too," Lars agreed. "She really didn't want us separating the family."

"Strength in unity."

"And control."

"There's something off about the timing," she said. "Even when Joaquin was tossing aside their alibis, he was lying through his teeth about last night."

"The movie, popcorn, and hot cocoa?"

"Yeah. Simple details. Believable. I think it happened, just not last night." And the itch she'd felt earlier as she'd driven away from her first meet with the family began to scratch toward the surface. Words and faces swirled, and events began to take shape. "No, there was no movie last night, no popcorn," she said, "because Beatrice left the resort for Christmas dinner, just as Daisy reported, and she never returned."

"Proof?"

"I met a young man at the resort this afternoon. He knew Beatrice. He said she was on her way to a party Christmas night. First dinner with the family, then off to a party. Beatrice and her sisters."

Her sisters. Saying it aloud, putting the youngest Esparzas together with their older sister at a time and place that correlated with the vic's disappearance, created a free-fall sensation in the pit of her stomach and a trickling of bile up her throat.

"Her sisters too?" Lars repeated, and she heard the dawning dread in his tone.

"And they were dressed up like princesses." The words were tight, her breath thin. She had missed it. Her first pass at the family had been at four o'clock in the morning, and it had been entirely reasonable that Sofia and Isla were sleeping. Besides, the mother had claimed the girls had colds. Plausible. Nicole had bought it. But now, a half day into their investigation, with pieces sliding slowly into place, a different picture was emerging.

"Fifteen fucking hours," Lars said.

Wasted time. It didn't bode well for the girls. If they were being held against their will, if the person who had killed Beatrice had the same intentions for the youngest Esparzas, Nicole and Lars were already too late.

"We never saw them," Nicole said. But had she known to look for it, she would have seen evidence of their absence—the three parkas hanging in the closet that should have been five. "And it didn't seem off. Not until now."

"Why didn't they tell us? When Beatrice turned up dead? Why not then?"

"Because Sofia and Isla hadn't," Nicole said.

"They had reason to hope."

"Or thought they did."

"Right."

And that explained the hold on the family, the restraint that Nicole had sensed from the very beginning. "We need visual confirmation," Nicole said. "If possible." She put the cruiser in gear and rolled forward. Snow crunched under her tires. "You're closer to the Huntington."

"Already moving," he said.

"I'm staying here." She cut a U-turn and headed back toward the boat ramps. "Call me after you've made contact."

"Will do."

"Get a visual. Ask them their names. Use their ski passes for confirmation." If they were wrong, that is—if the girls were in the hotel room, tucked into their beds with boxes of tissue and chicken noodle soup. And if they weren't . . . Her feeling of dread thickened. Instinct flared. How she wanted to be wrong.

"I know the protocol." His words were thick with breath, and she could tell he was outside then, jogging toward his cruiser.

"I know you do." She heard his car door slam shut, his engine turn over. Too little, too late. "You have Esparza in the box?"

"Waiting about as patiently as the second hand of a clock."

"Good."

She hung up and slid her cell phone into its holder on the dashboard. Snow plows had left upwards of four feet of drift, even at the entrances to the ramps—no one used them in the winter. Nicole cut across the mound at an angle. Her back tires spun, caught, spun again. She got out, used her miner's shovel to dig herself out, and finally pulled up to a metal pole and post. She used a heavy set of clippers to cut through the Schlage and then stood for a moment, pondering the sweeping shoreline.

She knew the terrain well. Eight years of crime and recreation around this lake had made sure of that. From where she stood, their crime scene was due west, lost beneath new snow. She thought about Beatrice out here, no coat, knowing she was in trouble. But smart—was she smarter than she was compassionate? Or had her soft heart betrayed her? She had turned and faced her killer. She had looked him, or her, in the eye—the markings on her throat showed that—but were her last words ones of love or fear? Had she pleaded for her life, for the lives of her sisters? Or had she realized it was already too late?

She climbed back into the Yukon. Lars was on rescue detail. Nicole had recovery, in case the Esparza children hadn't been kidnapped but had been murdered like their sister. Her men had combed the crime scene, fanning out in ever-increasing circles, but they hadn't known then to look for the bodies of two small children. Had they known the girls were missing, they would have expanded the search area, brought in more people.

Nicole moved the transmission into neutral and released the parking brake. The Yukon inched forward, tapped into the potential energy from gravity, and hit the ice at ten miles per hour.

In winter, the ice was thick enough, even at the center of the lake, to drive a car across the surface without fear of breaking through. Nicole allowed the Yukon to slow naturally. With little resistance, that placed her about fifteen yards from shore. She turned in a wide arc and straightened the Yukon. Lake Maria wasn't big—three-point-three miles long, less than a mile across at its widest—and people were generally too nervous to venture too far out. She decided it would take two sweeps, executed slowly, to complete the search. Still, kids were small and easy to miss. And with the new snow that morning, she was looking for irregular shapes that could be bodies. A rolled shoulder, the tapering of legs. She peered through the glass, adjusted the strobe lights, and tried to push away the feeling of defeat crouching in the shadows.

*　*　*

Her cell phone rang. The screen saver was a picture of Jordan—five years old and wearing a small red pail on his head. His smile was wide, and he was all about pulling you into his world. He was still like that.

She hadn't named him after Michael Jordan, but because she'd wanted a name that would work equally well for a boy or a girl. Reese, Taylor, and Peyton had made her list, but only Jordan was a place of miracles. The river, at the highest point of the season, had stopped flowing, had stacked up like a brick wall on either side of a group of believers, allowing them to pass through. And that did describe Nicole—she was a believer, in good and bad. She expected the unexpected. She was willing to be moved by love, although her son was her only proof of that.

She had circled the lake twice, then crossed its center in a series of switchback motions, and found nothing. Lars had already called—the Esparzas' hotel room was empty. He was searching the grounds, talking to people.

She took one last, sweeping look at the lake from where she sat, back on asphalt and above the tattered yellow ribbon her department had used to protect the body of Beatrice Esparza and its surrounding geography, then pressed the icon of Jordan's shining face and spoke. "How was the backgammon?"

"We played checkers," he said. "Mrs. Neal is pretty good."

"She didn't let you win."

"She swept me," he admitted. "Three games."

"And made grilled ham and cheese."

"Yeah. That was good. What did you have, McD's?"

"You know I wouldn't do that to you."

Jordan snorted. "You wouldn't tell me about it."

She had a healthy suspicion of fast food and wouldn't so much as park in the lot of a restaurant with less than an *A* in the window. She'd waitressed her way through college and knew the difference the alphabet made on her plate.

But sometimes calories, even if they tasted like a cardboard box and called her soldier cells into formation, were all she had time for.

"I had the double box tops with extra cardio-blocking cheese and curly cancer-fries."

He gasped and put enough drama into it that Nicole felt it. "That is so unfair."

"You'll live longer than me."

"I'll do that already."

"Occupational hazard."

"No, it's the lack of love in your life."

He wanted her to get married. Because he wanted a father, and because she needed a daily dose of "affection." He'd caught a show on *O* about longevity and its link to human touch.

"Thanks, Dr. Phil."

"I prefer to be called Dr. Oz. It's way cooler."

"Okay, Oz, what's up?"

"You need any more info on Morgan le Fay?"

"Why do you ask?"

"It's all around town," he informed her. "The dead girl and her father complex."

"Morgan le Fay had a father complex?"

"Maybe. She had a thing with Merlin for sure."

"The Great Magician?"

"Wizard. But yeah."

"What kind of thing?"

"You know, like, she loved him. It wasn't just about discovering his secrets."

As Beatrice had loved her father? She might have been at the heart of his secrets, and she might have died because of them, but when Nicole thought about Beatrice Esparza and her father, the *ew* factor did not kick in. She hadn't gotten that feel. Not from Dr. Esparza and not from Beatrice's mother either. She thought about the photo of Beatrice in the embrace of a much older man. A man who held her maybe too closely. There was affection in the image, and it was mutual. But possession? No, not quite.

"What did you hear?" *And from whom*, Nicole wondered.

"We talked about her at Scouts earlier. Some of the guys knew her from the resort." The winter season brought in the bulk of Blue Mesa's economy, with the influx of tourists carving through the mountains and dropping money in the restaurants and gift shops. The employment rate saw an increase and the locals were upbeat. Most of the jobs went to housewives and senior citizens, a smaller portion to teens and college students returning for the holidays. "The dead girl was all about her father," Jordan continued. "She spoke like he was a god, but they fought like dogs."

"Who told you this?"

"Jackson Lambert. He works in housekeeping."

She thought about going to see Jackson herself. "What did they fight about?"

"He wanted something and she wasn't coming across," he said. "It was weird, Jackson said. Like Beatrice held all the cards and the father was begging her not to play the deck against him. Those were Jackson's words."

13

Benjamin Kris loved snow. It gave him a kid kind of glee, that ribbon of excitement inside pulling tight as anticipation grew to an almost unbearable point. Snow meant a lot of things to him, all in the past now. It triggered a series of images: snowmen and forts and snowball fights; ant-hills on mirrors and powder stuck to nostril hairs; money—his first big score, fifties and hundreds cascading onto his prone and laughing body on the bed of a cheap motel on Valentia Street in Denver. Nicole. It was no surprise that she would be stitched into his imagination and into this little trip to wonderland.

She could have busted him; instead she'd slept with him. More than once. And every time it had been too good to talk about. But women couldn't be trusted.

The thought was sobering. Even Charlene had messed up. She had played when she should have been working.

He shifted in the seat and the leather crackled. They cruised down Main Street, USA, Charlene glued to his side in the back seat of the Durango—Montana's winter limousine. The shops had been renovated recently, painted earthy colors, and twinkled with holiday lights.

"Could be a Christmas card," he said.

"It's beautiful," Charlene agreed. But then, they had the heater pump-ing and she was bundled up in faux fur—at her insistence. Benjamin wanted to buy her the real thing, but she was a member of PETA and Women for Humane Cosmetics.

They approached the crossroads where the police station sat kitty-corner to the only bar in town. Such an easy walk to the tank, it could be self-service.

"Stop here a minute," Benjamin ordered the driver, a man he'd often used and whom he'd sent ahead of them by two days in order to secure the right ride and get acquainted with the layout of the town. Specifically the roads in and out of Toole County and the rolling stretches of land that could be used for the disposal of bodies and evidence—if such a need occurred.

Benjamin was an accomplished escape artist. The Magician's secret to that: he left no witnesses because he created none. He kept a quiet demeanor and frequented places for the rich and pretty, where he blended in better than most. When he had to speak, he was neutral. Otherwise, he smiled as much as the next guy but no more. He didn't smoke, nursed a drink, and never dabbled in the goods of his trade.

But Toole County was different. He was known here, by none other than the head of law enforcement. As the father of the sheriff's son, he had pull with her.

The thought was dark and settled on his brain like a cat teasing a favorite toy, and he laughed, enjoying himself. Catnip. Nicole was that for him. Tormenting her gave him an insane kind of pleasure.

"Benjamin?" Charlene prompted. "Why are we stopped in the middle of the road?"

He considered his next move. Contact. That he'd decided before the day dawned. But when and how?

He'd waited long for this moment. He'd mapped out scenarios in his mind—all the possibilities in Nicole's reaction and how he would handle each. He couldn't have been more ready.

He spoke to the driver. "Pull in at the police station."

There was an initial wave of hesitation—the natural response of a man who had spent his life doing wrong—and then the driver pulled forward, hit the indicator light to signal his intentions, and executed a clean turn into the parking lot adjacent to Nicole's office. And that made him smile too. He was looking at the product of Nicole's slow, downward spiral. She'd been on the fast track to captain and beyond, but she'd given it all up to raise their son in a safe environment, away from the violence and drugs of Big City life and the father who had played a role in creating him. That part wasn't so nice, but he was a changed man. While Nicole had taken a step down the ladder, Benjamin had ascended by leaps.

"Wait here," he instructed, and felt Charlene's hand tighten on his arm. "What are we doing here?"

Always, they carried out their business as shadows that moved across the wall. He understood her apprehension but pried her fingers from his arm.

"I want to say hello to someone," he said. He climbed out of the SUV and lifted the hood of his parka. The snow was coming down steadily, and he had spent time on his appearance.

The entrance to the police station had Nicole's name on it in bold black lettering.

He liked that. He'd bet Jordan was proud of it.

Inside, the lobby was warm and lit with fluorescent tubing. A woman in uniform sat behind the desk. She addressed Benjamin and he stepped forward, lowering his hood and pulling the top toggle of his parka open.

"How can I help you, sir?"

"Is Nicole around?"

"Pardon?"

"Sorry." He smiled—an easy slide of his lips that didn't seem at all practiced but reached his eyes and carried a wattage of charm that was neither too much nor too little. "The sheriff? Is she in?"

The woman cocked her head to the side and considered him. "Does Sheriff Cobain know you?"

"Old friends," he told her. "And I'm in town for a few days. If I come and go without dropping in on her and Jordan, well, that would be grounds for arrest."

That was lame. As a rule he wasn't a punster, but he was nervous. And he blamed Nicole for that. The last time he'd seen her, she'd put the cuffs on him and the flared tip of a loaded .357 to his temple. She'd threatened him with all the things she could do to him. All legal, and she had the goods. Before that, he'd been the one jerking her chain. He'd liked that a lot better. He'd liked that so much he was willing to walk into the lion's den just so he could pull her strings and watch her dance to his tune. Again.

The woman frowned, but before she could complain, he held his hands up in surrender. "Sorry. You've probably heard a thousand bad jokes just like that one."

"And that's all in one week," she assured him.

"Could you just tell her Benjamin came by?"

"Sure. You have a number?"

He watched her scribble his name on a pink memo pad.

"She has my number." He'd had a few hundred phones since seeing her last, all disposable and tossed away, but if she had wanted to contact him, she could have. Nicole was an excellent detective. Accommodated. He'd seen the plaque, the gold star. He'd even watched her hustle a few scumbags into the back of a car. He'd liked that about her, until she'd turned it on him.

He pulled up his hood and pushed out into the flurry of snowflakes and the rapidly dropping temperatures.

* * *

Lars was already at the station when Nicole pulled up, steam rising from the hood of his cruiser as the engine cooled.

Lars had questioned the help, from equipment rental to baristas, but no one had seen Mrs. Esparza or her daughters.

Daisy had seen only Joaquin leave. He'd had the keys to the Tahoe in his hand and strode through the lobby and out the doors without comment.

There was a lot of activity at the Spa, but Lars had followed the cleared, paved path from a back door, around the rustic building, and into the adjacent parking lot. It was possible Mrs. Esparza had left using that route. Possible that her daughters had been with her. But there were no discernible prints on the stone, and those in the snow beside it were too numerous and layers deep, such that it was impossible to know for sure.

No one had seen or heard anything. The family could be on the slopes. They could be en route to the station, hoping to connect with Dr. Esparza; they could be at the morgue for a parting moment with the victim. Or Joaquin and his mother could be searching, as Nicole and Lars and the entire department would be, for the lost girls.

"So where does that leave us?" he'd asked.

"Not knowing, but believing their kidnap is probable." They would work that angle with Dr. Esparza. They would do it in a circuitous manner, hoping the man would provide answers that led them to a confession of another kind.

She parked beside his cruiser and cut the engine, then pushed out into the thickening snow. She didn't have far to go before she found Lars, hovering in the lobby as he unbuttoned his parka and unwrapped the scarf from around his neck and ears, which were a persistent shade of flamingo.

"If a kidnapping, do you think Mrs. Esparza and Joaquin are delivering the ransom?" he asked.

"Depends on the currency," she said. She pocketed her skullcap and removed her gloves. "At this level, Big Pharm and the doctors who orbit it are in a totally different stratosphere. Money probably isn't it."

"Loss prevention," Lars said.

And she agreed. "Nueva Vida. And there's only one person still breathing who has it."

"All roads lead back to Esparza."

Nicole nodded. "We have a strategy," she reminded him. "Let's use it."

He waved her ahead of him, but they didn't get far. The desk clerk called them back.

"There's a message here for you, Sheriff." She pushed the pink memo toward Nicole. "He came by about an hour ago."

Nicole picked up the slip of paper and read it. A single word. A name. But it had a visceral effect on her. She felt the blood drain from her head and spiral to her feet. Years of practiced control kept her from wavering, even as her world tilted.

"He was here?" She heard her voice as if from far away. Small. And she hated that. Small was how he'd made her feel. He'd had a hold on her back then, until she'd turned the tables. Until she had slithered with the other reptiles of the underworld and gathered the evidence she'd needed to pry his fingers from around their son's neck and keep him caged as he belonged.

He'd admitted to uncivilized behavior. She knew him to be an animal.

Benjamin Kris. He hadn't left his last name, but he didn't need to. He hadn't left a phone number, but she already had it.

"You okay, Nicole?"

She felt Lars draw near. He tapped a finger on the memo, putting enough weight into it that the paper bent, and read the name.

"Who is he?"

"What," she corrected. "*What* is he."

"Buzz the door, Fern," Lars spoke over Nicole's head, then turned and led the way. He refrained from grabbing her elbow and escorting her, and she appreciated that. As they paced down the hall, then through a series of desks, she felt the blood simmer in her veins, beat heavily in her temples and wrists. Slowly, the roar of a lion was building in her throat.

When they reached her office, Lars stood aside and waited until she'd passed through to follow.

"What is he?" He leaned back against the closed door, his cheeks still flushed from his time outdoors but his eyes steady.

But she still hadn't decided what to tell him.

"It's a personal matter."

"You're afraid of him," Lars said. "In six years, I've never seen that from you."

She wanted to deny his words, but that would make her a liar.

"He hurt Jordan," she said. "And I let him. Until I found a way out." A way that was still viable. So why was Benjamin here now?

"He's your ex."

"That implies too much of a relationship on our part. He's Jordan's father, and let's leave it at that." She had defied every reasonable doubt when she'd become involved with Benjamin, and she'd paid for that in numerous ways. But he no longer had that kind of hold on her, she reminded herself. "We haven't seen him in eight years."

"Why is he here now?"

She walked around her desk and sat down. She placed her hands on the calendar blotter and stared at them. She felt the slight tremor moving through them, but it wasn't visible. Her fingers were slim, the nails short and buffed and covered with a coat of clear lacquer. They weren't the hands of a killer, but they could have been. She'd done many things with her hands, more out of love than ignorance. But she would have killed Benjamin to save her son. She'd made that decision before their last confrontation. She had laid it all out for him, the evidence that would send him to the state pen for twenty-plus, and next to it a full chamber in a .357 she'd bought off the street. "It'll take one shot, no doubt between the eyes," she'd told him, and he'd known she was an expert marksman. "The rest will be for the hurt you inflicted and the hate that's burning in my belly." And then she'd offered him an out. The decision was easy, and Benjamin had never made bones about it—if anything took too much effort, he wasn't interested. "Door number three," she'd told him. "We never see you again." And she'd opened her hands in a gesture of freedom.

A freedom he didn't deserve. He'd killed a man and Nicole had watched him do it, but he wouldn't have spent a day behind bars. The courts didn't like video evidence and she'd had little more than that to offer. Nicole would have been portrayed as a spurned lover, an officer of the law who must possess questionable morals to have involved herself with a drug dealer and possible murderer. She would have had no credibility and her eyewitness testimony would have been scrapped. She would have lost her job and possibly her son. And when she remembered that, the decision she'd made eight years ago softened around the edges.

She'd heard from Benjamin four years later in the form of a check— one hundred thousand dollars. In the memo line he'd written *child support*. It had ignited an anger in her. A spark of fear. Both emotions were unwanted. Benjamin had no right to think of Jordan as his son. The insinuation that he did, she received as a threat, one that brought back searing memories of the harm he had caused.

Her response had been as brief. A home-burned DVD delivered by personal messenger. It was forty-seven seconds that documented the end of a young man's life. Benjamin entered the scene with the gun already in hand. He walked swiftly toward his target, extended his right arm, and pulled the trigger when just three feet separated them. As the body fell, folding at the knees before it pitched forward, Benjamin kept walking, sliding the gun into a coat pocket, rolling his shoulders. At one point he turned toward the camera. It was a clear shot, even at ten times the resolution. He'd received her message and hadn't contacted her since. Until today.

"If anything happens to me," she told Lars, "or to Jordan, I want you to come and get this—" She opened a side drawer in her desk and reached into the back. She pulled out and held up a plain white envelope. His name was scrawled across the front. There was a key inside and nothing more.

He took it in his hand and weighed it.

"Safe-deposit box?"

"At the credit union," she said. "Your name is on the POA."

He raised an eyebrow.

"I added it a few months after I met you."

"But never told me about it."

"I didn't think it would come to this."

"You think he came here to kill you?"

"I don't know what to think." She took the envelope and replaced it, then sat back and considered Benjamin's motive for turning up in Toole County. "Benjamin is a drug dealer," she revealed. "High class. Mostly Vicodin, because that's easy to push and Benjamin doesn't like to work. For select clients, he's delivered on Valium and Ritalin."

"A white-collar scumbag?"

"When I knew him, he was making that arduous climb from street vendor to retail. As far as I know, he's prescription drugs only now." She caught and held his gaze. "People die around him, Lars." A thread of queasiness squirmed through her stomach, but it needed to be said. "Jordan could have been next."

She watched anger draw the features of his face taut.

"How'd you get tangled up with him?"

"I was a different person then." Reaching. She'd thought about it a lot, and that was the best description of who she'd been. She'd been flailing in the water, surrounded by the sewage of a crooked department and trapped by a code of loyalty she'd thought would snuff the life out of her. Benjamin hadn't seemed like such a bad guy compared to all that. In fact, his crimes, up until that point, had been mild compared to those of some of her colleagues. "And I didn't know who he was. Not at first."

Lars nodded. "Why the move to prescription drugs?"

"Cocaine meant dealing with a seedy lower class, and Benjamin felt he was above that. He liked things clean. He liked a certain type of person, and he surrounded himself with them."

"He wanted to drive to work in a Mercedes and lunch with people who could locate Ghana on a map?"

"Exactly."

"What's in the box?"

"A treasure map," she told him.

"X marks the spot?"

Nicole nodded. "There are several of them."

"That's a lot of evidence."

"And still maybe not enough."

Lars nodded. "He knows you've got it?"

"Of course. I gave him options," she said. "I wanted to kill him, but we settled on a deal we could both live with."

"So maybe he wants to change the terms."

Nicole had already come to that conclusion. Blue Mesa was small. It didn't even show up on most maps. You had to have a reason to come here.

"Don't let him get to Jordan," Nicole said. She heard the warble in her voice and hated it. "If it comes to that." If Benjamin killed her and left Jordan unprotected.

Lars pushed away from the door and stepped into the center of the room. "He'd have to get through me to get to either of you."

Nicole swallowed the emotion gathered in her throat. She held Lars's gaze. "Thank you," she said, "but I don't deserve it." She troubled over her next words and decided on simplicity. "He killed a man, Lars, and I watched him do it. Hell, I filmed it and several other criminal acts he'd committed along the way. Evidence," she assured him. "I needed to get Jordan away from him, and Benjamin wasn't budging. He had a cop in his back pocket and did everything he could do to keep me there."

"Why didn't you turn the evidence over to the DA?"

Nicole shook her head. "It wasn't enough. There were no guarantees Benjamin would go to jail." She felt her composure slipping. "He beat Jordan. Badly. There are photographs of it." She nodded toward the envelope and the key to the security box.

"Your word is enough for me," he said. "And as far as your decision goes, court is always a crapshoot. Juries are unpredictable and video evidence is no slam dunk." His gaze grew ponderous. "He has stones coming back here. I don't like it."

"Me either."

"Don't let your guard down."

"No chance of that."

"Where's Jordan now?"

"Home with Mrs. Neal. I've added my address to patrol. A car will cruise by every hour."

Lars rolled his shoulders and nodded. "Okay," he said, and moved them back into the case. "You think he's involved with Esparza?"

The thought was stunning in its simplicity, and Nicole sat forward and chewed on it. "Prescription drugs and doctors is not a farfetched match."

"Add the Big Pharm companies . . . Maybe Benjamin continued his climb up the ladder."

"He had big dreams," Nicole said, and she knew Benjamin's work ethic—do enough and a tad bit more so that he looked committed, a team player, when all he really wanted to be was the captain. "Yeah," Nicole said. "Could be."

14

"**N**ueva Vida." Nicole spoke the words slowly and watched the doctor's reaction. Surprise made the muscles in his face stiffen. His eyes flared. His fingers pressed into the edge of the table. They sat in the interrogation room. Lars watched from the two-way mirror, and all of it was being recorded on video. "Your great discovery," she prompted.

"Yes. It will be great, for many, many people."

"What is it?"

"Can you imagine a world without cancer?" he posed. "I can. Cells that stop fighting each other and begin to champion each other instead? Yes, it's possible. It's probable. The reality is coming."

"You found the cure for cancer?" She knew there'd been many advances in the area, but it was still the number-one killer of Americans after heart disease.

For a moment, his face was animated. He opened his mouth to speak but then thought better of it, his daughter remembered. Grief stirred in his voice as he admitted, "I made an important discovery. More than one, actually. Science is like that. You find the right key and it opens many doors."

"Stop talking in riddles, Dr. Esparza."

"Not just cancer, Sheriff. Not just one disease, one life, one save," he assured her. "I found life in death. A way to heal without radiation, without chemotherapy. I have engineered the perfect cell. And I have replicated it outside the laboratory."

And pharmaceutical companies would be the biggest losers. Cancer was a billion-dollar business.

Nicole said as much to the doctor.

"It isn't good for them," he agreed. "Most of them."

She wondered how much life went for.

"You found a company who wanted to do business with you."

"More than one," he agreed. "I gave my notice at the hospital."

"Conflict of interest?"

"That, and the pay is better."

"Beatrice didn't like it."

What wasn't there to like about a cure for cancer? Selling it at a premium few could afford? The greed Joaquin had spoken of?

"My daughter would have made a better doctor than me," he said. "Did you know that? My Beatrice wanted to follow in my footsteps. AP classes in the sciences in ninth grade." His voice filled with pride. "She was set on it."

"Why better?"

"She was moved by matters of the heart."

"Unlike yourself, Dr. Esparza?"

"She was still young and hadn't developed balance. She didn't believe that life must be measured in degrees."

"That not all could be saved," Nicole posed.

"Exactly," he agreed.

"Beatrice was compassionate."

"Yes. To a fault."

"Explain that, please." Nicole sat back and folded her hands in her lap—settling in for the long version.

"If she didn't grow beyond her ideals, the medicine-for-all pledge she took, she would have squandered her talent in a free clinic in some barrio."

"Similar to the circumstances of your youth?"

He wasn't surprised by her observation. He didn't question or challenge it. He had waited in the box more than two hours and had probably wondered what his family was saying about him.

"Yes."

"And you didn't want Beatrice going there?"

"Absolutely not."

"Because you had climbed out of that black hole . . ."

His lips thinned, but his voice remained steady. "Beatrice was born in an American hospital. She was born a citizen; she didn't have to fight to become one. She knew nothing about having to struggle as an outsider."

"And it wasn't okay for her to want to reach a hand down into that hole and haul someone to their feet?"

"A person must climb out on their own, use their own quickness of mind and body, rely on their wits to truly appreciate where they land."

"Appreciate? Don't you mean contribute?" she asked.

"To society? Yes."

"And to family," Nicole pressed. "Isn't that the Esparza creed—contribute to the advancement of the family position?"

"It's a reasonable expectation," Esparza said.

"And you're never too young to do your part." She heard the challenge in her voice, and Esparza responded to it.

"You don't understand because you have no base of reference."

Nicole smiled into his insult. "The American caste system." She sat back. "I'm one of the forty-seven percent." Middle class.

He acknowledged her reality with a nod.

"And your position, Doctor?"

"Now or tomorrow?" he asked.

The smugness in his tone squirmed under Nicole's skin. She drew a breath to clear the irritation from her voice.

"Your contribution is that big? It will make a significant change in your family's standing? You will leave your mark on the world?"

He leaned forward, his fingers slipping from the edge of the table. His hands settled in his lap. His gaze became sharp, capable of puncturing a hole through stone. "Few people," he insisted, "will have done more."

Nicole felt his intensity. It escaped from his pores. It was suffocating. She drew a breath and eased her body back in the chair, and she smiled to indulge him.

"So you're right up there with Einstein and Ford?"

"My place is certain."

"And Beatrice?" She gentled her voice around the girl's name. "What was her contribution?"

"It would have been huge," he assured her. "But we will never know it now."

The last word fell like a coin down a wishing well, tumbling and flashing until swallowed by the darkness. She let the silence stretch until she was sure he felt the possibility of an endless drop.

"How did you replicate this cell outside the laboratory?" she asked.

His breath hit his teeth, a sudden, choppy stream of air. Only then did she realize he'd been holding it. "That is not public knowledge," he said.

"Beatrice was involved in that, wasn't she?"

"She was helpful."

"Helpful?" Nicole chided. "She was more than that. She was *it*. Walking, talking proof that your discovery worked, or didn't."

"You're suggesting I used my daughter as a test subject, but that's not possible."

"Because she didn't have cancer?"

"Because it is against the rules, of medicine and of common decency."

"You don't play by the rules, Dr. Esparza. Rules frustrate you." Joaquin had described a sudden transcendence: Esparza had been ruing his limitations one day, boasting about his achievements the next. No middle ground. No time balanced on the edge of possibility. "You cheated the system, didn't you, Dr. Esparza?"

He opened his hands in offering. "Think what you will," he invited.

"Your daughter was proof of your cheating."

He didn't comment. No swift denial. No flicker of offense in his expression. He stared beyond Nicole's shoulder and studied the wall.

"What function did she perform for you, Dr. Esparza? What contribution did she make to your discovery? Because she did something, gave something—along with her life—to Nueva Vida."

"She did, and she will be publicly honored for it. Everyone will know my daughter's name. I will make sure of it."

"I don't think Beatrice would like that." Nicole leaned forward and tapped her pencil against the table. "You see, I've learned a lot about Beatrice in the past"—she gazed at the clock on the wall, just over Esparza's left shoulder—"eleven hours, and one thing everyone seems to agree on, you included, is that Beatrice didn't care about glory. She cared about people."

"I do as well."

"But not everyone will benefit from your work," Nicole posed. "With one company holding a monopoly on . . . this super cell . . . it will go only to those who can afford it. True?"

"At first."

"Beatrice hated you for that."

"She did not hate me. We disagreed."

"What is the exact nature of your discovery, Dr. Esparza?"

He shook his head. "That will come to light at the right time."

"How did Beatrice become involved in it?"

"Curiosity," he said. "She would not leave me alone about it. She wanted to be a part of it," he insisted.

"So you let her?"

"Eventually, yes."

"In what capacity?" Circuitous questioning. The verbal equivalent of the battering ram. If she asked enough times, he would eventually say more than he wanted to. She waited and watched his shoulders give a little, his wrists weaken so that his hands fell away from the table and into his lap.

"She made the ultimate sacrifice," he said. "Like you said, she died for it."

"You're lying."

"That's an occupational hazard," Esparza pointed out. "The police always think people are lying. You also believe there's nobility in the pursuit of justice, but I doubt you recognize there's also futility."

"Something went wrong with the proofing, didn't it, Dr. Esparza?" He blinked and drew in a breath that bottled in his septum with a delicate purl. "Yeah, we know about that," Nicole confirmed. "Your round table. But it didn't go as planned, and Beatrice was upset. She called her mom, crying. She asked her to come pick her up. Not you. Your wife, but definitely not you."

"Beatrice loved me."

"Your wife told me she went looking for Beatrice and that she called you." Nicole leaned forward. "Seven times."

The doctor remained silent.

"She was frantic."

"She had no reason to be," he returned smoothly.

"You can say that? Even now?"

"Someone murdered Beatrice. My cure did not kill her."

"I think it did. But we'll know for sure when we take a look at your lab and your notes, when the autopsy on Beatrice's body is complete. So why don't you just tell us, Dr. Esparza? What was Beatrice's involvement with your super cell? What did you do to her? Kill her or cure her?"

"The world will see the contribution was worth the personal sacrifice."

"You confessed to killing your daughter. We can subpoena the information."

The tension in his features eased. His lips turned upward just slightly. Smug, but he probably didn't think so. He lifted a hand and tapped the side of his head. "The information you seek—it's all up here. How do you subpoena that?"

"You must have it written down somewhere."

"You may or may not think so."

"Who did you sell it to, Dr. Esparza?"

"You speak of it as a done deal."

"It's not?"

He shook his head. "Have you heard the term *silent auction*?"

"There's a bidding war going on?"

"It takes only the interest of one of the Big Six to draw the interest of the others."

"They got a whiff of the wind," Nicole said. "They knew change was coming. That it could destroy their companies if they weren't a part of it." She folded her hands on the table and looked him in the eye. "That placed you, and your family, in a very powerful yet very dangerous position."

"Montgomery had it worse." He ran his fingers along the edge of the table, watched them. "His home was broken into many times, his lab even more. He was followed, 'invited' to clandestine meetings—attendance mandatory, of course. His life was threatened daily. He collected the notes that detailed his demise and mailed them to a former student. He died two days later. A witness said he walked fully clothed—topcoat and trench boots—into Lake Ontario."

"Why are you telling me this?"

"I took precautions." He looked up and smiled at her. His lips were weak and trembled. "I made it known. Do you know what a Chinese puzzle box is? You must slide the tiles in a specific pattern in order to unlock the deepest recesses of the box. That is where I stored my knowledge." He tapped his head again.

"Then why is Beatrice dead?"

"I trusted, for the wrong reasons."

"Did someone try to get to you through your daughter?"

"No, Sheriff. My daughter wasn't for sale."

Lars entered the room then. He stood behind Nicole's chair and stared down at Dr. Esparza.

"You talk of your daughter as a saint."

"I loved her."

"You nailed her to the cross," Lars corrected.

The words caused a ripple of unease to move across the doctor's face, but he said nothing. Lars walked around the table and sat down on the edge of it, close enough to Esparza to really make him feel small.

"The chairlift operator remembers you, Dr. Esparza. He confirms your participation in the moonlight run."

"I didn't lie about it."

"Well, you did, didn't you? You were on the mountain thirty minutes tops. One run. Up the lift, then down the mountain. That stood out with the lift operator because he saw less of you last night than any other night. Your usual? Four runs. So where were you the rest of the time?"

The doctor leaned into the little space between them and opened his mouth to speak, but Lars raised a hand.

"And your wife lied about it too. She was covering for you. Why?"

Lars pulled a notebook from his shirt pocket and leaned back to catch the overhead light. He read his notes, then lowered the book. "You had an alibi. You both did. And convenient, too, that it was each other. But your wife flushed hers, and in doing so, yours as well.

"You went to the moonlight run, but you were done by nine o'clock. And that leaves a lot of empty time on the clock. In fact, that gives you opportunity." Lars stuck him with his eyes. "Where were you?"

Esparza didn't answer.

"Let's move on to another lie, then," Lars suggested.

Nicole agreed. "Augmentin. We did a little research, Dr. Esparza, and found out two very helpful pieces of information. First, oncology frequently prescribes the medication. It's used for skin sores and lesions, such as a patient would develop during a course of chemotherapy. Did you forget about that?"

"I haven't had much use for the medication," Esparza returned, but Nicole could see fissures in his stoic facial expression.

"Second, children often outgrow their allergic reaction to penicillin."

"And some children who react to penicillin don't to Augmentin," Lars continued.

"Why did Beatrice need the Augmentin? At a dose"—Nicole clarified—"that is within normal parameters for a child cancer patient?"

"Did you ask my wife?" Esparza suggested. "She cares for the children when they're sick."

Esparza's muscles were pulled so tight that his back wasn't touching the chair.

Nicole leveled her gaze on Dr. Esparza. "The moonlight run skirts Lake Maria. It brought you close to where we found your daughter. Were you there, Dr. Esparza? Did you watch your daughter take her last breath? Do you know who killed her?"

"No." The admission released a set of slowly tracking tears.

"Why did you confess? Who are you trying to protect?"

His lips trembled then, and his chin wrinkled with an attempt to maintain some control.

"I don't know."

15

Benjamin carried two cell phones this trip, his personal and one that all the players in the game could call. The auction was digital, and no one was certain who was participating. They could only guess. As the auctioneer, Benjamin knew them all. He had a personal favorite, and it wasn't the woman paying him three million dollars for inside consideration. He wasn't new to this. Geneva Sanders would gladly slice him down the middle and leave him for dead, so she had paid up front, the full monty. And Benjamin, being the superior planner and with a lust for sweet revenge, had made an annotation to his will before leaving Atlanta. He had named Nicole beneficiary to that bundle of money should something happen to him. And he had left specific instructions so that she would know exactly how the money had been garnered, the when and where. It would forever be tied to the death of their son.

It was fortuitous that Blue Mesa had its very own turbine farm. There was something about wind that set his sails. The sheer force of it, probably. The ability to harness it, certainly. Few people could. Not without the help of canvas or fuselage. And he had paid well for the right information. Benjamin was the kind of guy who liked to make an exit. An exclamation point, that's what he was. Only this time, it would act as a sword as he cut Nicole's world to ribbons.

The phone rang again, and Geneva Sanders's name scrolled across the screen. Benjamin continued to ignore it. All work and no play was never his way. Now that was an epitaph. He'd have to remember that.

There was a knock at his car window then, and this startled Benjamin. He'd always been an avid daydreamer. It was his escape but also his place of greatest creativity.

He jerked his head back and turned toward the sound of rapping knuckles. He'd had the engine turned off for more than a few minutes, and the cold air was collecting on the glass. Still, he could make out the face and uniform of a Toole County sheriff's deputy. Benjamin turned the key just enough to roll down the window.

"Problem, sir?"

"Check-engine light," Benjamin said. "It's a rental, so no telling what kind of miles were put on it. Thought I'd let it rest a bit."

"There are better places for it," the officer recommended. Behind him, the blades of the turbines spun, and the air was choppy and rocked both the officer and the SUV.

"I don't know a lot about cars," Benjamin said. "Do you think it'd make it back to the hotel?" Benjamin named the resort he was staying at, and he had the parking tag hanging from the rearview mirror as proof.

"That's just another few miles," the officer said. "Unless you're out of oil or radiator fluid, you should be good to go."

"Topped off this morning," Benjamin assured him.

Another gust of wind swept through the fields and blasted them.

"That's some wind farm you have there."

"Yeah, but not without its trouble," the officer said.

"Oh?" Benjamin returned. "I don't like the sound of that." Though really his heart was doing cartwheels just thinking about what he could do with just a pocketful of that power.

"Turn the engine," the officer suggested, and Benjamin did. They both peered at the dash, waiting for a red warning light that wasn't going to show.

"Guess she's ready to go," Benjamin said.

The officer nodded. He gave Benjamin a considering look. "I'll follow you," he said. "A mile or so, to make sure you're good."

Benjamin expressed his appreciation. Window closed and back on the road, he laughed at the sweet irony as he led one of Nicole's finest away from the scene of what would be their son's untimely death.

*　*　*

They gave Esparza a moment to compose himself. They gave him a bottle of water and a box of tissue and space. But they had their limits. They wanted a viable conversation with the doctor, and they needed him responsive. Inside five minutes, Nicole was back in her chair, not rubbing knees with Esparza but close.

"Your wife called you last night," Nicole began.

"Yes, much later in the evening."

"Did she know Beatrice was dead?"

"She knew something terrible had happened."

"Because Beatrice had called her?"

"Yes. And because Beatrice was hysterical. My daughter was at times unreasonable. Theatrical, even, but she was never hysterical."

"And what did you do?"

"Nothing."

"I don't believe that."

His gaze distant, he crossed his arms and leaned back against the chair. "My wife called me seven times. Beatrice and Joaquin ordered cable and brewed hot chocolate in the coffeemaker. My sweet little ones have colds. My discovery, it will change the world."

His voice was an even monotone, no pitch but distant. The doctor was slipping away.

"What is that?" Lars asked. "Are you recapping events, or are you reciting your lines?"

Esparza didn't answer. Nicole watched his body vibrate as a tremor ran through him.

The man had lost his daughter and possibly his career. And he'd had a hand in their demise, Nicole was sure of it.

She needed to pull him back and reached for the large envelope on the table. She opened the flap and let Beatrice's cell phone slide out onto the table. It had been processed for fingerprints, and a backup had been made of all the data. The techs were at work tracing numbers, looking for image matches in the cyber world of Beatrice's extensive photo gallery. One image in particular. Nicole held the phone in her hand and pushed a few buttons, then turned the screen so that the doctor could see it.

"Who is this man, Dr. Esparza?"

The photo was the one of Beatrice snuggled up to the side of a man her father's age. She was smiling. The man's hand curved around Beatrice's side, resting in the innocuous dip at her waist.

"A colleague," he replied.

"He a touchy-feely kind of guy?" she asked.

"He's a doctor and handles himself with decorum."

Nicole turned the phone so that Lars could see the photo. He shook his head and eyed the doctor.

"I have a daughter myself. She's fifteen. And that picture makes me uncomfortable." He jerked his chin toward the phone. "Who is he? A name this time."

"Why? This photo was taken at a family gathering. We were celebrating Bea's graduation from junior high. That has nothing to do with my work."

"Then you won't mind telling us his name," Nicole pushed.

"He a close friend?" Lars asked. "You said family gathering, and Beatrice's graduation from eighth grade is certainly an important moment but not a real ticket seller."

"He is close, yes."

"Beatrice seemed to know the man. Quite well," Nicole pointed out.

"Look at her," the doctor implored. "She is happy. Beaming with it. Why involve my work in this?"

"But you said this was family," Lars challenged. He glanced at the cell phone, now sitting on the table between them. The man with Beatrice was younger than Esparza, but not by much. He was Caucasian, with dark hair just starting to go silver at the temples.

"It is both."

"Who prescribed your daughter Augmentin?" Nicole pressed.

"Someone who doesn't know her very well," Dr. Esparza returned. "But Beatrice didn't take it."

"She was compassionate but not foolish?" Nicole asked. Esparza's thinking was like a puzzle, and he was spilling the pieces onto the table. It was her job to build the edges, turn the pieces, and make them all fit.

"There's a difference, and she was growing. Her mind and her emotions maturing."

"And she was bound to turn your way."

Esparza nodded. The act was curt, singular, like a period at the end of a sentence. It held arrogance and pride. But not hope.

Nicole shifted gears.

"Is it easy to put another doctor's name on a prescription?"

"It is one minute at the computer."

"A computer in your office?"

He nodded.

"We won't arrest you for the murder of your daughter," Nicole began. "We don't have enough evidence for that. But we can arrest you for obstructing justice. And we'll find out who he is anyway. We always do."

"And when that happens, we'll look at him hard," Lars said. "*Interfere* and *involve* won't come close to describing the scrutiny we'll put this man through."

"And we'll do it because you tried so hard to hide him."

"We don't like secrets, Dr. Esparza," Lars pointed out. "We like answers. That's how we measure your willingness to cooperate. By the swiftness and accuracy of your answers. And time is running out on this one." Lars looked at his watch.

"Our tech guys will score a match sooner than later," Nicole confirmed.

"You're right," the doctor said. "Beatrice was not in favor of my recent decisions. She didn't understand them." He lifted his hands in frustration. "How could she? She was a child."

"You're referring to the sale of your research to the highest bidder?" Lars pressed.

"Yes."

"Who's the highest bidder?" Nicole pursued. "Is it this man? Is that why you're working so hard to keep him out of this?"

"He's a possibility," the doctor allowed.

Lars's cell phone chirped. He looked at the doctor. "What do you want to bet that's the name we've been looking for?"

Esparza's lips thinned, and a white ring rose up around them.

Lars nodded. "So be it." He pulled his cell from his pocket, but before he could answer it, the doctor spoke up.

"Dr. Michael King."

Lars pressed answer and spoke into the phone. He murmured a few words in response and stood up, pacing away from the table. The doctor watched him go.

"Your daughter didn't come back from Christmas dinner, did she, Dr. Esparza?"

"She went to a party," he confirmed. His face was beginning to show the stress, fracturing in places so that Nicole could see the fear and ruin running beneath his skin.

"Sofia and Isla too," Nicole continued. "They went to the party, didn't they?"

Esparza nodded. He paled, and the tremor she'd noticed earlier turned into a strumming. Nicole heard his teeth clack together and watched his elbows and knees twitch.

"Dr. King," he whispered. "He had a small party. A few girls over to spend time with his daughter. She isn't like our daughters. Not as capable. She has a neurodegenerative condition. It's a slow deterioration of mind and body. She is wheelchair bound and has the intellect of a six-year-old child."

"Dr. King is here? In town?"

"She wanted a slumber party. For Christmas. A kid like her, he said, didn't get a lot of invites. And not a lot of girls RSVP'd. That's what he said. Could Beatrice do their hair, their nails? That's what he wanted, for his daughter, a small slice of normal."

"Where is Dr. King staying?" she persisted. "Dr. Esparza?"

"It was the only wish in her letter to Santa." He opened his hands and laid them on the table, searching his palms for some clue into the future. "Beatrice volunteered for the job. She wanted to do it. She was drawn to kids like that. Kids who are different.

"They wore fancy dresses, and Beatrice did their hair in ringlets and rhinestones."

"Where are they?" Nicole demanded. She felt her heart race, the breath wispy in her throat. Esparza was unraveling. She didn't want that to happen with the information still locked inside him. "Where are your daughters, Dr. Esparza?"

"Dress-up. Hair and makeup. All little-girl things to do. Disney movies and popcorn. That was on the agenda. I asked, you know? That's what a parent does. A good parent asks, and I did."

Nicole sat forward and snapped her fingers two inches from the doctor's nose. He blinked and his eyes cleared. His lips trembled.

"Where are your daughters?"

He looked up, and this time his eyes were searching, imploring.

"He has them. But he's promised to return them unharmed."

16

D r. Michael King did not exist. Nicole had used a wide age range in her search, tapped into the Social Security database, and culled 1,117 Michael Kings with assorted middle names living in the United States. Of those, seventeen were doctors. None of them resided in or owned property in the state of Montana. Nicole had an officer working phone and internet. So far, none of the images produced matched the photo on the victim's cell phone. Nicole had reached across the border and asked for a similar search, with particular interest in the province of Alberta. Communication between the United States and Canada was historically a slow process, so Nicole didn't break her stride—she next charted territories for the search teams that were already assembling. A kidnapping brought with it an urgency that was universal among law enforcement agencies. Nicole had offers of manpower and equipment coming from as far afield as Texas, Florida, and New York. There was a protocol in place, one Nicole knew to work—she pulled from the agencies closest and kept the others on the back burner to dip into as necessary. An aerial approach would do nothing for them at this point, so she kept the helicopters grounded.

She'd left Esparza in the box with a deputy, allowing him to stew in silence, but returned for one more pass before she left the station and took her position in the search.

Esparza's face assumed a stillness that she was beginning to recognize. He was a man searching frantically for the seams of the nightmare that had engulfed his life. If given the opportunity, he would peel back the canvas and step into a new reality.

One where he starred as the celebrated doctor and scientist. Where his beautiful daughter stood beside him, but off-center. The proud prodigy. The indulgent father.

"When did you start to worry?"

"I didn't," Esparza admitted. "I was there, at King's. That's not protocol, and I had to leave before the proofing began, but I met and mingled with some of the bidders. Two had come in person; the others joined by conference call."

"You saw your daughters?" Nicole pressed. "Sofia and Isla?"

"Yes, and Beatrice too, but she would have none of me. She had agreed to the party the night before but not to the round table."

Nicole heard the door behind her open, and Lars step in.

"The party was a way to get Beatrice to the proofing?" Nicole asked.

"Yes, but it was for King's daughter too."

"And once Beatrice was there, she couldn't leave," Lars said.

"That's right," Dr. Esparza agreed. "It was the only way to get Beatrice to the proofing."

"Because she was no longer agreeable," Nicole pursued. "Beatrice refused to cooperate."

"Yes."

"Because once you accepted an offer, Nueva Vida would become a top-shelf cure."

"It would trickle down, but slowly," Dr. Esparza explained. "First available only to the wealthiest."

Silence.

"So maybe you're right. Maybe Beatrice did hate me."

"And this was all last night? Christmas night?" Lars asked.

"You were at King's last night, and each of your daughters were present?" Nicole pressed.

"Yes, last night. But I left at nine forty. I had to. King and Gatling, they would take a tissue sample from Beatrice, package it, and transfer it to the lab. And Beatrice's job was done.

"Soft-tissue sarcoma," he explained. "Healthy cells have uniformity. Cancer cells are bigger or smaller, and no two ever look the same."

"Thanks for the lesson, Doc—" Lars began, but Esparza ignored the intrusion.

"But it didn't go down that way. King didn't wait. Why would he? His daughter is dying. He split the sample, after I left. I'm sure of it. One look through the microscope and he would know."

"Know what?" Lars demanded.

Esparza looked up and regarded them mildly. "Beatrice didn't have cancer."

"And she should have?"

"That would have been ideal."

"Why?"

But Esparza wasn't finished with his train of thought. "And then I left. King said I should go, and I did. That's how transactions of this type are carried out. The principal player isn't allowed near the live tissue sample."

"You left without your children?"

"Yes."

"Why?"

"King insisted." The words left a gaping wound in Esparza. In them, he saw and acknowledged his inadequacies. His chin trembled, and liquid welled in his eyes. "I left my children but took Nueva Vida with me."

"Why did Beatrice need to have cancer?" Lars asked.

"So I could cure her, of course." He sniffed and brought a tissue to his nose.

"How would King and Gatling get a sample from Beatrice if she wasn't willing?" Nicole asked.

"We're doctors," he said. "There are ways of safely assuring compliance."

"Rohypnol?" Lars asked.

"Yes," Dr. Esparza said. "That is one way."

"Did King or Gatling have Rohypnol at their disposal?"

"King. He had everything at his fingertips."

"And you saw this? The Rohypnol?"

"Last night? No."

"Because you left?"

"Yes."

"In fact, you don't even know if King got the sample."

Or if a crime had been committed. So far, Esparza had given them nothing to incriminate himself beyond bad intentions and poor parenting, and neither was a cause for arrest.

"I am only guessing, but it's a good guess."

"Doctor." Nicole called for his attention. "You need to tell us. Where is King staying?"

"I told you, I don't know. He sent a car. It was dark, and I sat in back."

"You must have seen something. Anything that would give us direction."

Esparza considered her words, and his eyes cleared as he thought back to the night before. "It was on the lake. More than a mile from town, no more than three." He nodded. "Yes, I'm sure of that."

Nicole sent Lars out with orders to change the perimeter of their search. Then she sat down opposite Esparza.

"You have an opportunity to help," she said. "It's too late for Beatrice, but maybe not Sofia and Isla."

He considered her words, and they strengthened him. "What do you want to know?"

"How long have you known King?"

"Two years in February."

"How did you find him?"

"He found me," the doctor revealed. "I put it out there. I let the community know I was close, that I had the breakthrough at hand, the one I've been working toward my entire career, and they came knocking."

"By *they*, you mean the pharmaceutical companies?"

"Yes, the Big Six. And a few others, smaller companies wanting to become giants."

"Company names," she demanded.

He listed them, and Nicole recognized most of them.

"These are reputable companies," she said.

"Of course."

"Is Dr. King affiliated with one of them?"

"Yes."

Esparza named the company, Magellan, and Nicole felt her confusion deepen, because she knew the name. She knew Magellan was a trusted company, but she made a mental note to make contact herself.

"What is his position within the company? He must be pretty high up if he's calling all the shots."

"Chief executive officer."

"And is that the norm? Send the CEO to broker the deal?"

Esparza shook his head. "It's a team approach, usually. The CEO and their top scientists arrive, determine validity, and if they're encouraged, incentives are doled out accordingly. After that, I would be introduced to the board, tour the facilities where I would be working, and meet their in-house scientists."

"But with Magellan it was different?"

"It was all King, all the time."

"Why?"

"He made himself the point man. And he's the boss."

"Have you toured Magellan?"

"Yes."

"Met with the scientists?"

"The initial pass. I presented, they listened, and they were intrigued. Then King and I got to work. But the official meet and greet, that doesn't come until they put their name in the hat. Tender a serious offer. And I accept."

She passed a pad and pen to the doctor. "The company's headquarters. Their physical address, phone number. And King's cell number too."

She pushed back her chair and stood over the doctor. She waited until he could stand the weight of her gaze on him no longer and looked up.

"How much?" she asked.

"Bidding closed at midnight," he said.

Maybe at the precise moment Beatrice Esparza had lost her life. How much had she been worth, Nicole wondered. "The price?"

"Fifty-five million." A cold chunk of change.

"Did you accept?"

"I have until nine o'clock this evening to decide."

"What are you waiting for?"

"My children."

"Was King the highest bidder?"

"No."

"Why?"

"He can only offer what the board agrees upon. He came up short, and it was significant."

"And what does that mean to a man like King? Losing you and your discovery after he'd invested so much of his time and resources?"

"It was as much personal as professional for King. Maybe more so."

"Because his daughter needs what you have?"

"Yes. And she needs it now."

"Before FDA approval?"

"Now," Esparza repeated.

"And because you'd used your breakthrough on your own daughter, King thought you would use it on his?"

Esparza ignored her assertion. "He planned to appeal the trial design requirements and open an early phase of clinical studies that would include his daughter."

"Is that done?"

"Often. More so with cellular and gene therapy products than with drugs."

"So he had a reasonable chance of success?"

He nodded. "The FDA is pliable."

"This is a kidnapping, Dr. Esparza. Your daughters for the cure. That's how we're working it." Nicole pushed the notebook closer to Esparza's hand. "You're staying here," she said. "We have a tactical team searching for your wife and son and a trained negotiator on his way from Missoula. We're preparing a search of the vacation homes along the lake."

They were starting narrow and close—all homes within a mile of where Beatrice's body had been found. That put them in the middle of the grid, according to the parameters Esparza had given them.

"The highest bidder," Nicole said, and nodded toward the pen and notebook. "Company name. CEO. Anything else we should know about them."

He started writing, and Nicole strode toward the door but stopped and looked back at Esparza.

"Did King kill Beatrice?"

He looked up but shook his head. "She was his only hope."

17

They made use of snowmobiles and snowshoes, horseback and four-wheel drive. The new snowfall measured four and a quarter inches—any remaining evidence at their crime scene was buried. The tracks leading them to Beatrice's body were no longer viable. The time on the clock was running thin. King had had the girls nearing twenty-four hours. Numbers showed them that the victims of kidnapping rarely survived to first light.

Civilian volunteers traveled in pairs with instructions not to pursue. If a knock wasn't answered in a home clearly occupied, they were to report it by radio and move on. If the door was opened to a man resembling the photo of Dr. King, they were to issue an invitation to that evening's choral presentation of *The Night Before Christmas*. Show no surprise, no recognition, no fear. The small group of citizens culled for the job were trained military or first responders. There were twenty-four of them, mostly men, many of them retired. Law enforcement worked solo. Nicole borrowed from local and regional departments until she had a total of thirty-eight parties on the search. They fanned out from the Lake Road, a point parallel to their crime scene, and moved east, away from town and into the suburban tracts from which Beatrice had most likely fled. Several homes were known to be empty, the windows dark and the driveways neither plowed nor shoveled in several snows. They checked those off and moved them to a list of least likely. The homes where lights blazed but there had been no answer to the knocking of the searchers, she made her priority. And while she searched, she thought.

Beatrice Esparza running, chased and brought to a stop on Lake Maria. The killer taller than Beatrice. He had lifted her off her feet and looked into the girl's eyes as she died. Killer and watcher . . . male and female . . . it seemed most likely from the prints left behind. Evasion, lies, once-tight alibis rendered useless.

Dr. Esparza. Joaquin. Mrs. Esparza. They'd each had motive and opportunity. And at that moment, techs were measuring shoes in the Esparzas' hotel room. UGGs had been found—size eight—belonging to Alma Esparza. But there were probably a hundred more pairs fitting the evidence in hotels scattered around Blue Mesa.

Was Alma Esparza the watcher? It didn't hurt Nicole to think so.

Or maybe Joaquin, cast into the shadow of his sister, the shining star, had tired of being overlooked and underappreciated? Of being—though the eldest—held in constant comparison to a little sister who did every-thing better? Jealous, enraged, and broken, had Joaquin eliminated the source of his pain?

Or had Dr. Esparza killed his daughter, his discovery and all it prom-ised lost when Beatrice refused to cooperate?

Michael King had access to roofies, but with his daughter's life on the line, he'd had every reason to keep their victim alive. Beatrice had been a live link to a cure. But if the man had been angered at being locked out of the bidding war and lost his cool, it was possible he had murdered Beatrice.

And if he had killed Beatrice, what of the youngest Esparzas? Were the girls still alive?

Nicole received yet another report of lights on, no answer, and turned the Yukon north. She traveled the Lake Road half a mile and parked in the street, engine idling as she slid from behind the wheel and regarded the house. Small, but perched atop a small rise with the front windows facing the frozen sheet of Lake Maria. The home had an unobstructed view of the lake, rare with the road passing between them. Nicole knew the house was a rental, a two-bedroom, single-bath, which made it low-budget when it came to tourist choices—still, it rented weekly for what Nicole paid out monthly on her mortgage. It never stood empty during ski or summer season.

This wasn't the place. It was too small for a man of King's stature, too open, and it lacked the feel of a crime scene. Still, she walked up the shov-eled path and rang the bell.

She heard movement, a shuffling of feet. The tread wasn't heavy, and she thought there were probably children behind the closed door.

"It's Sheriff Cobain," she announced, tapping the star pinned to her jacket just below her left shoulder. "It's okay to open the door." She was greeted with silence. "Look," she tried, "I'm going to step back so you can see me from the front window." She did so and removed her department cap so that her hair, mussed from the wool but still in its ponytail, was visible and her overall look less threatening. She was in uniform now, but she held up her arm and turned toward the street, where the Yukon stood in the gray afternoon, light bar turning and exhaust pluming at the back. "That's my police cruiser." She tapped her left shoulder. "This is my badge. That's a gold star." The metal was cold, even through her glove. "I just need to make sure you're okay, and I need to see you and talk to you to do that."

Nicole watched a small face appear behind the window closest to the front door. Girl age eleven or twelve. Her top teeth sawed at her bottom lip and her eyes were flared, alert, moving over Nicole and the Yukon. Another child appeared beside her—male, maybe eight years old. The girl pushed him back. Nicole waved to her.

"Are your parents skiing?" she tried.

The girl didn't answer. The boy reappeared, smiling, and waved to Nicole.

"It looks like your parents prepared you well. Don't answer the door. Don't talk to strangers. I appreciate that. It makes you safer and my job easier."

The girl didn't crack, and the standoff was showing no signs of abating when Nicole noticed a white Subaru moving toward them, headlights on and defrosters pushing back the condensation on the windshield. It fishtailed slightly on the icy road, probably speed sparked from the flashing lights in front of the driver's home. It turned into the driveway, and a man stepped from the car before the engine was cut.

"What's wrong?"

He was tall, and his stride quickly ate up the distance between them. A woman scrambled from the car behind him and ran toward them.

Nicole held up her hands in a calming gesture. "Nothing is wrong," she promised. She even smiled a little as she said, "Your kids look fine, from where I stand." She indicated the front window where both children now stood, the boy bouncing on his toes, the girl relieved.

"They're your children?"

"Yes. Yes," the mother assured Nicole, and headed to the door.

Nicole followed, the father beside her. "I'm Sheriff Nicole Cobain, Toole County." she explained. "We're searching the area for two children." Missing children always softened people, and she felt the tension in the man's body slowly ease. "House to house along the lakefront. When your kids didn't answer the door for the first team I rolled out."

The mother had the front door open, and the boy rushed her. The girl allowed her mother to pull her in close.

"You guys okay?" the father asked. He stepped onto the front porch and held the door open so he could take a look at his children. The boy smiled at him and asked if he'd conquered the mountain.

"There are missing children?" the mother asked, turning to glance at Nicole.

"Yes, two girls, ages eight and ten."

The mother's face contracted, and the father looked out across the rolling hills and the wide expanse of the lake.

"How long?"

"Close to twenty-four hours."

His expression turned incredulous. "Impossible," he said. "You must know the rate of exposure and human mortality. If they've been outside this whole time—"

"We believe they've been indoors," Nicole said. "What do you know about exposure rates, Mr. . . . ?"

His lips thinned, the corner of one turning in as he chewed on it, but his gaze was level, considering. "Doctor," he corrected. "Dr. Martin Gatling. And left outdoors, the children could have survived six to eight hours in these weather conditions—with the usual winter clothing."

She felt the lock turn and the tumblers fall into place. Gatling. She had connected a dot.

"What kind of doctor are you, if you don't mind my asking?"

"My specialty is nuclear medicine."

Nicole had never heard of such a thing. She applied nuclear to two things—weapons and family—and she was pretty sure most ordinary people did as well.

She let her confusion ripple across her brow. "What is that?"

"I serve a very narrow field within the bigger scope of the discipline," he said. "Nuclear medicine is most often used to assess the presence of malignancy rather than biopsy for it."

"How is that done?"

"Instrumentation and radiopharmaceuticals." He tried to redirect her, "You said you were looking for two little girls."

She ignored his question. "Do you know Dr. Enrique Esparza?"

"Of course," Gatling replied. "He and his daughter—they're the reason we're here. Short notice too. Three days, and at Christmas."

Nicole felt her pulse kick up a notch.

"Who do you work for, Dr. Gatling?"

"Magellan Pharmaceuticals."

Ding. Another dot connected.

"And your supervisor is?"

"Why do you ask?"

"Is your supervisor Dr. Michael King?"

"Yes."

"Do you know him by any other name?"

"Other name?" His tone twisted with annoyance. "No. Why would I?"

"We believe Dr. King is keeping the children. The two missing girls, they're the daughters of Dr. and Mrs. Esparza."

18

Nicole was seated in the small kitchen of the home the Gatlings had rented at a moment's notice per the demand of Dr. Gatling's immediate supervisor, Dr. Michael King. Mrs. Gatling was brewing coffee. She looked out the window, her fingertips drumming on the granite countertop. Nicole watched her profile. The women's lips moved while she thought, sometimes shaping words, other times knotting while she frowned. She was a woman with something to say, but who worried about her words. Nicole hoped the silence would trouble her more. The doctor stood at the back door, removing his snow boots. He left them on the mat and walked to the table in his wool socks.

"Where is King staying?"

Gatling took his cell phone out of his pants pocket and began pushing numbers. "It's a big house, overlooks the lake." He found what he was looking for—a text—and read off the address to Nicole. "We were invited for Christmas dinner—" He snorted. "That was a fiasco."

Nicole took a moment and radioed the address to Lars. He and a wave of deputies were en route. She was familiar with the home. It even had a name—Big Horn—and was infamous in Blue Mesa, synonymous with waste and excess, an indulgence that threatened the natural environment.

Nicole was closer to it, just two minutes down the road from the Gatlings' rental, and she thought about leaving then and coming back for the interview. Heading out alone. But that would be stupidity. The grounds at Big Horn were wooded, the house nearly a fortress. And backup was on its way.

She clipped the radio at her shoulder and returned her attention to Dr. Gatling.

"A fiasco, you said. How so?"

"The guest list, for starters."

Mrs. Gatling spoke up then. She had turned to them and was leaning against the kitchen sink with her arms crossed over her stomach. "Dr. Esparza was there," she said. "And that was just one of the surprises."

"What was another?"

"Some guy named Benjamin and his lovely wife Charlene." Gatling's upper lip curled with the sarcasm in his voice.

Nicole felt her world tilt slightly. Benjamin and his wife, here in Blue Mesa, at the proofing. What was their involvement? She knew what Benjamin was capable of and added him and Charlene to the list of suspects.

"She wasn't lovely?"

"She was . . ." Nicole watched emotion flash across the doctor's face, but he finally settled on simple agreement. "No, she wasn't lovely, Sheriff. They were an odd couple. She stood about a foot taller than her husband, but he was definitely the alpha." He snorted at some private thought.

"Alpha?" That was an odd description, and she pressed Dr. Gatling for an explanation.

"He spoke and she barked," he said. Nicole felt her frown deepen, and he elaborated. "You know, something similar to the human-canine relationship."

Nicole raised an eyebrow.

"They wore matching identity bracelets," Mrs. Gatling added. "A cute idea, right? And they were beautiful. Platinum and jeweled, but not overdone. I asked her if I could take a closer look. That's when it got creepy."

"Creepy how?"

"She lifted her hand, and his came with it. You know what I mean? They were chained together. Like handcuffs. It took me by surprise. Martin says they're some kind of S and M thing. I laughed, because I was uncomfortable, and she smiled, but there was nothing funny about it."

It caused a stir of discomfort in Nicole too.

"Did she say anything?"

"She said, 'I belong to him.' After that we kept our distance."

"It was easy to do. We had our kids to look after and the house is pretty big," Dr. Gatling explained.

"How long have you worked with Dr. King?"

"Three years."

"And he's always been Dr. King?"

He paused, and Nicole could tell he was choosing his words carefully. "He's in a high-level position. He's the meet and greet. The detective and the charming host. And he has a mind for money and medicine."

"How does this connect to his name?"

He shook his head. "I would be surprised if King is his real name."

"Why?"

"They're chameleons. By job description, certainly, but they don't stay in one place too long. Turnover is high. They move on to another company. Maybe a start-up. Maybe a little fish that wants to swim in the big ocean. And change their names as it suits the circumstances."

"How long do people in King's position usually stay with a company?"

"Three to five years. Definitely no more than that."

Mrs. Gatling brought three mugs to the table and placed one in front of Nicole. She returned to the counter for the coffeepot and creamer, but she said over her shoulder, "And King has overstayed his welcome."

"Why do you say that?" Nicole probed.

Mrs. Gatling placed a pint of half-and-half on the table next to Nicole but said to her husband, "Tell her, Martin."

Dr. Gatling shrugged, discomfort in the movement. "He was going rogue. Maybe. Definitely he was extending himself beyond traditional expectations."

"In English," Nicole requested.

"King was working Esparza alone. He allowed liberties with our lab and equipment I've never seen before."

"Did he say why?"

Gatling shook his head. "But he was excited. King really thought they had something." He hesitated, and Nicole waited. "He needed it to be something," he confided. "Something big."

"Because that was all that would save his daughter?"

"Yes. You know about that, then." Nicole nodded, and he continued. "That was it. The reason I thought King was giving Esparza liberties—they have a kinship of sorts."

"They both have daughters who are sick," Mrs. Gatling said.

"And they were both desperate for a cure," he added.

And that gave King plenty of reason to want Beatrice alive.

"Why are you here in Montana?" Nicole asked. "Why now, with King and Esparza?"

"To close the deal. I'm called in at only two stages in the process—the initial, when the pitch is made, and at the close."

"You're the closer?"

"No. That's King. My job is black and white, no speculation. I point out strengths and reasonable concerns."

"What was Esparza's discovery?"

More hesitation. "I know it's something at the molecular level. Something that controls cellular regeneration, only more."

"You don't know the exact discovery?"

"No. No one does. No one except Esparza."

"How can a deal close without at least King knowing?"

"He's closed deals with less than what Esparza has already given him."

"So why the delay here?"

"There's reasonable doubt."

"What is it?"

He hedged. "I signed a confidentiality agreement," he told her. "Telling you more will require a warrant."

She felt her lips tighten but changed direction to keep the information flowing.

"How well did you know Beatrice Esparza?"

"Not well. Yet. We met at King's last night, but the girl bolted."

"Why?"

"King didn't say."

"It had something to do with those people," Mrs. Gatling said. "The odd couple. They talked to her. Upset her."

"It was like watching sharks in a fishbowl," Dr. Gatling agreed. He shook his head, and disgust thinned his lips. "They'd approach her, say a few words, and she'd take off. Dart over to her sisters or King's daughter."

"And they followed," Mrs. Gatling agreed. "And her father wasn't any help at all."

"He kept his distance from Beatrice," Dr. Gatling said. "And she from him. There was definitely friction between them."

"You don't know what it was?"

Gatling shook his head. "No. Esparza wasn't supposed to be at the proofing at all. Direct involvement is against protocol. I got the feeling he was keeping a tight hold on his daughter and she resented it."

"Was he friendly with Benjamin and Charlene?"

"He stuck with King, but he did introduce them to Beatrice," Mrs. Gatling said. Some thought twisted her lips, and she shivered delicately.

"What?" Nicole probed.

"Nothing. I just don't like those people."

"But there's something," Nicole persisted. "Something that disturbed you."

Mrs. Gatling shook her head but said, "She touched Beatrice. Put a hand on her shoulder and stroked her arm, all the way down to her wrist. She did it like, I don't know, like ownership or something. Like she was petting something pretty."

"I saw that too," Dr. Gatling agreed.

"What did Beatrice do?"

"She shook her off," Mrs. Gatling said, and there was a note of approval in her voice. "Then she went straight to King. She complained. I could tell, because her arms were orchestrating it—you know how teen girls can get into the role?"

Dr. Gatling nodded. "King was sympathetic. He spoke to them. To Esparza too. I don't know what King said, but Esparza was offended."

"Oh yeah," his wife agreed. "He got real uptight. The man is all about posture," she added. "You know, body language can bludgeon."

Nicole hadn't heard the expression before, but she understood it. "And Beatrice?"

"King took her out of the room. He was concerned, had his arm around her, and it looked like he was taking her upstairs. I thought maybe to a bedroom. The girl needed some rest and we needed a tissue sample."

"And Dr. Esparza left too?

"He made a grand exit," Mrs. Gatling confirmed. She picked up her cup of coffee and blew on the liquid. "Right after King took Beatrice upstairs."

"And the couple?"

"They stayed," Gatling reported. "But they made themselves scarce."

"But you definitely saw them again?"

They both nodded. Then Mrs. Gatling said, "But not together. Not until they left."

"Yeah, he must have set her loose," said Dr. Gatling. "For a while he roamed around the party alone. He spoke some to King. He was on his phone a lot. Stepped out of the room for a while too."

"I know, because I made sure he was nowhere near my daughter," Mrs. Gatling said.

"And the woman?"

"She was laying down upstairs," Gatling said. "Benjamin told King she was ill."

Nicole nodded. "Did you see Beatrice again after that?"

"No."

"But the woman, Charlene, you saw her later?"

Dr. Gatling nodded. "They left the same time we did. They had a car and driver, and Benjamin had her bundled up—" He shrugged. "Maybe she wasn't feeling well. Her face was flushed. She had the chills."

"When did you realize Beatrice was gone?"

Gatling thought about it. "About an hour after King took her upstairs. I asked him about her. I had to remind him I was there to do a job. He said to give her twenty more minutes and then he would check on her. And he did, but when he came back downstairs, it was without the girl."

"What did King say?"

"That she was gone. He didn't know where, and he was upset about it."

"And she didn't turn up. We left at eleven thirty." Mrs. Gatling's tone tightened with disapproval. "King wouldn't let us leave before that."

"Because we were supposed to start the proofing," Gatling said.

"And King thought Beatrice would be back?"

"Yes."

"Was the couple there for the proofing?"

"They were the neutral party. They were supposed to broker the deal."

"They knew that the moment of truth was upon Esparza?"

"Of course. We all knew it," Gatling replied.

"What would you have done with Beatrice? If she hadn't left?"

"Proven the presence of malignancy."

"So that Esparza could cure her?"

"Yes. And he was going to do it fast. In days rather than months. And better. No radiation. No surgical intervention."

"How?"

"He didn't say, but it could be done through the cath lab, so I thought maybe he'd invented some kind of nano-cell."

"Nano?" Nicole questioned.

"Small but mighty. We have a lot of them at our fingertips already, but none that can do what Esparza claims his can."

"Did it alarm you that Esparza used his daughter as a test subject?"

But Gatling shook his head. "No. He had FDA approval. I saw the paperwork myself. He had his daughter classified as a viable subject—that's what got our attention initially. Approval of that nature is hard to come by. It gave him credibility with us. But the girl had cancer, and that gave the whole project an edge of desperation. Her father developed the cure. He was sure of it. Or he was blinded by need. It was hard to tell which, because King kept a tight hold on this one."

"How do you know she had cancer?"

"It was in the paperwork."

"Did you confirm it? Run tests to prove its existence?"

"That wasn't necessary. Not at that point. His cure worked in the lab and would be tested on Beatrice. Just as soon as we proved the malignancy."

"The reason you're here."

"Exactly."

"And there's promise in his cure?"

"Definitely."

"King told you this?"

"Yes. Esparza too. I saw his lab notes—what he'd give to us, anyway. I went through them myself, checked and double-checked every detail. Esparza's documentation backs up his claim. I left our first meeting believing."

"You no longer believe?"

He shrugged. "If he had something, if it was genuine, then why haven't we begun the proofing?"

"And if the tissue sample showed no malignancy?"

That seemed to stump him. He was quiet for a moment as he processed Nicole's words and thought about all the implications.

"You mean, if Beatrice didn't have cancer?"

"Yes. What then?"

"End game," Gatling said. "Do not pass go. Do not collect two hundred dollars."

"There would be no deal?"

"Because there could be no deal."

Beatrice didn't have cancer. And even if Esparza had a cure, if his super cell existed and did everything Esparza claimed it did, with no viable way to prove it, he really had nothing. And yet the victim had been sick, multiple times. Sick and then cured in a deliberate cycle. Nicole had seen it for herself in the girl's sport diary. She'd heard it from Joaquin and the mother. Was it possible that Dr. Esparza had given his daughter cancer just to cure it? The thought raised the bile from Nicole's stomach.

"Have you ever known Michael King to be in possession of Rohypnol?"

The doctor's eyes flared, and his mouth tightened. "I've never seen him have it in hand."

"But he could get it?"

"Easily," he acknowledged.

"Beatrice had it in her system," she told him. "How do you think that happened?"

Gatling stood, and Nicole could see she'd insulted him. His body and mannerisms became stiff. His voice too. "I don't know. We don't medicate patients to get their compliance."

"It's a pretty common practice."

"In a hospital. Not in the lab. Testing is voluntarily or not at all."

Nicole nodded and accepted his answer, and then she let him have it. "Beatrice Esparza is dead, Dr. Gatling. She was murdered. Her body was discovered early this morning."

Mrs. Gatling stepped closer. Her arms tightened around her torso. Her body vibrated with tension.

"She's dead?"

"Yes, ma'am."

"Murdered?"

"Yes," Nicole confirmed.

"And you think it was King?" Dr. Gatling asked.

"Let's talk about Beatrice's sisters," Nicole suggested, redirecting the conversation. "You saw them at the party?"

"Yes. Sofia and Isla," Mrs. Gatling confirmed. "Little girls, younger than our daughter."

"Were they still at King's when you left?"

"Yes. Yes, they were sleeping over," Dr. Gatling explained.

"And the girls never made it home?" Mrs. Gatling paled and blinked rapidly to push back tears.

"No, ma'am. We think they're still with King."

"But why?" Dr. Gatling asked.

"You said it yourself: Dr. King went rogue. He has too much to lose. And Magellan wasn't the highest bidder for Dr. Esparza's super cell, was it?"

"No." Gatling shook his head. "We bid, because everyone agreed there was promise in Esparza's cure, but we came up short."

Nicole walked toward the back door, thinking ahead. Big Horn House was less than a mile up the road, hidden behind belts of forest. It was a fairly new construction built in tiers so that each level jutted out farther than the one below it. This placed the top floor over the surface of the water, with a large party deck that the owner and previous occupant had used to exhaustion. It'd caused trouble in the community, from blocked views to pollution and flotsam in the lake. Nicole had pulled champagne bottles and even fine china to shore and written more than a single fine for it, but a county permit existed, and even after the owner grew bored and left for finer climes, the home had been a popular rental.

"We'll want to talk to you again, Dr. Gatling."

"We're leaving Friday."

"Where is home?"

"Dillon."

Just south of Butte. Three hundred miles southwest of Blue Mesa.

"Magellan's home base is in Dillon?"

"No. It's a satellite lab and a few administrative offices."

"Why? Is that normal, keeping the lab separate from headquarters?"

"Most pharm companies have the same setup. HQ with its main lab, smaller labs lost in the boonies or the urban jungle."

"A secret location?"

But he shook his head. "Hard to find, but not completely off the map."

She moved toward the back door but paused long enough to connect with Mrs. Gatling. "Thank you, ma'am."

She didn't tell them she was sending a deputy their way. That Friday would come and go and the Gatlings would remain tucked in the small rental, material witnesses to the crimes of murder, kidnapping, and medical malpractice.

19

The snow caught in the headlights, a swirling dervish as the wind cut through the trees and swept the powder from the full branches. Benjamin loved pine and evergreen and fir. His favorite was the blue noble, which was often harvested in this area of the world. For the past five years he'd ordered one from Winter Haven Farms, in Columbia Falls, Montana, which was fifty-seven miles west on Route 2 from Blue Mesa. The tree had arrived on December 15th, and he and Charlene had hosted a tree-trimming party that next Saturday. Mulled cider and popcorn strings, ornaments of blown glass, and an angel for the top. He was a man who thrived on traditions but had to make them himself.

While he was disappointed in Nicole's home—it was small and ordinary, something lost in the blink of an eye—he was impressed with its location. He understood the need for solitude, that it was a place where problems were solved and new ideas birthed, but he wasn't able to sustain it long for himself. He needed to move, talk, have fun, and there wasn't any life in a held breath.

"We should move on."

The words came from the driver, and Benjamin knew them to be true. He paid well for the advice, but he didn't always like it. His eyes cut back to the house, perched on a small, rolling hill, and he wondered if wildflowers grew in the fields around it in the short summers. Did Nicole keep a garden? Did Jordan? Benjamin had always wanted that. A small vegetable garden. But once he had it, he'd found that he was not suited for the work. The most he did now was watch from the second-story window as Rico weeded and harvested, loading tomatoes and broccoli and romaine into the cook's woven basket.

"Yes," Benjamin agreed.

Nicole wasn't home. The driver had a portable police scanner, and there was chatter about a murder out on one of the lakes. A kid. It was amazing, how slow the police were in picking up the clues.

He knew nothing about the missing sisters.

He gazed at the windows of the common ranch house—three bedrooms, two baths, probably—and wondered if Jordan was inside, in one of the lit rooms. If so, what was he doing?

Benjamin had a son. He didn't want one. He'd never really gotten to be a kid himself, and he lived his life now spoiling himself as much as he could. He had a lot of toys and a housekeeper who baked cookies and purchased his favorite treats from the store. But he found it convenient for business to announce that he had a family. A wife and son. In his circles, no one expected to actually meet them. Charlene was always a pleasant surprise.

"Yes," he said again, stronger. "Go." There would be time later for this.

The tires spun on the icy surface of the road for a moment, and the sky was so close with cloud cover that Benjamin felt like he was being condensed, pressed down to the level of the earth.

"To the resort?" the driver asked.

"I'm hungry, Benjamin," Charlene said.

Benjamin kept a package of pistachios in a coat pocket. He never shared these. He never allowed his stomach to be empty. People close to him thought he had ulcers. Benjamin never denied it, but he would never tell, either, that he kept the pistachios so that he never again felt the burning pangs of hunger. That more than anything else could pull him back into his childhood and into memories that weren't sweet.

"That bar and grill we tried the first night," Benjamin decided. It was barely four o'clock in the afternoon. Too early for dinner, but he had an errand to run first anyway. A solo venture this time. A king-of-the-mountain experience awaiting him. "I'll drop you back at the hotel, and you can dress for dinner," he said.

He sat back against the leather and turned his head for a parting glance at the small house perched on the small knoll and the small life Nicole lived inside it. And he knew he would come back for a closer look. Soon.

"I bet that trout is good," Charlene said. She leaned her soft body against his, and he tucked her hand into the crook of his elbow. Encouraged, she ventured further. "That was a tiny house, Benjamin."

"Small and tidy." And he hated that word. Tidy meant everything in its place, and he wasn't very good at that. Which was why he planned ahead. Why he had dump sites and escape routes mapped out. It was why he'd hooked up with Charlene to begin with—she was a natural with details. He saw the big picture and she made the pieces fit together, like a puzzle.

"We have such a big house," she went on. "And a backyard that goes on forever too. Jordan would love the pool and your car collection."

All the things he'd wanted growing up, but bigger.

"And maybe you'll meet your match at the foosball table. You think you can convince Jordan's mother to let him come visit? Wouldn't that be nice?"

Taking care of a kid wasn't nice. It was *give me this* and *get me that*. It was *I'm hungry. I'm wet. I want Mama.* It had been a huge hassle eight years ago. But the boy was grown now. Maybe it would be different. And it would be nice to torment Nicole. That was what he'd come for. Location for the auction had been his choice, so long as he could highlight the tangible benefits. And he was a big believer that all work and no play made Ben a bad boy.

"You want to play house, Charlene?"

"I wouldn't mind having a little boy, a mini Benjamin, to take care of for a while."

Charlene worked her hand down his arm until her fingers twined with his, but she said no more about it. She wasn't exactly a butterfly in terms of her attention, but she wasn't a badger either.

"I think I'll order the seared trout," she said, and sank back into silence.

20

French-curve swing gates forged from wrought iron blocked the entry to the home King was renting. The house had gotten its name from the big-horned bull silhouettes that decorated each grille. The setup was a show of wealth and exclusivity, and was not padlocked. When the county plow made it this far along the Lake Road, it cleared the driveways of citizens who paid extra for the service—but the gates had to remain unlocked. Nicole climbed from the Yukon, slid the latch, and opened the gate wide. She was the first to arrive.

The driveway was a straight shot for a hundred yards, then veered sharply west, toward the lake and through a copse of dense tree cover. The pines were frosted with snow, and drifts were piled up on either side of the drive. Shades of white and gray blended and added a layer of charcoal to an already darkening sky. The isolation wasn't lost on Nicole, nor was the fact that people paid extra for that luxury with reason. From Gatling's description of the man, it was a safe bet that King wasn't a recluse. He'd come to Montana knowing that the need for secrecy was paramount. Big Horn was the perfect place for clandestine meetings where medical advancements were proofed and bartered for.

The paved drive made a final curve before it broke into a secluded plot of land where the house stood along with several outbuildings, including a three-car garage and barn. Behind the house were the pool, changing cabana, and sauna. Nicole idled at the bend and pulled her cell phone from her coat pocket. She dialed Lars.

"How far out?"

"Four minutes. Wait for me."

He knew she just as often proceeded alone as waited for backup. The department was too thin to send personnel out in pairs. But they didn't deal with murder every day, and they handled kidnapping even less. The case was fraught with obvious danger, but vulnerabilities as well. Nicole had to assume that two children were, if still alive, held prisoner in the house. Would King find it less threatening if Nicole arrived alone?

She thought so. She also thought it was entirely possible that King had summoned Mrs. Esparza the night before, when Beatrice became uncooperative. *Good girls don't do this.* Don't do what? Rebel? Disobey their parents? Nicole did not believe that Beatrice knew more than her mother about the great doctor's cure. Had Alma Esparza realized that her position in the world could be about to skyrocket but teetered on the brink, depending on the cooperation of a reluctant fourteen-year-old girl?

Or was Nicole wrong about the mother? She wondered if the woman had made it as far as the home. Had she asked for her children? Had she connected with Beatrice, even for a few moments, and calmed her distraught daughter? Or had she found King and Beatrice and a situation she wasn't able to handle? And was that when the calls to her husband began?

Had she feared, or had she fought?

For herself, or for her children?

Nicole had experience in hostage negotiation. Some training from when she was with the Denver PD.

She shifted the Yukon into gear, and the tires spun on the icy surface of the road, a sharp whine, before they gripped pavement and the vehicle jumped forward.

The house was huge. Seven bedrooms, each with its own bath. A cook's kitchen and three family areas, including a game room and a formal dining room. The roof of the barn peaked behind the three-car garage. Pastures were contained by a white slatted fence and were empty of livestock. The barn probably held more toys than tools.

Nicole stopped where the driveway branched. With no tree cover, she was as exposed as a turkey in the gallows, but she climbed from the Yukon without hesitation.

Show no uncertainty, she reminded herself.

The guy who'd built the house had a thing for the number three. Three levels. The front facade had three pairs of French doors—two on the second level, one on the third—that opened onto expansive balconies. The roof was peaked thrice, once front and center, then once to either side, with those peaks being set back from the first. The home was elaborate, designed for show and entertaining, but with its stone masonry and leaded glass set in iron millwork, it was also a fortress.

Nicole glanced at each of the front-facing windows but saw no small faces peering out. The windows were not covered and reflected back, dark and empty. Stone stairs led to a double front entry. Her boots crunched in the snow as she advanced, but she never made it off the driveway. A set of French doors on the second floor opened, and the man from the photo with Beatrice stepped out. He wasn't wearing a jacket. His shirt, red and tailored, was open at the throat, and the tails flapped in the wind. His hair was dark and disheveled. He had a drink in his hand and gestured with it.

"Is this a social call?" he asked. He was smiling, but there was no joy or amusement in his face. The man's eyes were turbulent and bottomless.

She went with the truth. She kept her voice steady, strong, unrelenting. "No, not at all." Her pace even, she trod closer to the house so that King had to adjust if he wanted to keep his eyes on her. He put his hands down on the railing and watched. "I've come for the girls, Dr. King."

He watched her a moment longer, that smile like a bleeding wound, and then nodded.

"I wanted Enrique to come," he said. "You'd think he'd come for his children, right? I thought he would." And his voice was full of censure and rose and fell like the ringing of a bell. The Christmas lights, strung among boughs of holly from the veranda railing, twinkled first red, then green.

"He asked me to get them."

"Really?" King was surprised. He thought about her words, then shook his head. "No, Enrique is a man first, a doctor second. Father doesn't even make his top-five list."

And King seemed to find that offensive.

"He didn't come to you, did he?" he asked.

"Where are the girls?" Nicole returned.

"Enrique wouldn't do that." He shook his head, and that smile reappeared. "You almost had me. Hope sparked." His face twisted at that. "I hate it, you know? Hope. Keeps us fighting even when there's nothing left to believe in."

"What do you believe, Dr. King?"

"That Enrique Esparza is a coward. That my daughter will die, and very soon. She will die never knowing a single day of normal." His mouth opened, and Nicole suspected it was laughter that fell from it, but it was sharp and cutting and hurt her ears. "That's not much, huh? A father should want more than normal for his only daughter, right? But I would die to give that to her."

"Would you kill for it?"

Tears streamed from his eyes, and he nodded.

"It was easy. Too easy," he said, but he gasped and his words were fragmented.

Nicole's worry for the Esparza girls increased.

"Who did you kill, Dr. King?"

"Are you worried about Isla and Sofia?" he asked.

"Someone should worry about them," she said.

"Yes."

"Because Dr. Esparza doesn't?"

"And that's a shame. Perfect girls in every way. Healthy and smart, beautiful girls. Beatrice would have changed the world."

Past tense.

"You know Beatrice is dead," Nicole said.

"I do."

"Did you kill her?"

"I loved her," he said. "She gave up everything for my daughter." His composure broke with a short, wrenching sob, and then he continued, "She wanted to help Violet as much as I did."

"How did she die?" Nicole persisted.

"Loving the world and everyone in it."

"And Violet?" The girl who would never make snow angels. The Gatlings had confirmed Etienne's story.

"Hanging on."

"But without Beatrice—"

"My Violet will die." His hand shook, and he spilled some of the amber liquid from the glass. "It's a no-win situation. Seems like it was that from the beginning."

He turned and threw the glass, and it landed in the snow, far left of where Nicole stood. He hadn't been aiming for her, but her hand twitched anyway, and it was with controlled thought that she kept her arms at her sides, her gun holstered.

Behind her, she heard the crunch of tires on snow, the sharp whine of rubber tread searching for traction, as a department Yukon turned the bend and came into view. Nicole didn't turn but kept her eyes on King. She knew, though, the sound of the department vehicles, the feel of backup.

"Your cavalry," he said. "It's too late, you know."

"We're coming inside," she told him. "For the girls."

He looked down on her, his eyes for the first time deep, calm, reasonable. "They want to go home. I called, but Enrique wouldn't come."

"Mrs. Esparza came," Nicole said, and took another step toward the front doors.

"Yes, but only for Beatrice."

"She took Beatrice but not her youngest daughters?"

"Beatrice is a fighter. She's a Joan of Arc. And she wouldn't leave."

The clouds seemed to part then, a moment of shining clarity came to King's face, and he shifted so that he could look down on Nicole and connect with her gaze.

"I loved Beatrice. She was beautiful, heart and soul, and I used that. For Violet."

"And when she refused to cooperate?" Nicole pressed. "What then?"

"I decided to take what I wanted. I'd been doing it all along; it wasn't a big jump."

"The Rohypnol."

"Yes. You should have seen the look in her eyes. I had betrayed her. I had used her. And in that moment, she realized it."

"What happened then?"

"She ran. Before I could get the sample. Not that it would have mattered. Enrique wasn't selling to Magellan."

"Who was the highest bidder?"

"Who cares? It wasn't us."

He swallowed and choked, a wet cough that caused his nose to run. "I loved her."

"Beatrice?"

"Yes, but I killed her. She had what Violet needed and she wouldn't give it to me. And so I held her in my arms and looked into her eyes, and I crushed her windpipe."

With that, King reached behind his back and pulled a gun from his waistband. Nicole watched as time slowed. The tug on his pants as the barrel of the gun resisted, caught in his belt. The big hand contracting around the cold metal. The wide arc of King's arm as he raised the pistol—from this distance she thought a Sig Sauer. It was a smooth motion, completely without hesitation. The ripple of muscle from neck to shoulder to arm, and then the squeeze of the trigger.

Yes, a Sig. It blew cleanly through the man's skull, and he was down. Dead.

Nicole walked the twenty or so yards to the body, her arm hanging at her side, her gun clenched in her fist, drawn as he'd drawn his. Blood sprayed the snow and was beginning to spread in a large puddle beside his head. She pressed her fingers to his carotid artery, but it was purely routine. There were no signs of life.

She heard the crunch of snow under boots. Lars wore Sorels, ankle-high, laced and double-tied. Distinctive because everyone else wore department-issued Martens, so she didn't need to look up.

"Dead," she said.

"Was that a confession?"

Nicole stood and turned away from the body, the house, and stared beyond Lars's inquiring face.

He hadn't bothered with the driveway once he saw King wavering on the balcony and had parked the Yukon on the lawn, several yards behind Nicole. His coat was open, his cheeks already at a full flush with the cold. His breath plumed in front of him.

The front yard rolled into fenced pastures and beyond that a copse of trees. Camera-ready. It could have been a backdrop for a commercial featuring a rough cowboy and cologne. She followed the winding driveway with her gaze, into the trees, and picked up its thread on the other side. Her deputies were arriving in a caravan of SUVs with bar lights turning and the department seal emblazoned on the front doors.

"He killed Beatrice," Nicole said.

"Are we sure?"

"No." She shook her head, bit down on her back teeth. "He held her in his arms, looked into her eyes, and 'crushed her windpipe.'"

"He said that?"

"Exactly that."

She ordered the scene contained and left Lars to wait for the deputies, who were only a breath behind them. The front doors were not locked and opened onto a foyer with a sweeping staircase to the right and a living room to the left. Empty. Her feet echoed on the marble tile as she advanced, seeking the back of the house. And that was where she found them—Isla and Sofia and King's own daughter, Violet, wheelchair bound and upright with the help of belts and a headrest. Someone had shoveled snow into the sun-room, and the girls were taking turns making snow angels while Violet watched, her eyes sleepy but, Nicole realized when the girl shifted slightly and hooked her gaze, stubbornly aware.

And then the back door opened and the cold air blew in, followed by a lanky teen armed with a shovelful of snow. He wore a down jacket, unzipped, and a blue cap over dark hair that was just long enough to get in his eyes. He'd already noticed her; his eyes flared and his mouth pinched. He dropped the shovel and demanded, "Who are you?"

21

Kenneth King, aka Excalibur, refused to sit down. He'd taken off his coat and thrown it on the marble counter top. His wool cap remained perched atop his head. They had taken the kitchen. Sofia and Isla were in the living room with Lars, where they sat on the couch, legs swinging, unaware of the activity going on outside—Nicole had drawn the curtains as uniformed officers secured the house and grounds. Violet King was with her nurse. The woman had been sleeping in an upstairs bedroom.

"Was your father distraught?"

"What?" Kenny turned on his heel and paced toward her. "You mean like upset? Yeah."

"Why?"

He shrugged. "A lot of reasons."

"Start with one," she suggested.

So far, Kenny King was holding up. Frenetic energy hummed inside his wiry body, and she often had to ask a question twice before she broke through the white noise in his head.

"Violet," he said.

"Your sister?"

"She's dying. Has been since the day she was born."

"And your father wanted to do something about that?"

"He was driven by it. Obsessed with it."

"Your father mentioned she was declining."

His eyelids fluttered, and Nicole remembered the smile on the young man's face when he'd entered the kitchen with a shovelful of snow for the girls.

"She's lived longer than the doctors thought she would."

"What's her medical condition?"

"Primary mitochondrial disease. It's genetic. Lots of people look at her and think it must have been trauma at birth, but that's not true. They think she can't hear or see. But she does. Still."

And Nicole remembered the look in the girl's eyes when she'd first entered the room—alert, intelligent.

"How old are you, Kenny?"

"Seventeen."

"How did you know Beatrice?"

"We're friends."

"You live miles apart." With several states between them, it turned out. One of the first things Nicole had asked Kenny was his address: Kalispell, Montana.

"That doesn't matter. We talk, Skype, FaceTime, see each other at least once a month."

"Because your fathers were working together?"

"Yes."

"Were you more than friends?"

"She was too young for that. But maybe, in a year or two—"

He sounded like he was repeating the promises of a dead girl. "We have some of the text messages you sent her, Kenny. I think you loved her."

"No."

"You wanted more than friendship," she continued.

"Well, yeah," he said. "Beatrice was beautiful."

"But she didn't want you."

"Yet," he insisted.

"You think she was going to change her mind?"

"Yes."

"Do you know what she used as an icon for you, Kenny?"

"Excalibur," he admitted.

"She thought of you as her King Arthur."

"No, not me," he said, and his tone had turned, become snarly. "That was my father." He started pacing again. "It was more than just a play on our name. She really thought he was *amazing*."

"She said that?"

"Yeah, she did."

149

"So if he was King Arthur, what did that make you?"

"An extension of him, of course. You know, the sword of a knight is his pride or his shame."

"And which are you, Kenny?"

"My father loved me," he said. "That was one thing he was really good at, you know? He loved us."

His voice wobbled with emotion, and Nicole changed the course of her questioning, drew him away from personal loss.

"Did Beatrice's father love her?"

"Yes."

"But?"

"He loves his work too. He was divided."

"Were you here Christmas night?"

He nodded. "Bea came over to help with the girls. She was good at that kind of stuff—fixing their hair, telling stories—and she talked to Violet like my sister understood her, which she does."

"Your sister wanted a sleepover?"

"She still believes in Santa. She's thirteen years old, but really like five or six. She's never had a sleepover or friends. Everyone needs a friend, right?"

"Right," Nicole agreed, and then rocked his world further. "Your father confessed to killing Beatrice."

"My father?" He froze.

Reality chose that moment to come crashing down on him. His shoulders shook. He sank to his knees, his head bent, sobbing.

Nicole called for the EMTs. She put a request through for the unit psych. Nicole needed to speak to Kenny. He needed to process. He needed a soft place to land. She stayed with him, occasionally laying a hand on his shoulder so he'd know he wasn't alone. And she spoke, about the snow he'd brought inside for Violet and for Bea's sisters. The looks on their faces when he opened the door and pitched in that magic. He had delighted them and he had wanted to—that look had been genuine in the young man.

Talk of the girls seemed to wind past his turmoil. He quieted and rose to his feet.

"I love my sister," he said. "She's pure, you know? Like I don't think she ever thought a bad thing about anyone. She's like no one else on this planet."

"She loves you too. I saw it," Nicole agreed.

He nodded. The emotional fog was clearing from his features.

"Why do you think your father killed Beatrice?"

He shook his head, confused. "Bea was it. Our last chance."

"Was Beatrice Nueva Vida?"

He nodded. "I can't believe she's dead. I hear the words. I know what they mean. But that's not Bea, you know? She was meant to live forever."

"You and Beatrice have a lot in common," she said. "You love your sister as she did hers. You were born to be doctors. Joaquin told me your father was preparing you for that the same way Dr. Esparza was preparing Beatrice."

"Yeah. It's expected, you know? Those who have been given much are expected to do much. Our fathers agree on that. They're raising us that way. To do much."

Contribute. Carry on the family name. Elevate it. The creed of the wealthy.

"Did Beatrice resent that?"

"No. Absolutely not. She wanted it. She saw how other people lived, a lot of them without the medical attention they needed. People die every day from need of an antibiotic or simple surgery. Beatrice wanted to change that."

"Is that how you feel?"

But he shook his head. "She saw people as individuals. Their suffering. I see people globally. You can get stuck on the needs of the one. It's better to meet the needs of many."

He paced across the room and leaned back against the island. He crossed his arms over his chest. His nerves were jumping, and Nicole gave him the time he needed to regroup.

"Beatrice didn't think about medicine the way her father does. For her, it was as much about listening to a person as examining them. It was more about how a person feels and less about what's making them feel that way. She led with her heart, and medicine is science." But he was smiling, and Nicole could tell that he'd liked that about Beatrice.

"Sounds to me that Beatrice would have been a good doctor."

But Kenny disagreed.

"She thought medicine should be a calling, but it's really big business." He shook his head in a patronizing gesture that irritated Nicole. "She just didn't get it. Dr. E had something—something big—and Bea thought he should just give it away."

"But there are problems with his super cell," Nicole pointed out.

"There are always problems with great advancements. That's why he wants it in the biggest, most badass lab available."

"Your father's company?"

"That's just one option."

"If Nueva Vida is so great, why isn't it already in a badass lab?"

Kenny peeled himself off the counter and paced back across the room. Flurries had started again. He stood in front of the window and watched.

"My father's dead," he said. "And you think he killed Beatrice?"

"Yes. I'm sorry, Kenny," Nicole offered, but the young man was looking for something else.

"He shot himself? Really?"

Nicole nodded, but she was staring at the back of Kenny's head, and he wasn't following her reflection in the window.

"I was there," she said.

"Why? Did he tell you that?" He turned to her. "It wasn't just Violet. He's known from go that my sister wouldn't live long."

"He lost hope in Dr. Esparza's cure."

But Kenny shook his head. He wasn't buying it. "Sometimes you can borrow time. The wealthiest can even buy it. That's how Violet's lived so long. It's also what upset Bea so much—the disparity. Another kid like Violet, with the usual family resources, they get maybe two years. Five at the most. My father didn't lose hope in Dr. E's super cell; he lost hope that Esparza would ever sell it to him."

"Your father extended Violet's life expectancy because he got her the medical treatment she needed?"

"Cutting-edge medical treatments," Kenny clarified. "Violet has been the launch pad of a lot of different medical trials over time. But he was really counting on Dr. E's super cell."

"So what happened?"

"Bea told me the paperwork was bogus," he confided. A frown rippled over his brow. "She checked, you know? When she was getting sicker and her father was having a harder time curing her. By the third round, she knew something wasn't right. She was scared, but she was committed."

"What paperwork?"

"From the FDA. No clinical trial can start without permission, and no credible pharm company will work with a doctor who doesn't have the paper."

"Do you think Dr. Esparza had permission?"

He turned back to the window and pressed his fingertips to the cool glass. "It's not hard to counterfeit documents. You could probably buy a set online."

"Did your father think they were bogus?"

"My father wanted Nueva Vida for Violet," he said. "He wanted it bad. Bad enough maybe he ignored some things he shouldn't have. But in the end, if all of Dr. E's experimenting was without regulation, the FDA would never approve a trial based on the results of his work."

"And that meant Violet wouldn't get her chance?"

"Exactly. But if Bea wasn't in the picture anymore, if there was no evidence of Dr. E's success outside the lab, then maybe my dad could get the super cell into the human gene pool, open clinical trials that are legit."

Motive. If Kenny was right about Nueva Vida.

"Does your sister have that kind of time?"

He shook his head slowly. "It doesn't look like it."

"And that saddened your father too."

"Yeah. Nueva Vida has enormous potential, but medicine doesn't move at the speed of light."

She'd known as much. Anything she'd ever read about medical advancements put it at a snail's pace.

"What did Dr. Esparza do when Beatrice confronted him about the paperwork?"

"He told her he had preliminary permission. That he was extending himself beyond that, but with good results. And Beatrice could see he was right. But she could also see that with each round, she was getting sicker."

"And she wanted out?"

"She worried there would be a cancer the cure wouldn't fix."

"Because not all cancers are created equal?" she asked.

"Right, but Dr. E has gone a step above that. He created a cell impervious to the disease."

"A cell that can never get sick?"

"A cell that can never get cancer," he corrected, and he liked the idea so much that a smiled bloomed on his face as certainty infused his words. "Never."

"So why was Beatrice sick so much?"

"Clinical trials," he said. "Through the summer and fall. Sick and then healed. Dr. E had to do it, and then apply new data to the next trial, and so on. That's how he built his super cell."

"He perfected it on Beatrice."

"Exactly. The cell is synthetic—man-made—and doesn't exist naturally in the human body. Beatrice got sick because her cells are human in every way. And she was stage one."

"So Dr. Esparza gave Beatrice cancer?"

"Four times, to be exact," Kenny agreed.

"How?"

"He preserved cancerous tumors he removed from the body of his patients and implanted them in Beatrice. And then he watched them grow. Each trial he waited a little longer to launch his super cell. And each time the cell went to work.

"Nueva Vida is like a legion of knights, armored, prepared, on-the-spot execution. The moment a cell in the human body starts to go bad, it's eliminated before it can contaminate neighboring cells."

"Dr. Esparza told me Beatrice doesn't have cancer," Nicole said.

"That's right. He tried to do it again. Twice, actually. He implanted, each one larger than the one before, but they disappeared almost immediately."

"How?"

"Because he created an army of super cells inside Beatrice and they were waiting, already in formation. And he did it from one single cell. He got it to replicate. And that's Esparza's great discovery. A synthetic super cell that replicates like organic cells. No one else has ever done it."

"And the super cells eliminate disease before it can take hold?"

"They eliminate cancer," he clarified.

"Because the super cells were coded for cancer."

"One central code, boiled down to the deadliest commonality among cancers," he agreed. "Before Dr. E could even set up a microscope and take a tissue sample, the cancer was gone."

"Hours."

"Less."

"Beatrice was a miracle," she said.

"She should have lived forever."

22

Benjamin sat in the driver's seat, the window cracked and the heat pumping full blast into the cabin. He'd left Charlene at the resort to rely on the snack bar in their room. He'd left the driver to his own devices, which meant the man was filling in crossword puzzles at a small table in the hotel bar. Benjamin wanted to be alone with Nicole without an audience, and so he waited in the parking lot of the station, backed in so he could watch the vehicles as they arrived. So far, they'd been few, and none had been the sheriff's Yukon.

The windows were clouding, and he sat forward and flipped the switch to defrost. He glanced at the clock on the dash. Forty minutes. Irritation plucked at his nerves. Instant gratification had its high points, but anticipation had given him hours of imaginative play. He'd waited for this moment a long time. Eight years. Killing Nicole would be enjoyable but not practical. And not as much fun as toying with her. He wanted to give her a fright. And he wanted her to worry. Damn the video she had. That could be reduced to inadmissible after claims of tampering, editing, imposing his image onto the footage. What Nicole probably hadn't yet realized—her only viable witness to his crime was dead. And that made him smile. Not an accident. Not even a suicide. But a slow clogging of his arteries had produced a heart attack magnificent in its strength.

There being no witness weakened any case against Benjamin to a roll of the dice.

His cell phone rang, and he looked at it hooked to his belt. The calling number flashed at him in red. He knew having a woman for a boss would mean an increase in frustration. Women liked to talk. They stuck their noses into business that wasn't theirs and wanted details. Men were satisfied with a job well done. When evidence surfaced that a contract had been fulfilled, they pressed a button on a keyboard in a room far away and the electronic transfer of large funds was executed. Women held on to their purses with white knuckles. Callon had won the bid and Benjamin was owed a bonus, but the old bat was holding out on him.

He answered and resented having to do so. But you wouldn't know it by his tone or his words.

"Geneva," he said, his voice full of pleasant surprise. "I thought you were going to try the slopes this evening?"

She ignored his small talk. "I've spoken with Esparza," she said. "He's not cooperating."

"He's hurting," Benjamin said. "You knew killing his daughter would result in sticky emotions."

"He's a man of science."

"And a father," Benjamin said. He loved pretending that he knew what such a thing could do to a man. Personally, Jordan's existence had caused him nothing but trouble, and his death would be a relief.

"He needs to know things can get a whole lot worse."

"And you want this done in conversation or action?"

"A little of both," she returned.

"You have a list of dos and don'ts?" The woman had a lot of rules. They'd already broken one when Charlene used her hands to kill Beatrice. That had earned them a scolding—the woman didn't understand that the girl was fast. Rabbit fast. "Any preferences?"

"Yeah. Face-to-face contact. And whatever you do, don't kill the man. We want what's inside his head."

"No luck with his computers?"

"Wiped clean," she confirmed. "We believe he has his lab work on flash drive or media card. So if you're not able to follow directions on this, make sure you check every nook and cranny on his dead body for it."

"Of course."

"But it won't come to that," she continued. "Because you will follow directions."

"That's always the plan," he agreed, but he knew that sometimes changes were necessary. Like right now. Now was a good time to shake up the boss, make her appreciate what she had in him. "The police are looking for you," he told her.

A pause as time crackled across the line. "How do you know that?"

"They were in the lobby of our hotel this afternoon. They have pictures of you with the dead girl. But not just you. Looks like they have the whole bunch of you, all posing like you're family." He shook his head. Arrogance and intellect—the two did not complement each other. The Big Pharm players who had come to Blue Mesa intent on either buying or stopping the sale of Esparza's discovery had lost their common sense along the way. Geneva included. "That was a mistake."

She ignored the criticism. The woman had a way of never acknowledging personal faults.

"Esparza called that meeting. The big mix and mingle, let the competition see itself. It was his downfall, really. We all knew that if he had the goods, then we had to wrestle it from him as we have every other promising development that's threatened to undo us."

"Not all of you."

"King is out of the picture now."

"Convenient."

"Helpful," she corrected, then returned to the business at hand. "Meet with Esparza tonight so that he's ready tomorrow first thing. He needs to leave with us voluntarily."

She hung up without waiting for Benjamin's response, which she wouldn't have liked anyway and which would have been something along the lines of "Fat chance." Although he was practiced enough to deliver it in digestible words such as, "He may need a little more time than that. You know, he's grieving and all."

And then Benjamin laughed, because Geneva would understand that no better than he did and because at that moment Nicole was pulling into the parking lot.

Benjamin waited until she parked and then approached the Yukon in her blind spot, from the right side back end, and when she was standing and had shut the door, he stepped around to the driver's side and was quiet enough that he spooked her, drawing the desired effect.

"Hello, Nikki," he said, and she whipped around, pushing him up against her cruiser with the flat of her hand against his throat and pulling her baton with the other. The polished wood caught the light and gleamed, and Benjamin remembered, too late, the precision with which she could wield that weapon.

"Benjamin."

It was not said kindly. In fact, he thought she was enjoying this too much. That she might, in fact, take it further. But that wasn't her way, he reminded himself. She was intense but methodical. She didn't act in haste; she planned.

It was good to see the fear shredding the irises of her eyes, pinching her mouth. His smile grew until he was laughing. And then she brought her baton up with a fierce but economical motion that stopped only after it connected with his balls.

He bent forward, and he knew that was only because she let him. He didn't doubt that. Nikki was strong. If she'd wanted him pinned against the cruiser, writhing in pain, he would be there now. He gasped once, twice, then said, "That was close, Nikki." Close enough he would feel it for days to come.

She had exercised restraint. She hadn't incapacitated him, but instead had delivered a warning. A reminder.

He rose and laid a hand on the baton. "You can consider your message received," he said.

"I don't think so, Benjamin. The way I remember things, you have a thick skull and slower reactions."

But he wouldn't let her get away with that. "I was a match for you," he said. "In fact, I was winning in our little game called life."

"Not for long." But she paled and her mouth tightened, and he knew he'd landed a direct hit.

"How is Jordan?" he pushed. Too far, apparently, because Nicole brought the baton up again. He would have dropped to his knees, but she wouldn't let him. The weapon made contact with his jaw next. He heard the clack of bone, but it didn't shatter. Then she was standing close to him, the nightstick against his throat as she leaned both hands against the wood on either side of his head.

"You feel that, Benjamin? Not the pain. In a moment that will pale in comparison to your need for air. I think Jordan probably felt that way when you were kicking him in the ribs. I think the pain stunned him and he felt betrayed. Not by you; at some point he realized what you were. But by me, for continuing to leave him with you. And then, his heart breaking, his ribs hurting, he started to feel that fire in his lungs. You feel it now, don't you? I want you to remember it." She leaned heavier on the stick. And she was right. The burn in his lungs was worse than the hurt in his dick or his throat, which he thought she might really crush. "You see, Benjamin, how close, how easy it would be for me to kill you?"

He made eye contact, nodding slightly. Her weight shifted, a small give, and he could take a shallow breath, just enough to keep him from passing out.

"Nikki," he said, though he didn't recognize his voice. It was rough, dry, reduced from the smooth swagger he threw at the world.

"Sheriff," she corrected him. "Why are you here?"

"It's been eight years—"

"I can count, Benjamin." She toed his feet apart. "You're not here to see Jordan. He was never anything to you other than a means to get at me."

"I'm actually here about Truman." He could tell by the look on her face that he'd scored a hit. "Material witness. Only witness." He heard hysteric glee enter his voice. He loved that feeling—enjoyment at the expense of another. It was a pure rush. "He's dead, Nikki," he told her. "A bad heart. A very bad heart." Benjamin bided his time.

"Truman wasn't much of a witness," Nicole said. "I wasn't counting on him." As the man was a criminal and known associate of Benjamin's, his account would not have held a lot of weight in court. "Besides, he wasn't the only witness."

"You don't count," he said. "We both know that. Lovers. Bad breakup. Vengeance. A good lawyer could turn all that against you."

She shrugged but didn't seem at all confident. "Eyewitness testimony was a very small piece of the evidence against you."

"Gotta love the digital age," he said. "I have it from an expert in cinematography that videos can be altered without leaving a trace. A jury would be very interested in that."

Nikki didn't appear to believe him. "You want to take this to court?"

"Your case is cold," he said. "Less than seventeen percent of murders not solved in the first days are ever resolved. I did my research."

"Let's talk about why you're really here. Esparza."

Benjamin raised an eyebrow. Too bad Nikki knew his ways, believed every move was calculated for a definitive reaction.

"Yes, that Esparza. The one you mingled with at King's place last night. You and your not-so-lovely wife, Charlene."

"You're good, Nikki," he said. "You always were."

"What are you up to, Benjamin?"

"Business," he said. "I don't peddle in the small stuff anymore."

"What does a broker do?"

She surprised him with that. "Your source is good."

"Did you kill that girl, Benjamin?"

"You know killing's not my specialty."

"But you've done it before."

"Once."

"More than once," she said.

"Keeping tabs on me?" He smiled and made sure it was big and full of satisfaction.

She ignored him. A pretense, he was sure. "Why did Beatrice Esparza have to die?"

"What do you know about it?"

She shook her head. "You had opportunity, Benjamin. You had means."

"But not motive. You'll never find that. I didn't even know the girl."

"Some people kill for fun. Others for career advancement."

"You're reaching and you know it."

"You know what else I know? You accumulate people according to what they can do for you, and based on descriptions of your wife, I'm wondering, is she a good spouse, Benjamin? Or a good killer?"

"Why not both?" he said. "You know I have high expectations."

He slid an inch, and then two, along the cruiser, and she let him.

"It was good seeing you, Nikki." He smiled because he knew she hated that. She wanted him to suffer, always.

She stepped back but kept the baton handy. Her mouth shut. She stood her ground and watched him climb into his vehicle, gun the engine, and pull out of the lot. He caught a last glimpse of her in his rearview mirror. She stood with her coat open and flapping in the wind, her feet solid on the ground, unmoving. She wasn't the last man standing, which was probably what she was thinking. Benjamin was that. Always.

23

Nicole took the stairs two at a time, arrived at the top, and made a sharp left into the dimly lit corridor. She paced herself, or tried to. Forensics didn't like uninvited guests, even when it was the sheriff. Science took time. Tests couldn't be rushed. Results had to be confirmed. She knew she was the stick stirring the beehive and that there was no soft entry, but she strived for calm. She willed ease back into her muscles, stiffened from her encounter with her past in the parking lot not twenty minutes earlier. Benjamin had grown some stones.

Her pulse still carried the memory of that first frantic beat when she became aware that Benjamin was here. Fear had become a spark in her belly, and she'd had to keep dousing it with reason to keep it from becoming a bonfire. Benjamin wasn't here to take Jordan away from her. He couldn't do that. Benjamin was a drug dealer, and judges did not award the custody of children to known criminals. Anyway, Benjamin couldn't parent from behind a jail cell, and, she reminded herself, she had plenty of hard evidence to put him there.

Or did she? Truman was dead. Nicole had stopped at her desk long enough to find his obituary online. A witness to the sound of gunfire, to its flame against the night sky, to Benjamin's face, in profile, some fifty feet across a shadowed street and to his hasty retreat, Truman had given a statement to Nicole. She had filed it, knowing it was circumstantial at best. But a jury loved living evidence, a live play of Q and A. It had been one more seed in a planter's box. Now dried up and blown away.

She stopped midhall and pulled her cell phone from her pocket. Jordan had to know. If Benjamin had the balls to show up here, what else might he do? The connection rang twice and was picked up by Mrs. Neal.

"Checking in," Nicole said, after greeting the woman.

"All quiet here," Mrs. Neal promised.

"I hope it stays that way."

Nicole felt the shift in the woman's awareness before she heard it in her voice. "You have reason to think it won't?"

"I have a concern," she admitted. "A visitor in town. Jordan's father."

"I've never heard you speak of him, and I figured that's because he wasn't worth mentioning."

"Only as a matter of precaution," Nicole agreed. "Don't answer the door tonight."

"I'll check the locks now."

"I'm probably being overcautious."

"There's nothing wrong with that."

"I won't be back till late."

"That's okay. I took down that stack of board games you had in the closet. I think we're on for Sorry and Parcheesi."

Nicole smiled as an image of Jordan's disgruntled face simmered into her mind's eye.

"He puts up with me, doesn't he?" Mrs. Neal said.

"He adores you."

"For five minutes here and there." She heard Mrs. Neal call for Jordan, and then she said, "He's a good boy."

The best, Nicole thought.

"Hey, Mom."

His voice was light, not weighted by a single concern, and Nicole liked it that way.

"How was Legos?"

"Cool. Two hours, four hundred forty-three pieces, and every one of them had to be used."

She didn't know how the rules were made or what made them so challenging, but Jordan loved the planning and building aspects of Legos. He had already started lobbying for a two-week summer camp combo of engineering and Legos, and Nicole knew she would send him.

"What did you build?"

"That duel scene in *Star Wars: The Force Awakens*, with Solo and Skywalker on the laser bridge. I'm calling it 'Animosity Between Friends.'"

"Way cool."

"Yeah, but that's not why you called," he said. "And it's not even five o'clock. Too early for your check-in."

"You're right. I have ulterior motives." She paused and looked for words that would make the announcement easier, then cast them aside. Jordan knew to expect honesty from her and that sometimes words had bite. "Your father's in town."

There was stillness over the line as he processed that.

"In Blue Mesa?"

"Yes."

"Why?" The air had become thin in his throat, and it showed up in the feathery quality of his voice.

"I don't know yet. And I don't want you to be afraid. I want you to be prepared."

Jordan had only shadow memories of his father, more remembered emotion than actual time spent with the man. He feared his father, and it was a clawing in his gut that climbed up his throat—that was how Jordan had described it to her at seven years of age when he brought up his father in conversation. Nicole had validated his feelings by giving him small pieces of the past, gentling the words as best she could. But trauma had a way of settling in, of never allowing the mind and heart to erase it completely. The flashes of fear had lost their frequency, taking him by surprise less often, but were forever just under the surface.

"He came by the station," she told him. And had left his name. Benjamin had known it would make them spin. He'd probably driven by the house too, because he liked to watch people squirm, and he got off on it when he was the one pushing the needle through the spine of a butterfly. "I spoke to him. Let him know we aren't interested in a family reunion."

"A direct assault," Jordan said. There was more weight in his voice. He didn't want to be afraid of his father.

"Did you want to meet with him?" Nicole didn't like offering; it made her stomach tilt and put a buzzing in her ears. But maybe it would ease the terror that sometimes haunted her son.

Jordan seemed to consider it. The silence between them became ponderous for a moment.

"No," he said. "I have nothing to say to him, and I don't think he's here to see me."

"He's good at pulling the strings on a marionette," she reminded him. But yes, a bold move for Benjamin. And that made Nicole nervous. He wasn't here to see his son. He wasn't here solely for his connection to Esparza. He was here to poke Nicole and see how far he could push her.

Nicole had been honest with Jordan. She'd told him about his father, the drug dealer of the rich and infamous. A more appropriate job for a man who liked to watch people implode didn't exist. She'd also told him that it had taken her too long to pry the man's fingers from around their son's throat. She'd been a different woman then, under attack at work and vulnerable to Benjamin's charm. In hindsight, she remembered bruises she'd wanted to believe had come from toddling falls, and she had heard cries of hunger and distress she'd thought were the result of Benjamin's carelessness. But at the first concrete evidence of abuse, Nicole had launched into action. She'd stared at it until her eyes burned dry and her heart lodged in her throat. And then she'd vowed to do everything necessary to save her son.

Honesty. She relied on it to keep their world in balance.

"Knowledge is power. I'm telling you so you have that. He's in town, but I'm the one he wants."

"That doesn't sound good."

It wasn't. "He doesn't stand a chance," she assured him, and heard Jordan's next breath, drawn easier.

"Yeah. He must like punishment."

Nicole had told him about their last confrontation, leaving out most of the details, emphasizing the life-or-death decisions that had been made that day.

"I'm ready for him, Jordan."

"I know."

"And so are you, if it comes to that." Over her dead body.

"I'm a brown belt," he reminded her.

"Your father is a sapling in comparison."

Jordan liked that, and when Nicole said good-bye, it was with a lighter heart.

Her footsteps echoed on the linoleum. Forensics was at the end of the hall.

Arty saw her coming and left his place at the proton microscope and the purple cashmere sweater belonging to Beatrice Esparza under the red light to meet her at the door.

Her blood rushed with the threat of Benjamin's presence in a place he didn't belong, her place, but it was matched by the urgency to find and apprehend Beatrice's killer.

Nicole scanned her ID and waited for the door lock to release before she pushed through. Fingers tapped on computer keys and gases escaped applicators as tests were run.

"Good to see you up here, Sheriff."

"What do you have for me, Arty?"

Arthur Sleeping Bear was the head of forensics. He saw in numbers, in planes and angles and trajectories. He was the only person she'd ever encountered who could stand at a crime scene and predict to within millimeters the trajectory of a bullet simply based on the movement of the wind. He was fond of T-shirts that carried scientific slogans. Today's was *I have a Mind for Matter*.

"If I had something, Sheriff, you'd have heard from me."

She knew that many of his hunches became truths.

"Let me into your mind, Arty," she said. "Let's talk in maybes for now."

He didn't like to speak prematurely and was seldom moved to do so.

"You talk theories; we speak in facts," he reminded her.

"She was fourteen years old. He played with her. Let her think she could outrun him. And then he picked her up and whispered in her ear. I don't think he was singing lullabies."

His lips pursed, and the lines around his eyes puckered as he considered her request. He surprised her.

"Because it's a child we're talking about, Nicole," he said. "And because you appeal to my heart and not my head." He motioned her deeper into the room toward Beatrice's purple Prada bag under an ultraviolet light. Plastic covered a small area of the leather.

"A latent print that doesn't belong to the victim. But it's incomplete. From here, we might get lucky."

Nicole nodded.

"Come see this."

Three shallow pans each held a thick plastic bag of what looked like snow.

"We're letting it melt," Arty said. "Decompensation at an accelerated rate, given that it's inside and under the heat lamps."

"What are you hoping to find?"

"Skin. A piece of nail torn from a finger—victim or perp—or mucus from a running nose—that's far more common and just as easy to plumb for a DNA profile."

The techs had scooped the snow from around the body, from under her head and hands and feet. Eventually, all of the snow Beatrice Esparza had been lying on, and that from within a small perimeter around her body, had been shoveled into bags and transported in coolers back here to the lab. Their geographical location meant they had top-notch equipment and investigators trained in cold-weather anthropology.

Nicole walked toward the pans. A piece of Plexiglas stood between her and the active experiment. The scene was sterile. And, per protocol, a small camera bolted to the ceiling filmed every riveting moment of melting snow.

"I'll take anything I can get," she said.

"Then how 'bout this, Nicole," he said, and turned. She followed him to a small table and a microscope. "Take a look."

She did. The prepared slide showed irregular lines and bubblelike shapes.

"What is it?" She stepped back and looked into his broad face.

"The killer's spit. It froze on her face."

"How do you know?"

"Initial DNA study shows it's male."

King's? Probably; the man confessed. But the case wasn't closed until evidence proved it. And this could be it. That felt good.

"What else does it show?"

"The sample is small, but I think we'll get blood type. And from there, maybe a marker or two unique to the killer."

A break in the case. "How long?"

"Tomorrow morning. I have it running on an expedited schedule. I hear there's some evidence waiting for you downstairs," he said. "Unpleasant, but maybe it will light a path for you."

"What is it?"

But he shrugged. "It didn't come from my department. Computer forensics scored this one."

24

Snow angels. His sisters had spent the morning playing in snow that Kenny King had shoveled into the sun-room, and that made him a good guy in the sheriff's mind. Joaquin almost choked on the thought. Kenny had wanted more from Bea than friendship. She'd been a prize that all three had fought over—their own father and Kenny and his father. Each of them had wanted more from Bea than she had been able to give. But it was too late to mention that now. He'd stood in the waiting room at the county hospital, with his mom and his sisters, when Cobain told the tale of finding his sisters, safe and sound. She was impressed. He could tell, because for the first time since he'd met her, she smiled.

Sofia and Isla were fine. The doctors had examined them.

Kenny King had watched over them, had kept their spirits up. He was a good brother, and that was the only thing Joaquin liked about him.

Michael King was dead, as he should be. He'd chosen his daughter over Beatrice, and Joaquin wished King had died months, years, earlier. Before his family had ever had the chance to mix with him and his kind.

Kenny hadn't called the family or police because, according to Cobain, he hadn't known the girls had been held there against their parents' wishes. Just as he hadn't known Beatrice was dead. Cobain was the sheriff. She was supposed to dig deeper. So much for finding the truth, for delivering justice.

Joaquin sat in a chair in the small sitting area of their suite, his back to the window. The curtains were drawn, but behind them evening pressed against the glass. His father paced in front of the couch. His mother opened Styrofoam containers delivered from the grill downstairs and divided up food. Sofia and Isla sat at the dining table, drinking from cans of Coke.

Tomorrow they would talk to a psychologist at the sheriff's request. They would try to pry details from his sisters' memories that would help them find a killer. Joaquin didn't like it. He wanted it over. He wanted out of Montana.

The feds had been called; they had been en route, but the girls had been located before their arrival and had never considered themselves captives. The possibility of kidnapping was put in question. And in any case, the guilty had already taken his life.

But it wasn't finished. All Joaquin had to do was look at his father to know it.

"Enrique," his mother entreated. "Sit down. Eat."

Not because food was a source of comfort, of care, because his mother wasn't like that. Food was energy. And maybe that came from her childhood, when little was all they'd gotten, so what they chose had to work efficiently to sustain life. And the Esparza family was in trouble, the kind of trouble that drained a body's resources, fast. They were all to refill their tanks and soldier on.

"There's a way out," his father said. "I made sure of it."

"I don't see it," Joaquin said. He still didn't know everything Bea had known. His father's work was a threat to many, so the less anyone knew about it, the better.

"I told the police I never wrote down a single note. No formulas or lab reflections."

"They didn't believe you," his mother said. "That can't be done, and they know it."

"But maybe they believe I shredded everything. And, anyway, they will never find the truth if I don't lead them to it."

His father stopped in front of the covered window and rubbed a palm over his forehead. Then he turned and faced them. Weariness made his eyes heavy, his lips tremble.

"If I make my discovery public, the need to suppress it is gone. And we will be safe."

"Don't throw it all away, Enrique. We are in this together," his mother said. "Spread the pieces among us. Let us help carry them."

"You know nothing. You never did. Just me and Beatrice. We know where that got her. We know what will happen to me. And it ends there."

"King knew," Joaquin said.

"And he's dead."

"Yes," Joaquin's mother agreed, her voice reduced to a hushed whisper.

His father's cell phone rang then. A series of notes that rose in scale, like the crying of a rooster. And Joaquin watched him tense, his shoulders and chin rising.

"Who keeps calling you?" Joaquin wanted to know.

His father turned and headed for a bedroom and privacy, but Joaquin blocked his path.

"No more secrets," he said. "It's not about you anymore." This was about Bea and what they could do to help her now. "It never was."

His father was slow to respond. "Okay, Joaquin. This is where you step up. For your family."

His father held the cell phone in the palm of his hand and pressed speaker, and then he nudged Joaquin into a bedroom, away from his sisters, who already knew too much.

"Hello?"

"Dr. Esparza. I'm standing in the lobby of my hotel, and you're not here."

"I told you I wouldn't be."

"And I told you how important it is that you follow through."

"That is your opinion," his father returned.

"You have your girls back, Dr. Esparza. Now it's time to move forward."

It was a woman's voice.

"No. Not all my girls," his father returned.

"I wanted Beatrice to live. Remember? I was the one who asked you not to do this. Not to your daughter."

"And not to you," Dr. Esparza said. "You were more concerned about yourself and Callon Pharmaceuticals than you were about Beatrice."

Callon. Joaquin recognized the name and the woman's voice. She had been to their home but had refused to work with his father. Apparently, there had been a change of heart.

"Let's talk, Enrique," she said. "Why not let Beatrice's life count for something big?"

"The cost is too high," his father said. "I will not meet with you. I will not give you my work."

"Beatrice is dead. Will you feel any better when thousands who could have been saved are buried beside her?"

"Nothing can make me feel better, or worse." His father hung up. He silenced his cell phone and dropped it in his pants pocket. Then he resumed pacing.

"Callon was the highest bidder?" Joaquin asked.

"Yes. And according to the rules, I am to hand over my work to them, but more than that, I am to work beside their scientists and re-create the super cell in their lab. Not so they can save lives. No. All this so they can save themselves."

"How? What will they do with Nueva Vida?"

"Squash it. And me along with it."

25

Charlene sat across from him at the tall bistro table. She'd ordered white wine and a salad that included seven of the super foods—antioxidants and slow-release proteins. She speared a forkful.

Benjamin was irritated. He'd thought a lot about his meet with Nicole in the weeks before he'd left for Montana. He'd made it the stuff dreams were made of. Only it hadn't gone down that way. Nicole wasn't afraid of him. She was as strong as she'd been on that last day in Denver. Maybe more so. Nicole wasn't a woman who trembled. She didn't flinch. Nicole was a fighter. She was everything he was not, and he hated that about her.

Across from him, Charlene lifted her wineglass. She breathed in the bubbles from her spritzer and rubbed her nose. He used to think that was charming, but today everything was off. And it wasn't just Nicole. Things were shifting with the Big Pharm players. He answered only to one, and she'd given him loose rein. Until last night, when everything had gone to hell.

Killing the girl hadn't been enough. She was the evidence. Evidence that could be replicated. They had needed to take out the father too. He'd suggested that but had been ignored. And now the dominos were falling. Benjamin didn't like that. He was a believer in eliminating small problems before they became big.

"You're not eating," Charlene said. It was true. It was 5:40, and he didn't like dinner before eight o'clock. Outside, the sky was in full darkness, but that made no impression on his body's clock. He had work to do later that would interrupt his usual routine. A job they hadn't planned, a meeting he didn't look forward to. Esparza. The whining doctor. But Benjamin was king of the coax. He'd get the man into a state of agreement, or he'd kill him.

"You need to change," he told Charlene.

She wore an outfit that started as a halter top and flowed into pant legs that were loose and liquid. He liked what the material did when she walked. He liked the way the top exposed her shoulders. But it was wrong for their destination.

"What?" A small frown rippled across her face.

"People will remember you. We need to blend in," he said. Their success here depended upon their ability to get lost in the crowd.

When he'd planned the Big Pharm round table, he'd convinced himself that he could pull off the biggest deal of his career right under Nicole's judgmental nose. But he wanted her to know he'd done it. That he had the intellect and the balls to do it. And his weakness for her esteem might have fucked up the whole operation. That made him mad.

"She got away from you, Charlene. That wasn't good."

"No."

The plan had been to kill Beatrice Esparza in King's house and tuck her into bed like she was sleeping. Charlene had suggested the master bedroom, to cast further aspersion upon the man. He'd be to the police not just a sore loser but perhaps guilty of child abuse. It would put just enough shade on the man; the police would have to dig deeper while Benjamin and the remaining round table packed up and scattered, back to life as usual.

"Tell me again how that happened."

"She was arguing with King, and she ran."

But there was more to it than that. Charlene was terrible at harboring guilt. She couldn't look in his eyes. And she was full of excuses and platitudes. And diversions.

"The ME's going to find the marks," she said. "But he won't know what they are. Not beyond surgical scarring."

They weren't worried about the bruising left by strangulation. Murder was trivial in this case. This had always been about Nueva Vida.

"He'll know, if Esparza talks about his work." And even if he didn't. The incisions on the girl's body would be investigated. By then, of course, there would be no one left to blame.

Certainly not him. His job was to broker the deal. To make sure the bidding was carried out and that Geneva was the winner. He'd done that. The only thing that remained for him to do was deliver Esparza. Then Benjamin's reputation as a top-shelf drug dealer would be solid. And that would happen tonight. A country-bumpkin ME wasn't going to pry the secrets out of Beatrice Esparza's body before midnight, and by then Benjamin's bank account would be busting at the seams and he would be floating above the clouds. He picked up his smartphone and tapped into his favorite flight app. Kalispell to San Francisco to Hawaii and eventually Bora Bora. He selected and paid for a single seat in first class.

26

"What do you see?" Nicole asked.

Lars walked back to midtable and tapped a photo. "Surgical scarring," he said. "It has to be. Thin, straight, all the same width and length."

"Nicely done, right?"

"I'd let this doctor fix my face," Lars agreed.

He let his eyes drift over the glossy photos, pulling four of them from the pile and arranging them side by side. "Strange, the way the incisions are arranged. Almost like someone is keeping score."

Yes, on what had turned out to be the hip of the young lady.

"You call MacAulay?"

"Yeah. He confirmed the markings. All surgical."

The ME had accompanied the body back to the morgue in the early-morning hours and prepped her for storage. Then he had gone home to bed and had approached the victim fresh that afternoon, after his morning office hours. He would get back to them when he was done en suite. Meaning he would do a thorough exam that took a painstakingly long time and then summon her.

She stepped back and took in the photos as a whole. They had come in slowly from the forensic techs, pulled from a locked cache on the victim's cell phone. Each was dated and time-stamped, so arranging them accurately was not a problem. After wading through the images, discarding those that didn't seem to have relevance to Beatrice's murder, they were left with thirty-two shots that told only part of the story. There were gaps, days and weeks of the vic's life not represented in the pictures.

But the photos made some things solid for Nicole. They showed her the greed and power that had surrounded the girl leading up to her death.

Many revealed the same polished, suited men who Nicole believed were players from the Big Pharm round table, and she had sent these photos out to deputies, hoping to find them among the skiers and holiday revelers. But nothing yet.

She moved six pictures so that they were grouped together. Michael King, an older, suited woman, and four men who appeared in multiple shots over several occasions. Each of them posing with their victim. "What do you think of this?"

"The round table?"

"I think so."

The night of Beatrice's eighth-grade graduation. What should have been a family gathering to celebrate their victim's accomplishments had been turned into a pony show.

Nicole tapped the image of the older woman with Beatrice. She had a solid build, with short hair styled away from her face. She wasn't smiling. Concern filled her eyes.

"Who is she?"

"Someone who refused to play the game?" Lars guessed.

"Why do you say that?"

"They're posing but not touching." No arm around a waist, inches of air space between their shoulders. "And the woman's frowning. She's worried about something."

"Maybe this is the woman Joaquin spoke of." The grandmotherly pharm exec who had dismissed the idea of working with Enrique Esparza. "Maybe she changed her mind when the cards were on the table. When she realized there was too much at stake not to play.

"We need to find her."

"A priority," she agreed. "What do you think about this?"

She walked to the end of the table and removed another photo. It had been taken on the mountain four days ago. It showed Dr. Esparza, skis and poles and bright sunshine. He was talking to a couple. Benjamin and Charlene.

Nicole knew that Benjamin was five feet seven inches tall. Charlene towered over him by about eight inches. In the photo she looked at Esparza, neither giving nor receiving any emotion. She didn't care that Esparza was unhappy, disagreeable, or anything else. Benjamin was smiling. "A meeting of like minds?" Lars said.

"Except Esparza doesn't seem to be in agreement."

"No. He definitely looks defensive."

"I believe Kenny," Nicole said. "Esparza's documents were forgeries."

Nicole had a deputy working on it. The FDA, being a government office, meant a lot of waiting, but she wanted the certainty.

"And that wasn't the limit of his deceit. What do you suppose they're talking about here?" Back to the photo of Esparza with Benjamin and Charlene.

"What everyone in their circle was talking about: Beatrice."

"But what specifically? Why meet with Esparza prior to the proofing and auction?" Was it even allowed?

"Maybe there was a favorite, and it wasn't King," Lars posed. "Wouldn't be the first time a dark horse entered a race."

Made sense. Nicole knew Benjamin was an easy sell if the money was right and the workload light. "No honor among thieves."

"If Esparza gave his daughter cancer," Lars began, "then he cured her too."

"I'm waiting for MacAulay to confirm that."

"But listen to this," Lars said. "Esparza implanted his daughter four times. That keeps with what Kenny said too. And if each time the cancer sample was bigger, a different kind, a tougher-to-beat cancer, that explains why the vic got sicker for longer as the months passed." As Joaquin had reported and the girl's diary entries seemed to reflect. "So even if Esparza carried out his medical trials without government approval, he had a viable cure for the disease. A cure that could, potentially, apply to other diseases." He hooked her gaze, his own hard and penetrating. "Maybe what Esparza has is the base cure for every human ailment."

The thought was staggering. Improbable. And the discovery perhaps already lost.

"Do you think he wrote it out? Scientists keep journals of their work, right? They hypothesize and test and have to put results somewhere," she said.

"He made a point of telling us that it was locked inside his mind. One of his precautions. But there's no way he could come up with something so big without keeping a record of it."

"So we move this away from the family?" she posed. "We start digging into those who would be hurt the most."

"Big Pharm," Lars agreed. "This group." And he slid the photo of Esparza with Benjamin and Charlene into the pile.

"We need to find the other players," Nicole said. "At least the two who are here in Toole County."

"One of them must be the highest bidder," Lars said.

"And maybe with Benjamin's help."

Her gaze lingered on the older woman. She was different from the others. Worried, on edge. Angered? "I'd like to talk to her."

*　*　*

Nicole passed cold storage for the small suite of rooms that held MacAulay's morgue.

He looked up as she approached. "I expected you sooner."

"You take a look at King yet?"

"I did." He turned and leaned back against the table. "He didn't kill Beatrice."

And that gave Nicole pause. "He confessed."

"He lied."

"You can prove that?"

"Three-quarters of an inch," he said. "The pads of the thumbs that choked the life out of Beatrice Esparza measure exactly three-quarters of an inch."

"But King's don't," she followed.

MacAulay shook his head. "Not even close. King was stocky, with thick hands. The pads of his thumbs measure one and one eighth of an inch. I took several impressions, different angles. There's no wiggle room there."

"Damn."

The killer was possibly male, but not King. The killer was five feet ten to six feet three inches. He weighed no more than 165 pounds. And he had slim hands.

Had it been jealousy or rejection? Either could result in murder.

Or was it fear of financial ruin?

Of their current pool of male contestants, that made their killer either Joaquin or Kenny King.

Or Benjamin and his wife, Charlene, hired by the Big Pharms. Not just broker but executioner too?

"And the perpetrator wasn't wearing gloves. This was skin-to-skin contact."

"How do you know?"

"Latent print." And he smiled. "In the bruise pattern. They're never admissible in court, and there isn't enough to provide an identity pool. Just enough so we know the killer used his bare hands."

"Who am I looking for, MacAulay?"

"A pharm company not in the running," MacAulay posed. "Or one that wants to keep the status quo. A family member who didn't believe in what Beatrice was doing. Or was jealous that her altruistic ways outshined the behavior of an average human being."

"Strangulation is personal."

27

Patience was not a virtue. Not in a homicide investigation.

Patience allowed a lead to run cold and a case to enter deep freeze. They were on a collision course with the midnight hour, and statistically speaking, that meant their chances of finding their killer would take a nose dive. Nicole sat in the driver's seat of the Yukon with the engine idling and steam from the exhaust billowing around the vehicle. Sometimes you had to slow down, like when a thought was bordering your awareness. Exactly what she hadn't done in the Esparzas' hotel room, when she should have noticed the absence of the girls' coats in the closet Mrs. Esparza had flung wide open.

It was 5:40, and in the dead of winter that meant the sun was already hidden behind the mountains and the sky was a sketch in charcoals. The lights inside the station were a somber yellow glow that didn't quite reach Nicole where she remained with her vehicle, her memory playing a deadly game of hide-and-seek with her consciousness.

Her conversation with MacAulay had her reaching back into that hotel room. Had her rummaging through images like they were snapshots in her hands. But which of his words had triggered that search, and what in particular was she looking for?

Strangulation is personal.

And she supposed that was true. Unarmed, an assailant could be reduced to the menial labor of murder. Some probably preferred it, got off on proximity and the power of taking life. But it wasn't the norm. It wasn't efficient. It wasn't choice.

Nothing personal . . . Joaquin's words tangled with MacAulay's.

Beatrice. Nicole's mind suddenly lit on it. There had been no outward signs of the victim's presence in the living space the family shared, except for her journal. No snow boots at the door, sweaters thrown over the back of a chair. No books or magazines that would appeal to a teen girl. No jewelry taken off and left on the coffee table. No sign of Beatrice at all.

And yet she was remembered by hotel staff. She'd been a regular, passing through the lobby, drinking cocoa and roasting marshmallows on the patio.

Nicole needed back in that hotel room. She needed to confirm what she suspected, that when Beatrice Esparza disappeared, she'd done it fully packed and with no intention of looking back.

Nicole cut the engine and slid out of the Yukon. She walked into the squad room just as Lars was rising from his desk, cell to ear. He hung up, shrugged into his coat, and said to her, "Forty-five."

As in percent. Their chances of apprehending their killer fell by forty-five percent once a day stood between them and the crime.

Nicole nodded in acknowledgment. "Where are you headed?" she asked.

At this time on an average day, his answer would be that he was going home. Unless his daughter had a volleyball game, but then he would be slipping into his sweat shirt, Blue Mesa High School stamped on it with the raging-bull mascot breaking through the ball, and not into his parka.

"Judge Williams signed the order," Lars told her. "The kids will be questioned by a court-appointed child psychologist tomorrow morning."

"And you're going to deliver the order yourself?"

He nodded. "You want to come?"

"I was headed there anyway."

He held her gaze as he finished buttoning his parka. "Why?"

"I didn't see Beatrice Esparza in their hotel room," she said. "It wasn't just the absence of her coat, her purse. There was almost a complete absence of the girl."

Lars thought about that, nodding slowly. "Yeah. I didn't see anything that screamed teenage girl."

"Except her journal."

"You think she forgot that?"

"She could have left it on purpose. Some kind of statement. I don't think it matters. Not as much as the fact that she packed up and left."

"And what made her do so."

"Exactly." She turned and walked with him toward the door. "You drive, and I'll tell you about what I learned from MacAulay." They headed out of town and into the ski resort area, passing signs for Deer Run and Jagged Ridge as they waded deeper into the tourist hub. Lars already knew that King was not their killer. She had called that in. Now she told him about the suture lines and MacAulay's discovery—the crater where a cancerous tumor had been but miraculously disappeared.

"What did Esparza say about his discovery?" Lars posed as he searched his own memory. "Something about the bad cells having a change of heart and turning into cheerleaders?"

"Champions," Nicole corrected. "He said they championed the body."

Nicole settled into her seat. She wondered about Esparza's discovery. If he had found a way to turn back time and disease, certainly there would be more activity around the doctor. Protections and demands. Why wasn't he hidden away, like Oz, behind a shroud of secrecy?

"There's a flaw," she decided. "In Esparza's discovery."

"Always," Lars agreed. "Or getting it into clinical trials would have happened."

"But even with its flaws, it's big enough to stir up the pharm companies."

"They eat guys like Esparza."

"You think it's happened before?"

"They like to keep the tempo steady," he said. "When we were going through Amber's treatment and recovery, I got the feeling that there was a measured pacing with medicine, with discoveries and allocations—who got what drug and when. There are people deciding every day who will live and who will die, and it all comes down to money. A cure for cancer—" The thought settled on Lars in a deep frown. "That would shake up the world. A way to turn every sick cell into a super cell? Pharm companies would be reduced to aspirin pushers."

"All but the one who owned Nueva Vida."

"Esparza's lying," Lars said. "About several things." And he began to list them. "He has documentation."

"Or he would have been taken off the board already."

"Exactly. There's a reason they kept him alive."

And Nicole thought about Esparza's single text message to his daughter: *Cooperate.* Maybe she hadn't. There were rules in every game played, and maybe Beatrice hadn't followed them.

"And King is more than we think," Lars continued. "He's more than an interested party, more than a father who took a step off the deep end."

"Whatever the game is, it crushed him."

"You heard him," Lars said. "He lamented Beatrice's compassion. It broke him up that she had died on the board."

"Almost as much as it disturbed him that his own daughter wouldn't know a cure for her disease."

"I got that feeling, too. He was counting on Beatrice."

"And he was grateful."

"And saddened. He'd lost hope for his daughter, for Beatrice, and something else."

Nicole nodded. "And that something else was the breaking point. Guilt of some kind," Nicole posed. "But not about Nueva Vida. He felt good about what they were doing, but not how they were doing it."

"Maybe it caught up with him. The ethics. Desperation twists a person beyond recognition sometimes."

28

Montana had never been on their list. In the past, vacations had been all about getting outside and breathing in nature. Here, skiing was okay, but there were better places for it. The resort was rustic and one of the better places they'd ever stayed, in Joaquin's opinion, but he knew his mother and father both felt that it was less than they'd expected. This was not a hot-spot destination. Hard to even find on a map.

They were in Blue Mesa for one thing. And it had failed them. Failed Nueva Vida.

Now Montana would always be stained with losing Beatrice. It would be about mistakes, bad decisions, and greed.

"Sometimes, Joaquin, the desire to live life to the fullest clouds our vision." His father had admitted that he had been blinded by the need for more.

His father was remorseful. He'd cried for Bea. He'd sobbed, his shoulders shaking and his nose running, and in that moment he hadn't cared what the world thought of him. And it was in that moment that Joaquin realized that he loved his father, even though he despised his weaknesses. It was possible to feel both ways at the same time.

The thick carpeting absorbed his footsteps, and so he arrived at the second-floor conference room unannounced. His father sat in a chair facing the windows. Night was early and pressed against the panes. His laptop and cell phone sat in the chair next to him. His head was down and his hands were folded in his lap, but Joaquin could see that he was thinking. Small lines deepened around his eyes and his lips were pursed.

He looked up and caught Joaquin's reflection beside his in the window. And he smiled. It was soft and slow and it reached his eyes, and he opened his hands and invited,

"Come here, Joaquin. Come sit next to me."

He walked around the chairs and stood in front of his father, and he took the hand his father offered, not knowing what was going to happen next. His father was not a physically affectionate guy. He didn't demonstrate emotion.

"I know this is a fine time to say such things, but better too little too late than nothing at all," he said. He turned their hands so that Joaquin's was over his, larger, younger, stronger. "You are at a crossroads. Great things are expected of you, and you will make big decisions too soon. You will choose wisely, learning from my mistakes. That's the way these things happen. And I will be proud of you. You will respond from your heart. That is the biggest thing about you, Joaquin. Your heart. There is beauty in your care for others and in your sense of right and wrong. And as you grow, you will become less rigid in that. You will bend as the boughs of a tree, but you will not break. Because there is strength in there too."

Joaquin felt his hand tremble in his fathers. He sat down beside him, and he turned his hand so that he could grip his father's. It sounded like his dad was saying good-bye. His father sensed his emotions and spoke to them.

"I've had another call," he told Joaquin. "Geneva Sanders, Callon Pharmaceuticals. She wants to meet with me and I'm going."

"You're going to give them Nueva Vida?"

"Never. We will meet where Beatrice died because I want them to know the true reason we are together. They will expect the final notes on Nueva Vida. They will expect me to arrive, suitcase in hand, ready to roll with them. Instead, they will receive devastating news. An end to many dreams."

"You've destroyed Nueva Vida?"

"No. Beatrice would not have wanted that. But I am giving it away. As she asked me to do."

He nodded toward his laptop, closed and silent now.

"I've downloaded it on the laptop," he said. "I've attached it to an email that I sent to a small pharm company with a big reputation for integrity. I've given all to them, except the final sequence in the code that opens all possibility. I've written a second email to a different pharmaceutical company. They will have to work together. They will have each other for checks and balances."

He opened his hand. A small SD media card rested in the center of his palm, and lines radiated out from it. Long life, as Beatrice had never had.

"If I give this to you for safekeeping, they will come for you too."

"They'll never know."

But his father shook his head. "If they think it's possible, they'll come."

Joaquin felt a heaviness lean against his throat. "I'll take that chance."

But his father shook his head. "If I destroy this, than there is no reservoir of knowledge. Nothing to go back to. The puzzle is incomplete. Scientists are good at chasing leads, but I wonder, have I left enough clues?"

He looked up at Joaquin, conflicted, and said, "Your sister can't have died for nothing."

"You're not going anywhere," Joaquin said. "You can answer their questions. Guide them through it."

There was a long silence that grew heavy and made the air thin, and before he even said his next words, Joaquin knew what they would be.

"Today I will die, Joaquin," he said. "I don't want you to be surprised by that. You will need to keep your mind clear, your actions precise. I am counting on you."

"You don't have to go."

"They will stop at nothing else." He lifted his hands, palms up, and gazed at them as though watching the highlight reel of his life. "I played the game. The stakes were high. I knew that going in, but was distracted by the payout. It would have been huge. Not just financially, but Enrique Esparza, he would be remembered by many here and many to come as the maker of miracles. I wanted everyone to know that. That I did it. That I rose to a position of power, that I was giving the world what no one else could—new life."

This Joaquin understood. Finally. And not because his father said the words, but because he'd given up the dream. "Don't meet with them. Tell them you gave it away."

"They won't wait. If I didn't agree, they would come for me. They would be here right now. They don't like liability, and they are big on canceling debts."

"With the knowledge public, they would have no reason to kill you. You said so yourself."

"I was wrong. All loose threads must be tied off."

"Fight this."

"I am fighting for Beatrice now," he said. "She will not have died for nothing, and that is the most important thing." He looked at Joaquin. "You will live your life, and you will have mountains and valleys, and you will be tested and true. I have no doubt about that. Look forward," he said. "That was my biggest problem, I was always looking over my shoulder. And the past was always gaining on me. Don't let that happen to you, Joaquin."

He opened his hand again, and the media card, a tiny piece of plastic and metal, rested in his palm.

"I'm giving this to you, Joaquin, not to keep but to carry. They are my notes, all my failures and triumphs on my way to Nueva Vida. Twelve years of work. Put it in your pocket as a piece of lint, but remember it when you get to the police. Sheriff Cobain—I like her, Joaquin. She is smart, determined. When you give her this, tell her what it is. Tell her it is not so much evidence as it is life."

29

Nicole returned from the Huntington for another pass at the evidence. She'd gotten nothing from the family. Dr. Esparza had accepted the court order from Lars and then had shut the door on Nicole's questions.

"Not now," he'd said. "Soon you will have it all, but right now it is time for family."

His tone had been somber. Fitting for such a time, but there was something else as well. A finality beyond the death of his daughter, maybe. It bothered Nicole, but she had respected their privacy. She'd had no other choice.

A secured manila envelope was waiting on Nicole's desk. It had a forensics stamp on it. Nicole sat down and used her finger to break open the seal. She pulled out a stack of neatly typed pages.

Lars knocked, then stuck his head through her door. "We have something," he said, and there was a beat to his tone that told her it was something solid.

"What?"

She noticed he had his coat in hand, so she gathered the pages she'd just emptied from the envelope. She'd have to read en route.

"Where are we going?"

"We found Geneva Sanders, CEO of Callon Pharma," he told her. "The woman in the picture with our victim."

Nicole pulled on her coat and followed him out of her office.

"That from the victim's locked file?" He nodded toward the envelope in her hand.

"Yeah. Her digital diary," she told him.

Would she find the tender words of a girl desperately trying to find her way? Or the agony that came with offering herself as a test subject, putting her father's ambition before her own? Maybe both.

"You drive," she said. "I'll read."

There were thirty or forty pages, and she skimmed through them. Each carried densely typed words; some pages bore doodles in fluorescent colors. There were photographs, and Nicole paused over these.

"Look at this." She caught Lars's attention before he climbed into the driver's seat.

It was an image of an incision, puckered and pink and still bearing the blue sutures used to close the skin. Beside it, another similar wound was beginning to fade.

"Why keep this one under lock and key?" Lars wondered. There had been several such photos in her open cache.

"Don't know." Yet. Nicole leafed through a few more pages and stopped, her hands clenching around the margins of the paper. "Damn."

Another photo, the same shot, only—Nicole searched for the entry date—a week later.

She heard a sharp intake of breath and a virulent swear slip past Lars's lips. It matched Nicole's sentiments for Dr. Esparza and his overreaching handiwork.

The incision was distorted. Swollen and bruised and leaking a yellow. Where the skin had been pink before, it was now a blistering red.

"Looks infected."

"Yeah, and we just found the reason our victim would take the Augmentin."

She skimmed for more photos but found only one. It was of Violet King and had been added to the victim's diary Christmas night, just hours before her death. Violet was wearing a puffy lavender dress with lace embroidery and her hair had been curled and pinned into an updo. The girl was smiling beautifully. There were no words with the entry, but a line of teardrops and hourglasses were stamped across the bottom of the photo.

Nicole climbed into the passenger seat and continued reading. Lars had already turned onto the Lake Road, headed toward the resorts, when she shared the next bit.

"She was tormented by her father's narrow-minded approach to medicine, but King's too. She has a whole entry here reflecting on King's use of his position and money that extended Violet's life. And she wondered if King's friendship with her family was based solely on their ability to help his daughter."

"A reasonable deduction."

She scanned through the remaining pages and realized several things at once. The vic had clearly defined boundaries. Sports were confined to the journal Joaquin had handed her and Nicole had read through earlier that day, like a log book. Hopes, dreams, and the obstacles to each were recorded in her digital diary. She'd written about her father and her hopes that he would come to see his patients as people. She felt it was the first step to seeing the world's population as deserving of an equal level of care. Some entries despaired that her father would ever reach that depth of compassion. She'd written about her mother. By far, they were the thorniest entries in the collection. More love than resentment, but barely. Her mother cared too much about material things. Things that would waste away. Beatrice had acknowledged at one point that her mother loved her enough to poke around in her business, although it was clear the victim had had more respect for her father, who didn't see much beyond his work, and when he did emerge from that, however briefly, his vision was blurry at best. Her siblings received little notice in the diary, perhaps because those relationships had been good, non-contentious. It seemed that the victim saved this space for matters that bothered her most. To that end, she'd made only two mentions of Big Pharm companies and their involvement on the fringes of her life. Beatrice didn't like to be paraded around like a show dog. She didn't want to be examined. She would allow that privilege only to her father and King.

"Listen to this," Nicole said, and began to read, "Dated December twenty-fifth. 'The Dynamic Duo showed up for cocktails tonight. Michael says they're necessary. The Big Six got together and decided an independent broker for dad's research was the only way to go, but they give me the creeps. The woman especially. She's touchy, and I mean the kind where she reaches out and puts her hands on people. And keeps them there too long. I avoid her. Michael says I should introduce myself. When I asked him if it was because I'm the product, he got all soft and sorry, which I knew he would. He doesn't like looking at me that way, and I like that he doesn't like it.'"

"Benjamin and Charlene," Lars said.

"Yes," Nicole agreed. She peered over the pages and through the windshield. They were scaling the mountain pass that would spool them out at the entrances of several swanky resorts. A sideways look captured the icy Lake Maria below them and in the valley next to it the turbine farm under tall vapor lighting. "Here's the other one," she said, and turned back to the pages, rustling through them to the very end.

"Geneva is here. And someone else. The guy from Axis Labs. I liked when they were silent. When we were working only with Michael. But now they get to have a look at me. Just a meet and mingle. I told my father no. Of course he didn't listen. Michael agrees it's the only way to handle these things. It's business. I don't have to talk, but it's preferred. I don't have to stay more than twenty minutes. Of agony. I'll hate it. Them staring at me, trying to look under my skin. That's what labs are for. Blood draws and biopsies. And that's what they'll get. Why do they need more?"

*   *   *

Sanders was staying at a five-star resort north of town, more than a mile from the Huntington and closer to the crime scene. Lake Maria was spread out behind the three-story chalet and was part of the ambience, with an oval skating rink marked by bumpers and over which were strung colored lights. Hills both west and east of the lodge were thinned of trees for tubing and sledding. An outside deck with bistro tables and butane heating lamps was a popular alternative to the indoor lounge with its inglenook fireplace and artificial heating. They found Geneva Sanders there, bundled into a down parka and sipping a latte. She was a short woman, sturdy in stature, and had a fleck of whipped cream at the corner of her mouth. She sat alone, a book on the table but closed. Nicole noticed she favored memoirs. This one of a fallen giant in the music industry.

Sanders noted their approach and didn't wait for introductions.

"Sheriff Cobain?" She sat up in her tall seat and offered her hand. Nicole took it.

"You were expecting us," she said.

"Yes. Your deputies recognized me from a photo on Beatrice's cell phone."

"And told you we'd be coming and why?" Nicole asked.

"Oh, they tried to be discreet about it, but I was in the lobby when they came in. And of course I had a few questions of my own. It's a little disconcerting, happening upon the police circulating your photograph."

Nicole nodded.

"How well did you know Beatrice?"

Sanders thought about that. "Not as well as I do my grandchildren, but certainly better than the daughter of a friend."

"Why?"

"She was our star pupil. And as is often the case, we had a lot more to learn from her than she from us."

"Then you know about Nueva Vida?"

"Almost from the beginning," she confirmed.

"But Dr. Esparza worked exclusively with Michael King."

"We're always snooping through each other's pockets, but that's the nature of the pharm business. In any case, Esparza gave Callon first pass. We declined, but we hadn't lost interest."

"Why didn't you jump at the chance of buying out Esparza's super cell?"

"Michael was far more desperate than us," she said. "For reasons I'm sure you've begun to understand. When business becomes personal the lines of protocol are blurred. Ethics are weighed against the needs of the heart."

"King paid for it?"

"He came across with the goods," she confirmed.

"Such as?"

"Equipment, gifts, financial support. In our business, it's called wooing." She grimaced, recognizing that the term was less than attractive. "Michael was cultivating a relationship with Esparza."

"With the expectation that Esparza would sell to him?"

"No, Michael would get an insider's look at the process. He would be given a few of the pieces but not the whole puzzle. Not enough to figure it out on his own. But it's understood by both parties that a sale isn't eminent. Michael knew there were several interested parties."

"Did you come to Blue Mesa for the auction?"

"Yes. Attendance wasn't mandatory, but we wanted a front-row seat for this. It could make or break many of us. We knew that. And by *we*, I mean pharmaceuticals collectively. From the Big Six down to the small little fish."

"Did Callon have something to worry about?"

"We all did," she said. "But we're better off than most. Unless you have a niche pharma, something this big would blow you out of the water."

"Does Callon have a niche pharma?"

"Yes. We hold the market on beta blockers. There are other companies that offer similar drugs, but none with the effectiveness of ours."

"So you didn't need Nueva Vida?"

"We wanted Nueva Vida," she said. "Without it we would stay afloat. With it we would prosper. But we didn't want it at the cost of our reputation and possible sanctions by the FDA."

"And that was possible?"

"Probable."

"And that's why you passed on Nueva Vida?"

She nodded.

"What changed?" Because she had come for the auction.

Her lips pursed. "Nothing, I think. We worried Esparza was using his daughter as a test subject for his nano-cell. He presented her as a cancer patient, but we had serious doubts about that."

"Because you never knew Beatrice to have cancer?"

"Oh no. The girl had cancer. In August. And again in October."

"How was that established?" Nicole asked.

"A blood panel, drawn by a neutral party. The sample was taken to a lab under watch, the results impartial. That's how these things are carried out." She sat forward, sipped from her latte, and paused over her next words. "So we knew Beatrice had cancer. We knew stage, had growth rate, and were present for the insertion of the super cell in December."

"Then what was troubling about Beatrice Esparza's cancer?"

"There were no records of other interventions. No chemo or radiation. Not even a round of Herceptin. In fact, no drug therapy at all. Esparza had the paperwork from the FDA, allowing a small clinical trial, but I doubted its veracity."

"Because he couldn't provide proof of other, failed options?"

"Exactly. And the FDA doesn't hand out invitations without evidence. If Beatrice had been treated at a hospital, by doctors other than her father, if there had been record of any such outside medical involvement, then we'd be a pack of rabid dogs after Esparza's super cell. But none of that exists."

"Are documents from the FDA easy to forge?"

"Easier to buy, I think," she said. "But who knows?" She shrugged. "The internet makes so many things possible."

"When was the last time you saw Beatrice?"

"Christmas night." She sat back, crossed her legs. "Did Enrique tell you about the proofing? It was our final step. A blood draw *and* biopsy. Proven clear at two months. We call it a double-sure. With the kind of money at stake, we need at least that much." She didn't wait for them to question, but sat back and confided, "Fifty-five million dollars. So the double-check was mandatory. It was to be done at King's place, out on the lake. Cocktails, hors d'oeuvres, and revelation."

"A biopsy completed not in a hospital?" Lars asked.

"You'd be surprised or aghast at the many places such procedures are done. In this case, sterile equipment and environment were all that was needed. Well, and an electron microscope."

"And you had all that?"

"King had a good setup."

"You saw it?"

"We all did."

Nicole and her deputies had been through the home. So far, they'd recovered medical supplies in the trash and a microscope on a bureau in an upstairs bedroom. A prepared slide was taken into evidence, specially packaged and delivered to Arty and company. No word yet on the type of microscope. Or on what the slide held, if anything.

"Was Beatrice a willing participant?"

"Definitely. She was proud of her involvement but resented the intrusion." Sanders shrugged. "Teen angst in the mix."

"Was she happy to be at King's?"

"She was happy with King," Sanders clarified. "She was happy to be a part of her father's great success—that's what she called it. But on Christmas, Beatrice seemed agitated. She refused to speak to her father, wanted nothing to do with the brokers hired to conduct the auction. And then her mother showed up—" Sanders's voice trailed off, and her mouth became grim. "A little late, if you ask me. I think if you'd asked Beatrice too."

"Explain that, please," Nicole asked.

Sanders paused to compose her thoughts. "I don't know Alma Esparza very well, so this is strictly as an observer. Enrique, he's the dreamer. Alma is supportive. She's loyal. But she also seems to have her feet firmly on the ground. She wants her husband to succeed, her children to obey, and her life to flow smoothly, from one pleasant shore to the next. She doesn't like turbulence, and so I felt she had very little patience with Beatrice's new-found independence and importance."

"Because it caused trouble?"

"Enrique spent more time with Beatrice than he did his wife or other children. To develop something like Nueva Vida, one must be obsessive. I imagine Alma was missing her husband, sparring with her daughter and distraught over the possibility that both were involved in a process that could harm Beatrice and shatter her family."

"Who bid highest?" Nicole asked.

"We did," she said. "We worried about Enrique's ethics, but this super cell, it has great promise."

"You purchased the rights to Nueva Vida?"

"The rights to Esparza's super cell and to him, as an intellectual property, until Nueva Vida is saving lives, and not on a small scale. Esparza will work with us for the next ten to twenty years."

Nicole thought about that. "It will take that long to effect the kind of change you're hoping for?"

"Medicine is a slow business," she said.

"Were you surprised when you heard Beatrice was murdered?"

"Shocked but not surprised," she said. "She was a beautiful girl, loved life, and so for that reason her death was shocking. But I was not surprised. Many people would gain from her death."

"Callon included?"

"Especially Callon."

30

A low, keystone garden wall separated the patio, with its bistro and fire pit, from the rolling grounds and trails. Alma Esparza sat with her back to the resort, watching her children play in the snow. The girls didn't show a lot of enthusiasm, and Nicole knew that they had been told about Beatrice's death. Children this young stood at the chasm of loss, trembling with fear. Nicole had read the articles, attended the conferences, watched it unfold in real time. Children needed to be surrounded by family, to be immersed in routine, to talk about their feelings. It was good to see Joaquin trying, reaching out to them in the ways he knew. He rolled snow into a large ball and carried it to where his sisters knelt and made it into the foundation of a snowman. Sofia and Isla patted and smoothed the ball to greater roundness. Their breath plumed in the air, and above them the halogen lamps caught swirling flurries in their light and held off the night. And Joaquin stood behind them, a steady presence.

Nicole's breath condensed against the glass, and she stepped back.

"A little bit of normal thrown into the blender," Lars said.

Nicole nodded. She didn't doubt that Alma and Joaquin and the little girls were feeling the sharp cut of a day without Beatrice. "I wonder where Esparza is?"

"Peddling his wares?" he guessed.

"Maybe."

She pushed through the door and stepped onto the resort's patio. A fire burned in the stone pit and several people were roasting marshmallows over it. A young woman was making coffee drinks and hot cocoa at the barista bar. Heat lamps sizzled in the moist air.

"You getting soft on Esparza?"

She thought about that. The man had been driven by greed, by the poverty of his youth and the desire to be someone who mattered. Human qualities, shared on some level by all.

"He didn't kill her," she said. Not with his own hands. "But his weaknesses did."

"What do you think about Sanders?"

"She was very cooperative, wasn't she?" Nicole said.

"You think too much?"

"I think everything she told us was the truth, but that she didn't tell us everything."

"What did she leave out?"

"Her own complicity."

Nicole let that drop and started across the patio. Lars was good at picking through shell fragments and formulating cause and effect.

Joaquin noticed her approach and raised his chin, indicating that his mother should turn and see what was going down. Nicole stopped behind her, close enough that she would have burst her personal space bubble, and waited for her attention, but she raised a hand to keep Joaquin in his place.

Alma Esparza wore her red, fur-lined parka and a wool hat and gloves. She turned, and her gaze found Nicole's. The woman had been crying. Salty tracks marked her smooth skin, and her lips trembled.

"Sheriff," she said. "Are you here to talk to me again?"

Alma Esparza shifted, preparing to stand.

"Don't get up, Mrs. Esparza." Nicole swung her legs over the wall and sat down beside her. She was quiet a moment as she took in the scene. Snow had an ambience, a hushed quality even beneath the current of laughter and conversation on the patio. "The girls look good."

Sofia and Isla had noticed the tension in Joaquin and stopped playing in the snow. They followed his gaze to where Nicole sat with their mother. She smiled, and they raised their hands and waved.

"Yes. It is better for them outside, with the fresh air and the snow. The room is too heavy with Beatrice's absence."

"She was close to her sisters." Hotel staff and family had commented on it.

"She preferred their company," Alma Esparza said. "Beatrice had a lot of friends, but she always made time for family."

Nicole turned so that Joaquin and his sisters were in her periphery and Mrs. Esparza was her focal point. She noticed that Lars had returned indoors. He had his phone in hand, was probably paging through his notes as he tried to form a path of logic to Nicole's theory—that Geneva Sanders was involved in the murder of Beatrice Esparza.

"Why are you here?" Mrs. Esparza asked. There was a river of desperation running under her words. "What could we possibly have now that you need?"

"Answers," Nicole said. "From the beginning, you've known more than you're saying."

"Because King had my daughters," Alma said. "And I thought they would all come home. I told Enrique that. Give him what he wants or at least make him think he's getting it. Then they can all come home."

"So what happened?"

Alma shook her head. "Enrique said it was too late for that. Even if they had gone through with the proofing, if King had solid proof of life, it would be too late because Nueva Vida would not work for King's daughter as it had worked for ours."

"Then your husband was testing his super cell on your daughter?"

"I believe that," Alma said. "But Enrique never said one way or the other. He never gave me a straight answer about his work. His family would know when the world did. It was safer for us that way."

"But you knew because Beatrice was sick."

Alma nodded. "I knew. I saw the incisions. He was slicing into our daughter and he would not tell me why, but I knew. I asked him to stop. Things had gone too far. But he said they were too close to stop now. And he was right; his discovery was working. Beatrice would get sick and then she was better. Better than ever before."

"Did you get the Augmentin for Beatrice?"

"Enrique would not allow any medications. Nothing that would compromise the validity of his trials. But one of the incisions was infected. Puffy and red and starting to ooze. Beatrice came to me. She showed me because Enrique would do nothing to help her. Nothing beyond a topical, and it wasn't working."

"Why Augmentin when you knew she was allergic to it?"

"Do you know what happens when an infection of the skin enters the bloodstream?"

Nicole knew basic first aid. "It's poison."

"Yes. And if that is not treated, if it gets to the heart—" She sniffed loudly. "She would die. Augmentin gave Beatrice a rash. She could deal with that."

Nicole caught a flash of movement in the corner of her eye and turned slightly toward it. Behind the glass doors, Daisy had approached Lars. She was talking, and he looked up from his notes to give her his full attention. His eyebrows peaked, and Nicole spent a moment wondering what the older woman was imparting. Would there be details that changed the direction of their investigation? That gave them greater insight into suspect or victim? She hoped so. She was always mindful of the clock and the diminishing odds of solving a murder. They needed a break that would propel them forward.

She turned back to Alma Esparza. Her eyes were focused on her son and daughters, but they were liquid and her loss was obvious.

"You went to King's house Christmas night." Nicole recalled her attention. "You went for Beatrice but not Sofia and Isla."

"They were playing and they were happy. Big girls at a big-girl sleepover."

"What did King say to you?"

"He would not let me see Beatrice. He thought I would upset her and the evening was too important for that. He kept me at the door and told Isla and Sofia to go back to Violet. There were still gifts and candies to pass out, he told them."

"And King asked you to leave?"

"Yes. He said he'd return my daughters after the proofing."

"But you didn't trust him."

"I knew what he wanted from Beatrice. I knew that he would stop at nothing to get it. It was the only way for him."

"And still you left?"

"Enrique was there. I trusted him." A flush crept up her neck and settled in her cheeks. "And Enrique told me to leave."

"Did you speak to Beatrice?"

She held Nicole's gaze and shook her head. "She wouldn't come with me." The confession fell from trembling lips.

"But you said she called. She begged you to come for her."

"Yes," she said. "But she had calmed down. She didn't want me there and she didn't want to leave."

"And your story, of following the Lake Road for hours and never finding Beatrice?"

"Was not true. I went to King's when I should have been on the slopes with Enrique. I didn't know he had lied about that until I saw my husband there, mingling."

"And what did your husband say, Mrs. Esparza?"

"He was not happy. He met me at the door and told me to go back to the hotel. To wait. It would only be a few more hours. At midnight it would be over and we would be back to our normal, together and enjoying our vacation. Business settled."

"So you left?"

She caught Nicole's gaze, hers steady and beseeching. "I beckoned to Beatrice again, but she would not come. She was mad at her father and mad at me too."

"Why was Beatrice mad at you, Mrs. Esparza?"

She looked away, at her children in the snow, at the trees and beyond, toward the lake. Her fingers worked the hem of her coat, pleating it, then smoothing it out. A repetitive motion she was aware of only at the edges of conscious thought, probably.

"There's something more you're not telling me," Nicole persisted.

"What?" Alma Esparza tried to deflect the question.

"'Good girls don't do this.' Does that sound familiar?"

She held Nicole's gaze and nodded. "I know you have Beatrice's cell phone. You know I wrote that to her."

"More than once. But I don't know why."

"And that's your question?"

"I think it's a pretty good one," Nicole said.

"I told you—"

"Yes," Nicole agreed. "You told me Beatrice was pushing back, rebelling as teens do, but there's more to it."

"Some things between a mother and her daughter are private."

"Nothing in a murder investigation is off-limits," Nicole reminded her. "You know my job is to look everywhere, shake the sheets, turn out the pockets. We find out a lot that way. Some of it connected to the crime, some not. I think your words to Beatrice are important, but more important is the reason you used them. That's what I want to know about."

"I am not happy about this," she began, "about my own behavior. Beatrice and my husband were spending so much time together, away from home, away from the family. And when they were present, they talked around us. It was like we had disappeared. We were pieces that no longer fit together."

"And you wanted your husband back?"

"Yes. And my life, the way it was before. That's what I wanted."

"It was enough for you," Nicole said. "To be the wife of a doctor."

"Yes. I had never dared to dream my life would turn out so good."

"When you were Beatrice's age and looking into the future?"

"Yes." Mrs. Esparza nodded and sniffed loudly. "Enrique worked long hours, but still we found time for togetherness. Until Nueva Vida."

"His work came between you and your daughter."

"Yes. I suppose I was jealous. Not so much of Beatrice, but of the time she spent with her father. And I missed him. Terribly."

"And so you and Beatrice argued."

"Sometimes so bad she left."

"Ran away?"

"Twice. Both times she went to Michael King. He pretended to understand her. He wanted her to think that, because Beatrice was giving up so much for him." Alma Esparza met Nicole's eyes, hers burning with certainty. "But it was a lie. He would sacrifice my daughter for his."

"Is that why he killed himself?"

She nodded. "He did not kill himself because he couldn't save his daughter. He killed himself because he did nothing to save mine. That is what I believe. He used her and cast her aside. You ask me why Beatrice wouldn't come with me? She loved her father more. Too much to let him down."

Alma Esparza sobbed.

"Enough to die for him?"

She nodded, shakily. "My husband is grieving. For Beatrice and for the decision to include her in his work."

"But that won't bring her back."

"No."

"'Good girls don't do this,'" Nicole said. "She'd run away again, since coming to Blue Mesa, hadn't she?"

"Yes."

"And you wanted her to come home."

"And I want Nueva Vida to never have been."

"Why didn't you go back for your daughters?" Nicole asked. "You knew the way to King's. You could have returned and gotten them, after Beatrice's frantic phone call. You could have called us for help."

But Alma was shaking her head. "I should have, but Enrique wouldn't allow it. For years he'd been working towards that moment. A few more hours was all he wanted. And the girls were safe. I'd seen so myself." She tipped her head back and looked Nicole in the eye. "Enrique assured me everything was fine. Better than fine. And I wanted to believe him."

Nicole held her gaze. She thought about how love and loyalty could be blinding. And about greed. Alma Esparza was as driven as her husband to bury her past.

"You're coming to the station tomorrow," she said. "The child psychologist, she's good. Gentle. Sofia and Isla will be safe in her hands."

"They knew nothing about Beatrice dying until we told them," Alma Esparza said. "They will be of little help to you."

"All the same," Nicole said. "We'll keep it brief."

31

Stepping into the resort, Nicole didn't cast a glance backward. She knew what she would find. Joaquin had approached them when Nicole stood, but she had wanted the young man to follow. She wanted him outside his mother's influence when she spoke to him. Inside, the air was dry and parched her throat. It stung her cheeks, and she pulled at the toggles on her parka until they were all open. She shrugged out of it and pocketed her skullcap.

Daisy had returned to her position behind the reception desk, and Lars stood with his smartphone in hand, sliding a finger along its screen as he scrolled and read. He felt her approach and looked up.

"What did Daisy have to say?"

"Dr. Esparza bought a stamp from her. He put it on an envelope with a Boston address and handed that to her to put in the mail. She wanted to know if I wanted it."

"A can of worms," Nicole said. Tampering with the mail was a federal offense, even for them.

Lars nodded. "She said the envelope was empty except for a small, hard piece of something. She suggested a photo card. She gets them a lot from her kids—pictures of the grandchildren. Daisy likes to scrapbook."

"You think Esparza took pictures?" No doubt he chronicled every step, every obstacle and triumph of his research, even though he denied it. Had Esparza scanned the pages of his lab notes? And if so, what was he doing with it? With Beatrice and King dead, he had to feel his own downward spiral. Had that led him to finally share what he'd been keeping in his iron fist?

"Of his greatest achievement? Yeah. Like you said, Esparza was full of shit. He wrote it down. All of it. That's what scientists do. They keep a record."

"Why is he sending it to Boston?"

"I looked it up. The address matches Lynwood Laboratories. It's a small start-up. They have a corner of the market in the manufacture of mitral clips. Microscopic clips used in cath lab procedures. Specifically the placement of cardiac stents. Reviews are favorable. The CEO announced a few days ago that the company was working on a synthetic valve that showed remarkable success in early trials."

"A fit for Esparza's super cell?" she posed.

"You think he's still shopping?" Lars asked.

"I think he's giving it away."

"The final act of a desperate man?"

"Something like that."

He nodded. "Your company has arrived."

Nicole turned. Joaquin was walking toward them, his skin flushed from the cold, the angles of his face sharp and determined.

"Thank you for coming," Nicole said. He frowned.

"You knew I would follow," he said.

"I wanted to talk to you alone."

"Why?"

"Your birthday is coming up, isn't it, Joaquin? March fifteenth."

"That's right."

"Not even three months," she continued, "and you'll be an adult."

"I am an adult," he said. "A date on a calendar doesn't decide that." His chin lifted a notch, and he spared Lars a look before he returned to Nicole. "What did my mother tell you?"

"What I already knew," Nicole said.

"Which is?"

She ignored the question and addressed instead the tension she found in his features.

"What are you worried about, Joaquin?"

He shifted and looked out the window. His mother continued to sit, her back up, and the girls pushed stones for eyes into the head of the snowman. "They're turning against each other," he said. "My parents. I've never seen that before. My mother has always been about supporting my dad. Loyalty was first."

"Her daughter is dead, and maybe your father had something to do with that."

"My father didn't kill her."

"No, but his weaknesses did."

"And you're going to prove that?"

"That's already done."

The declaration startled him. "How?"

"Greed. Approval. Those are two heavy forces behind some of the decisions we make. We call it motive. Your father was motivated by less-than-stellar qualities to peddle his discovery. Beatrice was motivated by approval—everyone who knew her agreed she was a people pleaser—but also by a very altruistic desire to help others. I respect that. I admire that quality."

"Because it's what you do?" he asked. "You help people, and you risk your life to do it."

The comparison surprised her, but Joaquin was right. "And maybe that's why I like your sister so much. That's a part of my job too, you know. I get to know the victim."

He considered her words and nodded slightly, his attention drifting again toward the windows and his family outside.

"Your father placed an envelope in the mail this afternoon." She could tell from the placid set of his face that this news was no surprise to him. "There was a media card inside it."

"He's given up," Joaquin said. "This afternoon he took steps to ensure our safety."

"The media card is a digital copy of your father's work?"

"It's Nueva Vida," Joaquin confirmed. "It stopped being about money and position and how he would be remembered. It's about Beatrice now."

"So he gave it away?"

"As my sister wanted."

"How does that ensure your safety?"

"The Big Pharm companies, they won't stop until they have the super cell. They call, they threaten. Together they would sit on the discovery, letting small pieces of it surface—measured increments that won't destroy their companies. With Nueva Vida in the hands of Big Pharm, more people will die and fewer will be helped."

"But Lynwood is a pharm company," Nicole said. "How can your father be sure they'll release it to the public?"

"He isn't sure. He sent one piece to Lynwood. Another to Axis Labs. Earlier, he gave an interview to the *New York Times*." He paused to consider his words. "And a final copy of his work is to go to the police. Not a complete copy, because no one person, other than my father, will ever hold that. But all together, the super cell will emerge, and it will be handled appropriately."

Nicole's breath turned thin and wispy as the enormity of Esparza's plan hit her. "Smart," she said. The newspaper would make sure the super cell was made public, the police would hold their copy as a reference point, and the pharm companies would eagerly receive the gift of a benefactor. Nueva Vida would make Lynwood and Axis the most powerful pharm companies in the marketplace, and Esparza had done it overnight.

"And strong," Joaquin agreed. "I wanted you to know that. He's strong too. In the end he did the right thing."

"But it's not the end," Nicole said. It was a new beginning. One with hope, promise, and new life.

"My father thinks it is."

And there it was again, a finality in Joaquin's voice. Acceptance. Resignation. The emotion that rode the tide after a battle was won but the human sacrifice had been too great. It put her senses on alert.

"Where is he, Joaquin?"

"He left the hotel."

"To go where?" she pressed. Montgomery had walked into a lake. Esparza had told her that. After he had mailed his work to a former student. Beatrice had died on the icy surface of Lake Maria. A knight's sword, after his death, was always thrown into a lake.

"He's walking. To remain still is to stand in the cross hairs, he said, and I think he's right." And the young man's voice wavered slightly until he brought his chin up and tipped his head back with resolve. "The next few hours are crucial."

He dug into his front pocket and drew out a small media card. No protective envelope. Not even a plastic baggie as a precaution. Black, a metal clip, a blue-and-white label. It was common, but what it contained would ripple across the surface of the earth and touch lives in every country, on every continent.

"He thinks you're trustworthy," Joaquin told her. He handed her the media chip. "We will find out."

He took a step back and began to pull on his gloves. He'd had a job to do, a role to play, and he was finished.

"The *New York Times* received an abridged version of his work. An emailed copy was good enough for them. That and the phone interview. But you—" He nodded at Nicole. "You need the hard evidence. That's how he said it. You need the proof in hand. And Lynwood and Axis need hard copies because they will replicate it, spread out the pieces among their scientists. My father knew all this."

And was methodically carrying out the dissolution of his life's dream.

"It's not the end," Nicole said again. "Your father will find life through his actions. Life freely given." As his daughter had wanted it.

Joaquin scoffed. "They will not let him live. He's the only living link to Nueva Vida. What he has stored in his heart and his head, there is no equivalent. The information on the microchip, it has no human connection once they kill my father."

And that made sense to Nicole. Big Pharm was Big Business. They would wipe out every possibility of success. A success that would destroy them. Esparza was the epicenter of it.

"It doesn't have to go down this way," Lars said. "Your father can have protection—"

"He didn't protect Bea. Not as he should have. He won't accept protection for himself."

"Let us help him, Joaquin," Nicole said.

"He has one wish left. To live for Bea now. To see her dream realized."

"Joaquin, before it's too late—" Nicole tried again, but Joaquin wasn't listening.

"He hates irony. My father. He will not give life and he himself lose it. To live under lock and key. To wear a Kevlar vest. He will not even tolerate a secret handshake."

"Your father took you into his confidence," Nicole said. "He told you about Nueva Vida."

"I know what it does but not how. He would not tell me that. I am the last of our name," he explained. "I must stay alive."

"Then you know that any inconvenience would be temporary. Once your father gave all he knew, there would be no reason to kill him."

"Nueva Vida isn't one cure. One save." Joaquin repeated words he must have received from his father. "It is the foundation of cure. It will change the world. There is no one better able to work that. But it will take his life."

"Then it's a lose-lose situation," Lars said. "If he dies, there is no one to steer the ship."

"Others must pick up where he ends," Joaquin said. "My father can't be persuaded otherwise."

32

Benjamin hung up the phone and turned to Charlene. Her eyes were sharp, focused on Benjamin. He didn't like the scrutiny. He didn't like Geneva Sanders, who had drilled him just now on the phone, and he didn't like that Charlene had watched and now felt pity for him.

"Do you want me to kill her?" she asked. "I think I should."

"I can do that myself." And he would enjoy doing it too, if it wouldn't fuck up his life as he knew it. Sanders was a bitch. No matter what was going down, nothing ever went right for her. It was hell, working for a boss like that.

Charlene had thought leaving the girl's body out on the lake was the thing to do. It saved time. King's round table was due to end at eleven and she'd needed to be back inside the house, tucked into her borrowed bed before Benjamin went looking for her. She'd needed to be present to say good-bye to their host. Benjamin wondered what exactly had happened when she chased the girl out of the house. Charlene had told him she had shown the gun to Beatrice Esparza, and she had promised to count to three before she fired.

Charlene liked a challenge, but she hadn't expected the girl to move so fast, to run a winding path that eluded her bullets.

That had been a mistake.

A bullet was clean. It was fast. It was aim, fire, and return to business as usual. Maybe Benjamin could trace all of his current problems back to Charlene's decision to go rogue.

Including Sanders current request—bring Esparza in alive and be ready to roll. It would be a quick drop-off. Sanders would have a car ready. They were getting out of Blue Mesa in minutes, not the hours Benjamin needed.

He didn't like being rushed. But Sanders was his open door. She was a damn skyway to the top.

It had taken Benjamin years to get in on the medical trade. He'd started peddling cocaine to med students and then to their mentors. From there, he'd taken the position of middleman, directing the supply and demand of Vicodin and oxycodone from doctors who'd learned to tap into their reservoir of prescription drugs undetected and delivering to some unlikely customers worldwide. Benjamin had gone global, and he'd become a millionaire doing it. He'd polished his look along the way. He'd cultured his voice. Now he looked the part. Benjamin had found his niche. The clientele were people he liked keeping company with. The money was hand-over-fist better than any other he'd ever made. He liked the cut of his suits, his Louis Vuitton shoes, the conversations that waned from vacation hot spots to chemical compounds.

He had no intention of losing any of it.

"You fucked up with the girl," he said.

"I chased her," Charlene said.

"And lost her, didn't you?"

"Yes. I'm sorry," she said. "You're right. You're always right."

Too little, too late.

A woman like Charlene was hard to find. She needed the strength of a man and a little boy to spoil. When the target wasn't moving, she was an excellent marksman. When the task called for it, she didn't mind getting her hands dirty. It wasn't like he could run an ad for her replacement, and he already anticipated some long hours when he would crave her company.

He stopped in front of her, used his knee to spread her legs, and stood inside that sweet space.

"You were perfect, you know that, honey?"

"Perfect?" Her voice was thin, wobbled only slightly. "That's good, right? Not many people can stake that claim."

He reached between them and withdrew the pistol she kept strapped to her thigh. It had surprised him the first time he held it, that it was so light. He'd doubted a bullet from this toy gun could do any damage, but Charlene had proved him wrong. Up close, the bullet penetrated the skull without hesitation. Inside it bounced around, tearing through gray matter. And when he held the blunt nose to her temple, he remembered that so small a caliber meant there would be very little spray.

Her eyes became fluid; her smile trembled. She whispered the word "Perfect," and then he pulled the trigger. Her head flopped into the palm of his hand. Blood and tissue and bone fragments hit the sheet behind her. Breath flared in her nostrils and skittered across his skin. Once. Twice. A third, final, stuttered breath, and then he wrapped her head in the bed-sheet and eased her to the floor, where blood seeped into carpet the color of midnight.

33

Darkness was complete by the time Nicole and Lars returned to the station. Streetlights illuminated small patches of sidewalk, and colored Christmas lights twinkled in store fronts. It was too cold to snow. The temperature on the dash said eleven degrees. They pulled into the parking lot, and Nicole scanned the cars and SUVs, looking for Benjamin even though his return wasn't likely. Benjamin had an MO. He laid low and licked his wounds while he cataloged every offense and created scenarios where he exacted payment in kind. He planned, although execution took effort, which meant it was often weeks after he made a decision that he followed through.

But she did see a black Escalade. A sticker on the license plate identified it as a rental, and Nicole knew she'd seen the vehicle before, parked at Big Horn—King's fortress away from home.

"We have a visitor."

Lars nodded. "King Arthur, Excalibur, and Morgan le Fay. How do you think Kenny felt about his father grooming our vic for medical stardom?"

"Pissed."

"My thoughts exactly." Lars pulled into a space and cut the engine.

"His size-ten hiking boot puts him in the lineup." And motive kept him there. Jealousy. More murders were committed through rage than any other emotion.

"You think he's a match for the gloves?"

The pair of men's gloves found under the tree, one on top of the other, like a Christmas present.

"Possible." Very. She would ask Kenny about them. Better, she would present them like they were his lost possessions. She told Lars the plan, and he called the clerk in the evidence locker and asked that they be processed for checkout.

"I'll get them," he said. "You going to put Kenny in the box?"

"He has something for us." Or he wouldn't be here. "Let's get that tucked away and then talk to him."

She pulled on her wool cap, shouldered out the door, and walked quickly into the station.

Kenny was seated in reception. He had a file resting on his knees, the papers inside disheveled and the edges poking out. He sat stiffly but turned toward the door when it opened and the cold air swept in. His mouth tightened when he recognized her. He stood but waited, clutching the file to his chest.

"Hi, Kenny."

"I have something here," he said. "Something you should see."

Nicole stopped in front of him and put out her hand for the file, but he pulled back.

"I want to talk to you first."

Lars came through the door next but ignored them. He took the stairs up, where the gloves waited for him.

"Okay, Kenny. Come on back," she invited, and led the way through reception and into the back recesses of the station to her office. "Have a seat."

But he didn't comply. He stood in front of her desk and shifted from one foot to the other.

"Remember when I told you Dr. Esparza wouldn't give my father the super cell?"

"I remember."

"So here's the proof. But there's more." He put the file down on her desk and opened it. "Look at this."

He spread out papers. They were email communications Kenny must have printed from his father's account. Most of them were brief, a line or two. Many were from Enrique Esparza and dated back more than a year. The bartering of a medical miracle. There were others. She recognized a

214

few of the company names in the URLs. All pharmaceutical. Her eyes caught on Sanders's name. She pulled the paper out of the fanned pile and read the brief message: *Don't be a sore loser, Michael.* It had been sent that morning.

Nicole used her fingertips to right the pile, then slid the papers back into the folder. They had something here. Context and implications, at least. She picked up the folder and moved across the room, opened a drawer, and tucked it inside.

"Thanks for bringing this in, Kenny. It will be helpful." She sat down behind her desk and invited Kenny to sit as well. "I'm going to look through it. My people will look through it," she promised. "But there are other things at play here that I think you can help us with."

"Yeah? Like what?" He sat down but not comfortably. His elbows rested on the arms of the chair, but his hands were restless. He rubbed the tips of his fingers with his thumbs.

"Remember those text messages, Kenny? We talked about them this morning?"

"So what? We talked, we texted, we Skyped. I told you that."

"And you wanted more. You wanted Beatrice, but she was busy rising to glory. Both her father and yours believed she would have been an excellent doctor."

He shook his head. His agitation increased, his feet pumping, his legs jiggling.

"It's true. They championed her."

"That's bullshit." His lips trembled, but it was more than anger or outrage; his feelings were hurt.

"Your father knew Dr. Esparza was breaking the law by experimenting on Beatrice."

Kenny snorted. "The law didn't apply to my old man," he said. "That's what he thought."

"What does that mean, Kenny?"

"Yeah, he knew. From the very beginning, and he didn't care. He knew the FDA would never allow it. And it wasn't the first time."

"You're talking about those cutting-edge treatments for Violet?"

"Some of them were taken straight out of Frankenstein," he said.

They were interrupted by a knock on the door. Lars opened it without waiting and walked in, the suede gloves, sealed in a clear evidence bag, tucked under his arm.

"Hi, Kenny." He held out his hand and waited for the young man to take it, an action that was noticeably slow as he adjusted to the intrusion. All of his anger seemed to escape through the opened door, and Nicole watched him deflate. His hands opened, his shoulders sank, and his breath expanded his chest unevenly, catching on the remnants of emotion.

"We didn't get to meet this morning," Lars continued. "I'm sorry about your father."

Kenny snorted and turned toward Nicole. "Who is he?"

"A police detective, Kenny. He's very good at his job. We'd like to share with you what we know." She moved her gaze to Lars and said, "Kenny was just telling me that his father has been breaking the law for years, all in pursuit of a cure for Violet."

"Yeah, and some of them were freakish," Kenny said. He would have sprung from the chair, but Lars placed a hand on his shoulder and lay the plastic evidence bag with the gloves on Nicole's desk.

"Take a good look at these," Lars advised. "Science is a wonderful thing, but of course you already know that. I hear your father was training you, getting you ready for medical school. Isn't that right, Kenny?"

Kenny's eyes were locked on the evidence bag, and his composure was shifting under the pressure. His voice became high, thin, desperate. "No. No, he wasn't. He should have been, but he was all about Beatrice."

Lars ignored his outburst. "Police work is a lot of things. But what we rely on most is science. We have tests and methods and even the psychology that predicts behavior, and you know what? It's solid. It's numbers, and there's nothing gray about those. It's tangible, we can hold evidence in our hands"—he raised the gloves under Kenny's nose—"and say things about them that are absolutely true."

"Have you heard of epithelials?" Nicole asked.

"Skin," Kenny said.

She nodded. "And we have equipment that will recover microscopic tags of skin for analysis, and from that analysis we will know—"

But Kenny jumped ahead. "DNA. I get it. So what? They're my gloves. I left them outside last night."

Lars nodded. "We know. You took them off because wearing them was awkward. You dropped something—a condom packet—small, slippery, and definitely impossible to pick up when you're wearing flippers."

"You took them off, set them aside, and left them in the snow," Nicole said. "Why did you do that, Kenny?"

"You're wrong," he said, but Nicole was already shaking her head.

"Evidence, Kenny. Facts. You knelt in the snow—we have impressions of that. We have your fingerprint on the condom packet. We have your text messages. You wanted her, Kenny, but Beatrice wasn't interested."

"So maybe you thought no one should have her," Lars offered.

"Who gave Beatrice the Rohypnol?" Nicole continued. "You or your father?"

"I did." He laughed. It was wet with tears and snot. "But she got away from me anyway. How sick is that? Even drugged, I couldn't get her in bed."

"She ran and you followed."

Kenny nodded.

"Beatrice had a head start, and she was fast," Nicole continued.

"She was slow and stumbling," he said.

An effect of the drug.

"And you caught up with her."

"Easy."

"And then what?"

"She told me she would never love me. Not like that."

"And you killed her?"

"I didn't mean to. I just lost it, you know? And I tried to fix it. I gave her CPR, but it didn't work."

"How did you do it, Kenny?" Lars asked.

"With my hands." He held them up, stared at his palms, and then buried his face there. "I choked her. It makes an awful sound. She gasped. She whistled. But she didn't change her mind."

"She was never going to love you," Nicole said, and Kenny looked up and met her gaze.

"Never," he said.

"And you told your father about it?" Nicole continued.

"I had to. He knew I took the roofie from his supplies. That I was looking for her. That she was gone." His eyes were glazed, and Nicole could see hysteria building in them. "He thought it was that blond freak. The broker. Because she was looking for Bea too, but I found her first. And then the woman came in and scared her away."

34

Next to his own home, Nicole's would be considered a cottage. And not a very nice one. Tidy, respectful, but no flair. Benjamin turned the SUV into the gravel driveway and started up the incline. His tires spun on the gravel, announcing his arrival, but who cared? Nicole had alerted them already. He was sure of it. She'd given the old lady who stayed with Jordan a list of instructions, no doubt: lock the doors, check the windows, don't answer a knock, a ring, a snarl from outside. Too bad he had a way around all that.

He parked in front of the garage. No need to turn the SUV around for a quick getaway. Nicole was busy. Two dead and another on the way. He'd disposed of Charlene. She wouldn't be found until the first thaw and by then would be completely unidentifiable.

Nicole had no idea who was next or she would have been here herself, armed and aiming for him.

He laughed, anticipating the moment when he brought Nicole's world to a screeching halt. Sanders had put him in a killing mood. The woman was impossible to please, and in that, she and Nicole were very similar. Nicole would suffer for it. She would know that Benjamin had their son and that he was up to no good. He wanted to be there when she realized that all hope was lost. In this case, it would pulverize her. Nicole would have little left to live for.

He pulled up his hood and pushed out into the cold. He was coming to hate Montana. Winter was only a wonderland from the inside out—gazing from a window with a fire crackling at his back. The consistencies were tedious—the temperature flowed between freezing and breathtaking, and snow looked the same no matter how it fell or lay on the ground.

He knocked on the front door. This was purely a courtesy and executed to further mess up their minds. Surely a drug dealer, a thief, a murderer, didn't knock on doors. By now, Jordan or the old lady would be dialing Nicole's cell. Maybe they'd even gotten through. He watched a curtain panel peel back from the living room window. Not close to the front door, but on the side of the house facing the garage and his SUV. He saw a blur of short, gray curls.

"Jordan," he called through the wood. "Daddy's home. Come unlock the door."

Nothing. As he'd expected. He pulled a slim LED flashlight from his pocket and walked around the side of the house. The electrical box was padlocked. Another expectation fulfilled. Nicole was a cop. Of course she locked up everything.

He lifted the hem of his parka and unsnapped his holster. He pulled Charlene's Sig Sauer out and stood back from the padlock. He was a good shot from five feet. Fifty/fifty at twice that. He didn't want to get hit by the shrapnel, but he didn't want to start a bonfire either. He settled on eight feet and aimed for the outer rim on the Schlage. He pulled the trigger, and the loop popped and slid from the box. Benjamin kept the flashlight steady, located the main breaker, and tripped it. The entire house, security lights included, went black.

Nicole would know from the street that something was terribly wrong. He smiled, enjoying the thought. Then moved on. He stopped at the long sidelight window beside the front door and used the butt of his gun to break it. He knocked out fragments of glass and pushed his arm through and turned the locks easily. Then he walked through the door.

"Let's try this again," he shouted into the dark, cavernous house. "Daddy's home!"

There was no response, and for a moment he damned people's predictability, though he knew it was useful to him. He aimed the flashlight into the corners of the living room, behind the sofa and an overstuffed chair. Nothing. He moved on, deeper into the house.

"Let's see. You're the child of a cop. I'd say she taught you to lay low, behind a locked door." He entered the kitchen and opened the pantry door, but it was empty. He moved into the dining area, swept the light under the table. "Nothing here," he called. He loved the sound of his voice. He loved fucking with people's minds. He turned into a short hall. Four doors. Three bedrooms and a bath. "Maybe you've burrowed under the things in your closet? Is that where you stuff your dirty laundry, son?" He tried the knob of the first door. It turned and he pushed it open. A bedroom. He stood on the threshold and checked the corners, waded slowly into the room, swung open the closet. Winter coats and rain boots. No kid. He knelt and checked under the bed. Dust and cobwebs.

He left that room behind and moved on to the next. Another bedroom, probably. The knob didn't turn. "Now that's a dead giveaway," he said. "Excuse the pun. 'Lock the door. Scurry under the bed.' Some of the worst advice ever given. Do you know how easy it is to pop a lock this weak?"

As an answer, Benjamin stepped back, canted left, and launched a roundhouse kick so that the heel of his boot delivered a direct blow backed up by his body weight and momentum. An object in motion and all that. But it focused about five hundred pounds on an interior lock. Sandbox play, really. He heard the pin spring.

"That's just a little trick your father learned early on in his career," Benjamin said. The door had swung open, bounced off the wall, and now came back at him. He held up his hand and caught it. "Back when I had to do my own cleanup. Your daddy has come a long way, Jordan."

He paused and listened. The darkness was total, the curtains in this room closed against any moon that might be in the sky. And the silence here was complete. No breath, taken or expelled. No involuntary shifting of muscle in a new and cramped position. He knew before he opened the closet door that he would find it empty. But he searched it anyway. Laziness when it came to personal safety was not a choice.

"Is this your room, Jordan?" He raised his voice, because he knew his son and the little old lady were not in this room. "I think so. Lots of Star Wars and blue jeans. Definitely not your mom's style. She always favored those tailored shirts, blazers that would hide her gun." He turned and let the beam from the flashlight fall over the room. Planets hung from fishing line, books were scattered on the bed and nightstand, Legos filled boxes that were pushed against a wall. Benjamin had never had such a room when he was a kid. Mostly he'd slept on the couch in the living room. A change of clothing had been a luxury. "I like your room, Jordan," he called out, then bent and lifted the bed ruffle under first one and then the other twin bed and found nothing but rolled-up dirty socks, scattered pieces of what looked like homework, and a single shoe.

He left that bedroom and walked quietly down the hall. "Are you in the bathroom, cowering behind the shower curtain?" he wondered, loud enough that he could be heard anywhere in the house. "Let's see."

He stepped into the bathroom, which was small. Maybe forty square feet. White toilet, basin, and tub; burgundy towels hung from the rack; exhaust fan, no window. Certainly Nicole had taught their son better than to seek refuge in a box with no escape hatch. But he swept an arm forward and pushed the curtain back on the metal rod with a scratching sound. Empty.

"That leaves one room, Jordan," Benjamin said. Glee made his voice light. It floated up from his throat like bubbles from champagne. He was getting closer. Soon he would have his hands on the prize. Nicole's raison de vivre.

The door to the master bedroom stood ajar, and he pushed it back with the tips of his fingers and stood on the threshold. Nicole's private domain. Thick carpeting and a full-sized bed in a lifted iron frame that was a complicated pattern of curlicues. No walk-in closet here, but double doors that slid back on a metal track. A small door leading to the master bath.

Didn't people know they could live better? he wondered. And then he heard a snuffling sound. The wet nose of an animal sniffing, panting. His hand tightened on the gun grip. He felt its beaded texture against his palm. He didn't like dogs. They were loyal and brave beyond reason. They lacked common sense.

He followed the sound with his ear, his head turning toward the right. Beyond the bed a wall with two windows, heavy curtains, and a swath of carpet. Were they huddled in the shadows? Seemed likely. But why hadn't they gone for the windows?

"Jordan, come say hello to your father," Benjamin demanded.

"No thanks."

The voice was calm, and bigger than Benjamin had expected.

"Well, that's polite," Benjamin returned. "Really. I'm glad your mom taught you to say please and thank-you. Didn't she also tell you it's a common courtesy to greet people when they come to your house?"

"Invited guests," Jordan agreed. "But you're not invited. In fact, we'd like you to leave."

Definitely coming from the floor on the other side of the bed, below the windows, which he could shatter with a single bullet.

"But I just got here, and I went to a lot of trouble to see you, Jordan." He took another step into the room, lifted the flashlight, and tried to illuminate the well behind the bed, but the beam touched only the wall and curtains. "It's been too long for a hug, and there's no picking up where we left off. I get that. A handshake will do. A 'happy to see you, Dad' would be okay."

"My mother taught me never to lie."

Benjamin shook his head, took another step. "I don't remember you so sassy, Jordan. No, I remember you whiny and crying and filling your diaper. You were not a pleasant baby."

He heard it again, the wet sniffling.

"What do you have with you, Jordan? A dog? Small, medium, or large? It's better you prepare me so I don't kill it offhand."

"A teacup poodle," Jordan said, and Benjamin laughed.

"Now, that snuffling sounds too deep for an animal that small. I'm guessing a Lab of some kind. Maybe a collie or German shepherd. It looks to me like your mom has done everything she can to give you an Opie kind of childhood."

"What's Opie?"

"Don't you watch Nick at Nite?"

"You do?"

Benjamin smiled. He loved challenges. So long as they were entertaining and required little effort. He was thinking he might change his opinion of fatherhood. "I like reminiscing. Thinking of the old days. Nothing like yesterday's TV to bring all that back."

"My mother told me you hated your childhood. That there was nothing good about it."

Benjamin felt a tic at the corner of his mouth. "That's where TV came in. I could reinvent myself every afternoon watching other kids who got it good."

He took another step forward. A second ticked by, two. And then his senses began to pick up movement. The air shifted, became dense and fraught with energy, and he turned because there was someone behind him. Definitely. But he was too late to do anything about it. A Louisville Slugger. Twenty-seven ounces of solid ash but, lucky for him, barreled by a pint-sized grandma. The bat connected with his upper arm. A solid blow. It knocked the flashlight from his hand, gave him a stinger, but did little else. Still, Benjamin ducked. He crouched and lurched toward the dark outline of the granny figure and caught her around the knees. She tumbled to the floor with a surprised gasp. But she didn't waste time.

"Run, Jordan," she commanded. "Run!"

"Stay, Jordan. If you don't, I'll kill her."

Jordan stayed. Benjamin heard him move, the rustling of his clothing and the soft whimper of the dog he had with him.

"You got that dog on a leash?"

"In the house?"

"Hold on to him. I'm a good shot, Jordan. Close up I'm a hundred percent."

"I've got him." His voice warbled a little. He cared about the mutt, and the old lady too, probably. "What are you doing to Mrs. Neal?"

"She hit me with a bat," Benjamin said. "I had to take her down."

"Don't hurt her."

"Too late for that."

"I'm fine, Jordan," Mrs. Neal said. "Do as your mother told you."

"Nicole? So you did talk to her." And that made his heart sing. "What did she say? Is she scared for you, Jordan? Did she sound breathless? Worried?"

"She said you were harmless," the boy returned.

Benjamin laughed. "Now that's not true. Your old man's a killer. She knows that. She's been a real bitch about it too. Really chomping away at your dad over it."

"And she's on her way," Mrs. Neal promised. "Her and about a hundred other officers."

"Toole County doesn't have a hundred officers," he chided.

"You know what I mean."

"Yeah, I do." And he didn't hide the smile in his voice. "I really rattled her, didn't I?"

"Nicole doesn't rattle," she informed him.

"She's the sheriff," Jordan said, and he was proud of it.

"So I hear." Benjamin stood and hauled Mrs. Neal to her feet. "No sudden moves, Granny." He tapped her with the tip of the bat he had wrestled away from her, but for extra measure, he rubbed the muzzle of the Sauer against her temple. "Double duty," he told her. "And like I said, up close I never miss."

He scanned the room, but the flashlight had gone out when it hit the ground. He figured they had maybe another ten minutes before Nicole and her posse made it here. They had to move fast now.

"Stand up, Jordan," he said. "You and that mutt are going to leave the room first. I want you to walk to the front door."

Jordan stood but kept a hand on the dog's collar. Benjamin could tell by the outline of his stooped body. "Hall, kitchen, living room, door. Just like that," he said.

Jordan followed his orders. Benjamin kept a hand on Mrs. Neal, and they walked a few feet behind the boy and the dog, but when they reached the front of the house and felt the cool air rush in, the old woman shouted again, "Run, Jordan! Make your mom proud."

Benjamin tightened his hold on Mrs. Neal's arm until he heard her back teeth grind together. To Jordan he said, "I'm a man of my word, Jordan. Remember that. You could make a run for it," he reasoned. "Save yourself and your dog, but that would kill Mrs. Neal. Can you handle that?"

"I won't run."

"Your word is good enough for me." He tried to remember the layout of the house. There was a door off the living room, a closet or laundry room. Either would do. "Put the dog in the laundry room and shut the door."

He needed a clear path to his truck, pulling a reluctant son with him. He needed to dispose of Mrs. Neal without the canine intrusion. And he needed to do it all in minutes. Nicole was on her way. And the damn Mrs. Neal was clairvoyant or astute, adding to his growing tension.

"She's almost here already," she said.

"Almost? No. She was on her way to the Huntington Spa. That's on the other side of town, and then a few miles of ribbon over the mountain pass. Police scanner," he explained, and smiled though she couldn't see it in the dark. "Now get walking."

She complied, but slowly, and she called to Jordan, "Bring our coats from the closet, Jordan." Sensible. Optimistic. Thinking forward.

He nudged her, because they had already wasted time on the dog and because she irritated him. Nicole had hired well. Most women would be hysterical at this point. He supposed that was good for him—made her easier to handle. But she had an air of superiority he didn't like. For that he pushed her again, with more force, but she didn't complain. She didn't put up a struggle. She slipped into her coat as she moved. He figured she was agreeable because they were walking away from Jordan and she liked that.

"You care about my son," he said. "And I appreciate that. I don't think I'll kill you. I will have to return in kind for the whack you gave me with the bat, but then we're square. Fair is fair and all."

"You sound like a child," she said.

"I never grew up," he agreed. He stopped at the front door, Mrs. Neal in front of him on the porch, and turned back to Jordan. "Hurry up, son. You waste any more time back there and I'll have to rush with Mrs. Neal. That wouldn't be good."

Jordan was obedient. As he drew closer, Benjamin stood back against the open door and let him pass. He kept a hold of Mrs. Neal's elbow and tapped the bat against the brick path as they walked around the house to the backyard.

"Why are we going back here?" Jordan asked.

"We need to put Mrs. Neal somewhere," he returned. "I told her I wouldn't kill her, and so I won't, but I'm not going to let her loose either." He led them across the back patio and into the grass. They came to a dog-house built like a log cabin. Benjamin tapped it with the bat. "What do you think, Jordan? A little too tight for our Mrs. Neal?"

"You can't put her in the doghouse," Jordan said. His voice had risen, and Benjamin liked that he was willing to fight for Mrs. Neal.

"Why not?" Benjamin bent and peered inside the open door. There was enough light from the moon that he knew what he was looking at, enough shadow that he couldn't read their faces, but Jordan's offense was clear in his voice. "Looks nice in there, but maybe a little cramped." He pulled lightly on Mrs. Neal's arm, and they advanced. A shed stood west, small at eight-by-ten feet and made of durable polyethylene. It had a chunky pad-lock on it. "What's in there?"

He felt Jordan shrug. "Bikes and patio furniture."

Benjamin nodded and looked down at Mrs. Neal. "Well, it looks like it's the woodshed for you." He felt resistance in her as he began walking toward the long, low trestle. It was made of sturdy plywood with a shingled roof. There were several doors that opened on swing hinges. "Your mother's going to love this, Jordan. She plays a mean game of hide-and-seek."

"You can't put her in there," Jordan protested. "It's too cold out here. She'll die."

Benjamin expelled a heavy breath and looked down at Jordan.

"What should I do then, Jordan? Kill her now?" He felt anger bunch in his muscles and exerted pressure on the woman's elbow, pushing his fingers between the bones at the joint, and was rewarded with her sharp gasp and the loosening of her knees. "But I promised her I wouldn't." He eased her down and looked over her head. "Take three giant steps back," he said, and watched Jordan shuffle his feet and put inches between them. His eyes had adjusted to the dark, and he could see that Jordan's face was pensive. He chewed his lip. "Don't worry, Jordan. Your mom will find her. She's good at this kind of thing."

35

Joaquin rocked back on his heels, fists pushed into the front pockets of his jeans. Air, so cold he choked on a deep breath, stole under his parka and chilled his skin. But he kept his place. He watched the big guy—Etienne—push the Bobcat out of the garage. He started it and let it idle and then stood back and waited for Joaquin's father to climb aboard. His father pulled on the helmet and adjusted the goggles over his eyes. His father enjoyed skiing. Downhill or cross-country. He'd been on a snowmobile before, but so few times and so long ago that Joaquin doubted he remembered how to work one. The equipment guy seemed to have the same concerns. As his father approached the Bobcat, the guy—built like a mountain—stepped forward.

"Let's go over a few things," he said, and then he pointed to the throttle and explained it. He took hold of the handgrips and showed how fast they responded to direction—like riding a bike. He bent over and pointed out the cut switch.

"And if I need to start it again?"

"No key," Etienne said. "You just push here"—a red button on the steering column—"and turn the throttle." He did it and the engine gunned.

His father straddled the snowmobile, and Etienne stepped back. "Machine must be back by eight o'clock."

Joaquin pushed back the sleeve of his parka and looked at the lighted dial of his watch. It was 7:10. He looked at the landscape. The trees were a darker shade of night against the sky. A sliver of moon cast a stronger glow than expected for its smallness, and a handful of stars were well out of reach. Clear skies finally. No chance of snow. His father would have an easy ride if he kept on the trail.

"What happens if it's not?" his father asked. "Do you send a search party?"

He'd meant it as a joke, but his voice was tight and Etienne took him seriously.

"We call your room. We look around the property. That's usually enough."

His father nodded. "I'll try to be on time."

His father's words were an assurance but also subtly dismissive. Etienne didn't move. He stood a few feet away from the Bobcat but still managed to tower over Joaquin's father. And he was troubled. Joaquin noticed the tension in Etienne's shoulders, the frown growing deeper on his face.

"Beatrice is gone," he said.

"Yes."

"She was my friend."

"I know." His father sat back on the padded seat and pushed his goggles up. He gave Etienne his full attention. "And you were a good friend to her."

"You didn't like that."

"I was wrong." He held out his hand. "I'm sorry."

Etienne looked at his father's hand but didn't take it. He seemed confused by the action or by Dr. Esparza's words as his face clouded and his voice became agitated.

"I miss her."

"Me too."

"But she's not coming back." Etienne wanted that to be a possibility, and maybe he wanted it so badly that he thought he could make it happen. Like some wishes did come true. Joaquin could tell by his tone, which was mostly wistful but torn in places by grief.

"Beatrice is dead, Etienne," his father said, and his voice was soft, steady. His father had had to say similar words before, lots of times, probably. Joaquin heard the ache in them.

He nodded. "The police told me that. I didn't believe them."

"They spoke to you?"

He nodded. "They found Beatrice on the lake. I told them she was on her way to a party and she looked like a princess." Etienne smiled with the memory, and Joaquin could tell it was pure. Etienne had thought Beatrice was beautiful. He had seen her heart and been drawn to it. That had happened a lot with his sister. He felt his lips tremble as he realized how much the world would be missing with Beatrice gone.

"Thank you, Etienne. You made her smile," his father said.

Etienne looked over Dr. Esparza's head at Joaquin. "You need a helmet and goggles. I'll get them."

"I'm not riding." And then Joaquin did something he never would have done but Beatrice would have. It was second nature to her. He reached out to Etienne. He walked around the Bobcat his father was straddling and came to stand next to Etienne. "My father wanted to shake your hand, to say he was sorry he'd misjudged you. I'd like to shake it for the same reason."

He held out his hand, and Etienne looked at it, then extended his own. It was an awkward gesture, and Joaquin realized that a handshake was a foreign thing to him, so he closed the gap and took the big hand and pumped it twice, then let go.

"That's how it's done," Joaquin said. "A handshake is important, Etienne. It means you're equal. The other guy's no better than you. You're no worse than he is."

"Equal is good."

Joaquin nodded. "It's the best."

The big guy nodded and turned back to Joaquin's father. "You need anything else?"

"Is there a GPS on this thing?"

"No. The trails are marked. Stay on them," he advised.

Etienne walked away then, his boots falling heavily on the snowpack. Joaquin waited until he was inside the garage and lowering the automatic door before he turned back to his father. He laid a hand on the steering column to get his attention over the purr of the Bobcat and the metallic crunching of the equipment door. His father looked up. His face was pensive but his eyes were lit with question.

"That was a good thing you did, Joaquin."

"Beatrice would have done it."

Dr. Esparza nodded. "We can all learn from her," he said. "We can make changes, even small ones, and that would be carrying Beatrice with us. That would give her life where there is none."

Joaquin wanted to remember those words. He wanted to sift through them and make sure he understood what his father was saying, but right now wasn't the time to do it. In forty-five minutes the resort would be looking for the Bobcat. In fifteen minutes his father had a meeting with Callon Pharmaceuticals.

"She'll be waiting for you," Joaquin said. "Sanders."

But his father shook his head. "It will be someone else. Someone she hired. Someone who will try to intimidate me. She doesn't know it's not necessary."

"You'll go with him?"

"Yes. Freely. I want to see Sanders. I want to watch her face when I tell her it's too late for her and for Callon. When she realizes life as she knows it is over."

"She never cared about Beatrice. Telling her won't change that."

"That's not why I'm doing it. She killed my girl, and I want her to know that she has lost everything too."

But Joaquin wasn't convinced it was a good idea. "It won't change who she is."

"But I will go anyway," his father returned. "Beatrice will hear my words, and she will know that I've changed."

Joaquin nodded. His father was set on a course. He was going to do this thing—meet with the Big Six winner, show her that he'd betrayed them all by going public with his discovery, make things right with Beatrice. He couldn't live with himself otherwise. He could die, though, knowing he'd done right by her.

Beatrice should have lived. His father's discovery was a success and his sister had been living proof of it. His father had thought the world would embrace Nueva Vida. He had not looked beyond his own greed, beyond his own rise to fame, and had been blindsided by the reaction of the pharmaceutical companies. Their game was to sustain life and to do it in the least cost-effective way possible for the patient. Sustain, not cure, and keep the cash cow fed.

"Are you ready?" he asked Joaquin.

"That's my line," he said.

His father smiled. "You are filling my shoes already."

But Joaquin shook his head. "I'll never do that. If I have to, if things work out that way, then I'll do what I can, but it will never be enough."

"You're wrong. You are more than enough."

36

Nicole knew the house would be dark. Benjamin had cut the electricity. That much Jordan had told her before he'd tucked his cell phone into his pocket, the connection open but words and movement muffled from that point on. She believed Benjamin had marched Jordan and Mrs. Neal outside and locked the woman in the woodshed. Her son was soft-spoken, but she'd heard his protest, Benjamin's response, and his flash of anger. But after that, very little.

She turned onto the state route and followed its soft curves. Her house, on its knoll, rose into view. She slowed the SUV, took the gravel drive faster than usual. If Benjamin was still here, then he knew she'd arrived. Maybe that would keep him in check. At least distract him with a new issue to handle. But her headlights swept over the silent house, the detached garage and the empty driveway. Jordan had described Benjamin's SUV—a Dodge Durango, black or dark blue. He'd come alone, as far as he and Mrs. Neal could tell.

Nicole cut the engine and wasted no time on the house but ran behind it, directly to the woodshed. She turned on her flashlight as she advanced.

New footprints had appeared in the packed snow. A piece of wood broken off a log had been slipped between the door handles on the shed, making it impossible to open from the inside. Mrs. Neal had been in there close to twelve minutes. Nicole had marked the time with the clock on her dash.

Nicole knelt, tapping on the roof of the shed as she did, and spoke to Mrs. Neal.

"I'm here, Mrs. Neal." She used the butt of the flashlight like a hammer and drove the wood out of the handles and opened the doors.

"He has Jordan," Mrs. Neal said, still curled on her side. Her teeth chattered and her lips were blue. "I heard two car doors slam shut, the engine start and the tires on the gravel."

Nicole helped Mrs. Neal out. Her limbs were stiff from cold, her joints sticky.

"Lars is working on it," Nicole said.

They would track Jordan using the GPS in his cell phone. Lars had already connected with the carrier. It wouldn't be too long before they had a flashing red dot on Lars's computer screen and he would direct her over the air until the visual came up on her computer in the cruiser. But she already suspected the general direction.

"He told Jordan that he wanted his son to see how Daddy did his job."

· Nicole nodded. Sounded like Benjamin. He liked to impress. He wanted people to think he was important. "Did he say where they were going?"

"A meeting. That was all. They were walking away then, and I couldn't catch all their words."

Neither had Nicole.

She kept her arm around Mrs. Neal and urged her across the snow and into the Yukon. Then she hustled to the driver's side, slid behind the wheel, and turned the engine. She hit the button for heat, moving it up. "It'll take a minute." She reached into the back seat for a blanket and handed in to Mrs. Neal. "Get that wrapped around you."

"He acts like a child."

"Always." Sometimes playful, other times with a temper that flared when he wasn't given his way or things turned against him.

"Do you think he'll hurt Jordan?"

"He already has." Nicole whispered the words, but Mrs. Neal caught them. She sighed, and it caught on a small sob.

"I was in a bad place," Nicole said.

She took the driveway too fast and her tires spun on the gravel; then she turned the SUV onto the state road, east, toward the lake, the resorts, King's rented home. There were many possibilities, but all of them clustered around the lake. Her cell phone was in its slot on the dash, and she pressed speed dial for Lars.

He answered on the first ring. "You got her?"

"Yes," Nicole said. "Benjamin has Jordan." As they had suspected. "You have his GPS open?"

"Not yet."

"Turn all the units back, toward the lake. Benjamin mentioned a meeting."

"Wish we knew where he was staying."

"Send a car to Sanders' resort. Have them get a bead on her."

"Where are you headed?"

She thought about that. She wanted Lars to tell her, to look at his computer screen and tell her exactly where Jordan was. "I'm dropping Mrs. Neal off at the station." Where an EMT could look her over, where she would be safe. "Then heading toward Lake Maria." Their crime scene. She felt its pull. All trails led back to it. "Or the Huntington." And she remembered the picture of Esparza with Benjamin and his wife, on the slope outside the resort. Acrimonious at best. Dr. Esparza didn't like Benjamin. Wasn't wooed by the charm or swayed by what-ever power Benjamin leveled. "Let me know as soon as you have the map up."

Lars' exclamation kept her from cutting the connection.

"I got it. Amber Alert is up." Which made it compulsory for cell phone companies to open the GPS signals of their underage members to police when a kidnap was suspected. "Lake Road," he said. "South side. Moving slowly."

Nicole turned the cruiser into the station parking lot and helped Mrs. Neal inside.

"I'm sorry, Nicole." Mrs. Neal was teary. She clutched the blanket the desk clerk wrapped around her shoulders. "I should have done better."

"No," Nicole said. "I should have."

She left then, back into the cold, into the Yukon. Onto the Lake Road. She pressed her foot on the gas and the engine roared and the SUV hopped forward to deliver. She hailed Lars.

"You have your internet open?"

Nicole looked at the computer screen on the console, positioned above the AK-47, which was positioned above the response kit—knife, flashlight, flare gun, handheld radio. As she watched, the screen flickered, paused, and then loaded the cellular map Lars was also looking at. It showed streets and geographical landmarks. The red dot was Jordan. It was flashing, which meant he and Benjamin were on the move.

"I've got it," she said. They were two miles outside town. She glanced at the speedometer. Eighty-eight miles per hour. Three minutes separated Nicole from her son. She would have to slow at intersections, when the road curved. Four minutes, then.

"I'm rolling," Lars said. "Coming in from the north."

From the Huntington. Where both Dr. Esparza and Joaquin were missing. Nicole had been on her way there when Jordan called. That meant she and Lars had Benjamin and Jordan between them. They would close in. But Nicole would arrive first. Protocol would have her waiting on Lars to catch up. To position herself so that they had Benjamin pinned, with nowhere to go. No moves to make. Except that he had Jordan, and that gave him cart blanche.

"I can't wait on you," Nicole said.

The silence snapped with the crackle of radio waves.

"No," he agreed. "I'm right behind you. Five minutes tops. I've called for backup, but they're still miles out."

Toole County spread far and wide.

Her eyes were drawn back to the computer screen, snagged on the red dot, blinking, moving, just a mile away. She cut the bar lights, not wanting to tip off Benjamin on her approach.

"Bring the Colt," Lars said. It was long range, and Nicole was a good shot.

She reminded herself that Benjamin hadn't come for Jordan. It had never been about their son, only in how Benjamin could use Jordan to hurt her. To torment her. And he would have to keep Jordan alive to accomplish that.

"He's alive," Nicole said.

"And he's going to stay that way," Lars promised.

37

His father wasn't comfortable on the Bobcat. His hand tightened on the throttle so that the engine burst forward with speed, and then he loosened his grip and sometimes glided into a stall. Joaquin stayed behind him. Fifty or sixty yards. A slice of moon illuminated the surface of the lake and made his father a small, shadowy figure. He tried to match the sound of his engine to his father's, to hide inside his starts and stops, but that was almost impossible. His father didn't seem to notice he had company, though. He was focused. He had a plan and he was determined to see it through.

Joaquin thought he would die doing it. He'd said as much and his father had agreed. He had asked his father to change his mind, but hadn't begged him. To turn away from all of it. To start again.

How did you walk away from a discovery that would change the world? Or a daughter who had died believing it would?

His father came to a measured stop. He sat upright, his feet on the rails, but moved his head, scanning the lake. They were near the home King had rented but closer to the place where Beatrice had died. A thin ribbon of yellow tape fluttered in the wind along the shore, attached to wood spikes, but tattered. Above that, the land rose like the gentle swells of an ocean until it reached the joggers' path, lit by sodium lamps, and beyond that and through a thin stand of trees, the road.

Joaquin didn't see anyone and neither did his father, who stood and began a deeper sweep of the lake with his eyes. Joaquin cut the engine on his Bobcat and the headlight extinguished. He was swallowed by darkness but ducked down anyway and tucked himself against the snowmobile so that he was consumed by its shadow.

His father wanted to do this alone. He refused to allow more harm to come to their family.

He had been carried away by the great meaning in his discovery, had dreamed of parades in his honor and the Nobel Prize. People would know his story, from a street kid in Mexico City to Nueva Vida, and he would be a hero. He had wanted that. He had needed to be king of the mountain so that he would feel some small measure of achievement. Of worthiness. He had thought Nueva Vida would be his defining moment and didn't realize, until it was too late, that his actions as a father would bring him the most glory.

Joaquin respected that. His father had made a mistake. Several. But more than he'd wanted his super cell to work, he'd wanted Beatrice to rise above death.

Above them Joaquin caught the flare of headlights as a vehicle slowed along the Lake Road. He watched it bounce over the snowbanks the plows had left behind on the shoulder of the road and stopped. For a long moment, there was nothing else. Then the headlights cut off. His father had noticed it too, and he sat down, opened the throttle, but was slow to release the brake. The engine whined sharply and then he shot forward, skidding on the ice so that the Bobcat veered left before his father straightened it out.

Joaquin waited. He counted to ten by thousands. He looked up and saw that his father was almost a hundred yards away and that Sanders, or her point man, was descending the embankment, carrying a flashlight. The beam was small and flickered with each stride of the person. Still, if Joaquin could see it, then his headlight would be noticed in return. He decided to move forward slowly. Blindly. And that presented a problem. The Bobcat was designed with automatic safety features in place. One of them prevented the rider from extinguishing the headlight with a simple switch.

He popped the shell on the steering column, pulled the glove from his right hand, and felt for the wiring. Snowmobiles were not new to him. He preferred them to skiing or sledding or tubing and every winter spent a considerable amount of time on them. Still, he realized pretty quickly that he was going to have to risk using his flashlight. There were too many wires, they crossed over each other and it was impossible to follow any with certainty. He knew the headlight would run directly to the battery. But he had to see it.

And risk being seen. The thought made him breathless. Dizzy. His father was meeting with the person who had killed Beatrice. His father was sure he would die doing it. Joaquin didn't want to think about that. He had done a good job pushing it out of his mind. He wanted to believe his father could release his research, vindicate his sister, remove the threat from his family, and live through it all. And he had followed him, thinking he could help.

And he could, if he kept his mind clear, pushed back the fear, dealt with each moment as if it was the only one that existed.

He reached into the deep pocket of his parka and pulled out the flashlight. It was a Maglite, heavy duty, made of aluminum but weighed more than a pound. It had a textured hand grip and was a foot long. The metal chilled quickly and seared his palm. Still, he held it firmly and thought about the best way to use it. Settled on pointing the beam toward him and away from his father and Callon. He cupped his hand around the lens as an extra measure of concealment and positioned it two inches above the console. Then he pressed the button, blinked against the sudden brightness, focused on the battery and traced the wires with his eyes. The orange one. It went from the block to the headlight. He tugged on it, wished he had a pocketknife, but he'd never been into that Boy Scout kind of stuff. It took three strong pulls before the wire snapped free. He extinguished the flashlight and dropped it back into his pocket.

Three seconds. Maybe five.

He sat back on the Bobcat's seat and looked over the handlebars. His father had stopped, was idling only a few short yards from the shore. The approaching figure was gaining fast. Joaquin pushed off, kept the throttle even, knew he would have to cut the engine when his father cut his and listened for it. He was within sixty yards when it happened. Joaquin cut the engine, dropped his helmet on the seat, and continued on foot. At forty yards his father rose from the Bobcat and stood beside it, the headlight bright. Beyond it were the shadowy figures of a man and boy stumbling down the slope and onto the ice. At thirty yards, the man and boy stepped into the light. At twenty yards, the wind was strong enough to catch his father's words and toss them back to Joaquin.

"You brought a child with you?"

His father wasn't happy about it. His voice was filled with dismay and then anger. "Why would you do such a thing?"

The man shrugged. "He's my son. I'm thinking of turning this into a family business." He laughed, but it was short and sharp.

"I am not his son," the boy said. "My mom's the sheriff."

Joaquin felt his heart skip a beat. He moved closer.

"You took the sheriff's son?"

"He's only telling you half the truth," the man said. "You have the research, Doc?"

His father remained silent. He hadn't been expecting the people responsible for killing his daughter to arrive with a child. And he didn't know what to do about it. Joaquin could feel his indecision from where he stood. Noticed the way his father shifted on his feet.

"I'm not here to turn over my work," he said.

"But that was the plan. Sanders gave me the update, Dr. Esparza. You agreed. And fifty-five million dollars is a lot of money. You won't get a better deal." His voice was reasonable, smooth. Joaquin took another step closer.

"I'm not looking for a deal. Not anymore."

The guy changed tactics, his words became about understanding. "You're upset about your daughter. We all are."

"You killed her," his father accused.

"Not me," he said. "I knew about the decision, of course, and I did nothing to stop it. We both know why." He took a step closer to Joaquin's father, pulling the boy along with him. "You know why Beatrice had to die. You had to know from the beginning. But maybe you hid from it. It was easier that way. Only a monster could look their child in the eye every day knowing that what they were doing would kill her."

"She was a success!"

"Exactly," the guy agreed. "And that's the last thing the Big Six want. Proof of life. Where's the research, Doctor?"

"It's too late for that," his father said.

"You know how this works," the guy continued. "Baby steps. There's a lot of money to be made, and lost."

"You mean there's a lot of money in dying. For the Big Six."

"That's what I mean." The guy pulled a gun from his coat pocket and Joaquin felt his breath thin, felt his lungs seize. His father noticed it too, but he remained steady on his feet. "And the longer it takes to die, the better. You thought you could change that?"

"I did change that," his father said.

"Your research, Doctor."

There was a long pause, and then his father raised his arm and made a show of looking at his watch. "Yes, too late. You see, Benjamin, I took precautions. Did you think I wouldn't? Did you think I would allow you to kill my child and run away with the spoils?" He shook his head. "No. Right about now my research, all of Nueva Vida, every note, formula, technique used in its development, the complete details of its success, are being devoured by those who will do everything to make it real."

Benjamin froze and then his hand twitched. His hold tightened on the boy, who tried to twist away from him.

"You sold it to someone else?"

"No. I gave it away. And I gave it to more than one person. I gave it to scientists and to journalists. I gave it to the police."

"You gave it away?" Benjamin couldn't believe it. And then he did, as Joaquin's father nodded and, Joaquin imagined, gave a smile of supreme satisfaction. And then he saw a burst of orange light, like a flame, extending from Benjamin's hand and igniting the black night. And then he heard it, the sharp crack against the sky. His father's arms fell to his sides as he crumbled to the ice.

Something happened to Joaquin in that moment. He felt, but from a distance. He acted on thought, not emotion. He shied away from that. His survival instinct kicked into overdrive. He stood on the ice, his knees weak, his hands trembling, his heart teetering above a deep canyon of grief, and he chose life. He chose action. It was instinct and he followed it.

Benjamin, the man who'd shot his father, pulled on the boy. The sheriff's son. Benjamin bent over his father's body and rummaged through pockets. It was dark, the man's flashlight little help. Joaquin stood more than twenty yards away, but he knew there was nothing to find. His father had left it all behind. Then the man stood and shot his father again. The cracking of the gunshot skittered across the ice. And that's what snapped Joaquin out of his stupor. It burned in his chest. He opened his mouth and roared. He was calling to his father, although he knew he was too late for that. He stumbled backward, ran for his snowmobile, and gunned the engine. He didn't care now who heard him, saw him, knew he was there. And he headed straight for the man who had murdered his father—and probably Beatrice too.

Benjamin turned toward the sound, pushed the boy onto the idling Bobcat, and climbed on behind him. He lost a few moments as the boy struggled. And a few moments more when a pair of headlights appeared on the Lake Road above them. He pulled his gun from his pocket again and held it to the boy's head. Joaquin felt his stomach clutch as he remembered its orange burst of flame and the sharp crack that had split the night in two, and his father, falling to the ice. But there was only the sound of their Bobcat engines. Benjamin turned and grabbed the handlebars. He pressed on the throttle. The snowmobile leapt forward.

Joaquin followed, slower. His father's body was unmoving, a patch of darkness on the ice. He stopped and knelt beside him. He turned his father's head so that he was looking up at the starlit sky, but there was no breath from his lips, no sight from his eyes. His face was remarkably peaceful. The skin translucent, unmarred, the dagger of beard under his lip crystal with frozen spittle.

He took the glove from his right hand and placed his fingers over his father's mouth, under his nose. To be sure. No breath. He waited. Placed his hand on his father's chest, where he'd been shot, and felt the wound. Warm still. He looked down and watched his father's blood stain the ice, Joaquin's jeans, and his boots. So much blood. He was aware of the snowmobile in the distance, the hum of the engine fading, and knew he needed to follow.

No more death. His father's last wish. And Joaquin knew the man who had murdered his father had no plans of stopping there. The sheriff's son. A kid. Younger than Beatrice had been. No more death. He clung to those words as he laid his father down and climbed onto the Bobcat.

38

Nicole drove the department SUV off the Lake Road and down the snowy banks, breaking sharply before she rolled onto the glassy surface of Lake Maria. The tires slid on the ice and she kept a soft, steady pressure on the gas pedal. She glanced at the GPS screen on the computer, at the flashing red dot. They were on the move again, not a half mile ahead, not yet off the lake, but approaching its shoreline. Beyond their position, the Lake Road continued to the north, though its winding turns were tighter, the woods there dense and holding the cold temperatures longer. Black ice was thicker on the road, stayed longer, and caused more accidents. Not a mile down the road, the trees thinned and then opened abruptly into a valley populated with turbines. Most of the resorts were perched at the top of those mountains and had cross-country ski and snowmobile trails, sledding and tubing slopes—but all of them well away from the energy farm and the fierce winds that circulated there. Her best guess, Benjamin was headed for one of those trails.

Nicole's headlights and strobes had a span of one hundred-fifty-five feet. Her gaze swept over the surface of the lake inside that perimeter and she almost missed it. A body. Black parka and pools of inky darkness.

She opened the radio and hailed Lars. "Location?" she asked.

He was at the lake. Two minutes behind her.

"There's a body out here," she told him. "An adult, maybe," she said. "Dead?"

"Probably." She had sensed the absolute stillness of the body. "I can't get close enough." Not without moving the Yukon through a series of wide turns that would eat up time Jordan didn't have. "Inside our crime scene," she told him.

"It's not Jordan," he said, and she appreciated the conviction in his voice.

"Definitely not." She'd seen booted feet, but they had been too big to be Jordan's. And the shape of the lower legs had been longer, fuller than her son's. "I'm continuing on."

"I've got this," he returned.

Nicole took another look at the computer screen. The flashing dot had turned at the shoreline. Not onto the road, but below it, in the shallow dips running parallel. Benjamin didn't know that Jordan had his phone on. That Nicole was tracking him through the GPS. He was staying off the road to prevent detection.

She thought about returning to the road. She could move faster, but if Benjamin spooked and went back across the lake, she would lose time and distance.

Lars called her over the radio.

"It's Esparza," he said. "Dr. Esparza. Best I can tell, two gunshot wounds. Massive blood loss. And someone's been swimming in it. Knelt beside him. Footprints and a handprint."

"How long dead?"

"Minutes." There was a pause. "Blood is ice at its thinnest, still liquid at its deepest."

He told her about the Durango parked at the side of the road. It matched Benjamin's rental, make, model, color. A unit was securing it.

"Jordan was in it," he said. "Star Wars stocking cap left on the back seat."

Nicole felt her heart take a nose dive. Confirmation. It didn't matter that she'd already known. That she'd heard it go down. They now had tangible evidence that connected the victim to the perpetrator. That identified Jordan as the kidnapped. And that caused bile to crawl up her throat.

"How far out are you?" Lars brought her attention back to the call.

She'd closed the gap some. The screen showed she was point-two-six miles from her son. "About a quarter mile."

"More units are coming in," Lars said.

"Send one up to the resorts," she said. "Benjamin is going to need another vehicle. One that will get him out of Blue Mesa."

"On it." She heard Lars make the call, and then he returned with, "You think Esparza was out here to meet Sanders?"

"Maybe he thought so, and got Benjamin instead," Nicole said. "I think Esparza chose the place, and that he knew what he was walking into."

"Like that scientist he told us about. Montgomery."

"Exactly like that."

"Then Sanders hired Benjamin," Lars followed her thinking. "And he wasn't a neutral party."

"Callon Pharmaceuticals and Sanders," Nicole said. "Joaquin was right. There was no way his father would survive this."

* * *

The north side of the lake was colder, the air sharper. Joaquin had pulled the cowl up over his chin and cheeks, but the wind drew snot from his nose and even behind the goggles his eyes teared. But he followed. He gained on his father's killer. He had the advantage of no headlight. Three times Benjamin had stopped, cut his engine, and listened for Joaquin. After the first time, he'd realized invisibility gave him power. It gave him strategy. He'd watched the progress of the Bobcat, listened to its purr, the engine downgrading as it slowed to its next stop, and had cut his engine in time, drifted over the ice soundlessly until air and ground resistance stopped him. And then he had sat motionless, careful not to give away his location by even stirring in his seat. It made Benjamin nervous, and he'd stopped one more time before ascending the banks of the lake and pressing the Bobcat full throttle down the side of the road, over the moguls created by the snowplow. Joaquin followed in the wake of his rails. Every fifty yards, a streetlight illuminated a cone of geography. Joaquin was careful to stay out of the spotlight, skirting the edges, but remained on their tail.

Benjamin wasn't as experienced with the snowmobile as Joaquin, and that helped. The guy plowed through standing drift, causing the engine to slow and sputter. He hit hillocks head-on, and the Bobcat jumped and shuddered. Joaquin took them on an angle and glided over them.

Up ahead the curves in the road were cut like diagonal hash marks, and Joaquin anticipated that Benjamin would slow down. Snowmobiles were not known for their dexterity. He loosened his grip on the throttle, fell back several more yards, but Benjamin kept going. He hit the first curve and jerked the handlebars, and the tail of the Bobcat slid across the bank and hurtled into the road, completing a 360 before it rocked to a stop. But he didn't wait. He gunned it and hit the next curve only slightly slower. Joaquin listened to the whine as the engine protested.

He looked behind them. There were headlights on the lake, a vehicle crossing and closing the distance between them. And further away, a police cruiser had stopped, its bar light rolling. Had they found his father? Did they know the sheriff's son could be next? Their snowmobiles had left fresh tracks—had they picked up on those?

Joaquin turned back to the road. He watched the Bobcat in front of him bounce over the uneven snow, catch air, and then wallow when they hit ground.

He wasn't surprised when the Bobcat rolled. When the riders slid across the road and slammed into drifts. He thought it would have happened sooner. Joaquin cut his engine and removed his helmet. He dropped it in the snow and started walking. His target—the canted headlight of their Bobcat. As he walked, he watched the beam of light bounce and realized Benjamin was trying to right the machine. That wouldn't happen. It weighed eight hundred pounds, and even if he had gravity on his side and got it back on the rails, it wouldn't start. The metallic shrieking before the crash made that clear. At least to Joaquin.

He kept his feet on the ice as much as possible, where they made a scraping noise that was lost on the wind. He lengthened his stride. He didn't know what he was going to do when he arrived. He couldn't stand in front of a killer and ask for the kid, or he'd be in the same place as his father and Beatrice. But he couldn't let him get away with the sheriff's son, either.

Benjamin gave up on the snowmobile and started looking at the road, turning in a tight circle. He pulled the boy along with him, then down with him when he started peering at and sifting through the snowbanks. He was looking for something. Something important.

The gun. It had to be. Joaquin hoped it was. And he kept walking, added a little torque to his stride. He wasn't afraid of the little man. Not if he was unarmed.

Joaquin didn't know how to fight. Not really. A few years in karate until he became a teenager and his interests changed had taught him about pressure points and the positioning of hits. But he had never used them in real life and it had been a long time since he'd practiced them in the dojo. They were a dim memory. But at least he had that. For his father, for Beatrice, that would be enough.

He felt their loss pumping through his blood. He saw again the flash of orange and his father's body, collapsing on the ice. Heard Benjamin's mangled cries of frustration before he fired again, standing over his father, wanting him dead. And rage poured from Joaquin's eyes in tears. He wiped them away, wipe under his nose, and ratcheted his stride another notch.

He pushed emotion away. Stomped on it with both feet. He was stepping up, as his father expected. He was carrying on the name, and Beatrice and his father with it.

He wouldn't let this man kill the boy. He made that decision the way his father had made the decision to come here tonight, knowing that in saving the boy, he himself might die. He felt a flame of protest—that wick of life inside him flare—and he squashed it with determination. Some things were just wrong. Bea had taught him that. Death, when it could be prevented, was one of them.

Loss was many things. Fear, sadness, anger, despair. Anger was easier for him to deal with, and in this case, had better odds for getting the desired results.

By the time he reached the Bobcat, Benjamin and the kid were gone. He followed the road through its last curve, listened to the whopping clap of the turbines he knew were on the other side, felt their draft even before he left the protection of the mountains.

The valley glowed. The wind farm was well lit and everything in it was white, from the massive foundations of the turbines to their metal blades, which had to be a 100 feet long. Benjamin and the kid were less than 50 yards ahead. They'd stopped and stared at the tilting blades, the wind pulling their hoods out behind them, ruffling their hair, plastering their parkas to their bodies.

It was a dangerous place. Any back draft would pull you straight into the blades. So maybe he should have expected what would happen before the night was over.

Benjamin stepped forward, pulling the sheriff's son with him, held up a strand of barbed wire, and ordered the kid to crawl under it. They argued about it. Joaquin could tell even from where he stood. The kid was nervous. Scared. His body was as tight as a bow string. He shook his head. Tried to shake Benjamin off, but the guy was menacing. He took a fistful of the boy's jacket and jerked him off the ground and up to his face and shouted words Joaquin couldn't hear, then pushed the boy under the fence.

Tall sodium lights spaced thirty feet apart cast a glow that reached just beyond the fence line and flooded the vast acreage. Joaquin stood in darkness, at the lip of light, and watched Benjamin drag the boy deeper into the turbine farm.

There were only two reasons he would do that. To elude or to kill. Joaquin wondered if he had recovered the gun, or if he'd left it behind with the crashed Bobcat. Maybe he thought he could wind his way through the towering mills, tuck himself behind the concrete foundations, which were massive—taller than Joaquin stood and as big around as the barrel of a small airplane—and elude capture.

He watched the killer and the boy as they approached the first turbine. One hand on the kid, the other empty. He could have the gun stashed in a pocket, but Joaquin didn't think so.

The draft was stronger here. It came off the mountain and howled around the trunks of the turbines. Wind ballooned their parkas and the boy stumbled.

No one in their right mind would go in there. Maybe Benjamin was counting on that.

Joaquin followed, scuttling through the barbed wires on the fence. He was in full light then. If Benjamin turned, he would see Joaquin. But what could he do without a gun? Still, he hurried across the snowy field, a third set of footprints.

His sprint cut the distance between them, and Joaquin could hear them now. Benjamin was impatient, unrelenting. The boy was rebellious.

"Move faster."

"I am."

"You're still trouble, Jordan," Benjamin said. "You were a whiny baby. Always wanting something. And now you're a crybaby kid."

If Benjamin was Jordan's father, then Sheriff Cobain had made a huge mistake.

Joaquin kept his shoulder plastered to the base of the turbine and walked around it, the wind clapping in his ears. He moved until he could see them again. They were halfway between stalks. Jordan had slowed considerably, dragging his feet in the snow, and Benjamin was pulling him along and complaining about it. And then the boy planted his feet. The man, not expecting it, lost his footing and came to an abrupt stop, sliding and pitching forward.

"I'm not going in there," the kid said. "People die in there."

"People die out here," Benjamin said, and Joaquin could tell from the way his voice leaned heavily on Jordan that he was saying the kid could easily become the next victim.

He pulled on the kid's arm and dragged him several yards before Jordan dug in his heels again and they both stumbled.

"Why are we here?" the kid asked.

The man stopped and looked down at the boy. "Your mother is a bit of a bitch, Jordan. She's done a few not-so-nice things to me, and I need her to know how I feel about that."

"Write her a letter," he suggested.

"That didn't work." Benjamin shook his head, a little sad about it. "I even sent a check. You know, back pay. Once I made it big, I wanted to make good on child support. You know what she did with it?"

"Deposited it in my college fund," Jordan said, and it surprised the man. His eyes flared.

"She told you?"

"She's told me everything about you."

"Really? Did she tell you she knew I was hurting you but she did nothing about it?"

"That's a lie. She tried to get me away from you, but you fought her. You filed papers with the court."

"Because I love you, Jordan."

"Another lie."

"Yes," Benjamin agreed easily. "I don't think I've ever loved anyone, and it's too late to start now." He pulled Jordan another yard or two, then put his hand on the boy's shoulder and squeezed. It must have caused a quick, sharp pain, because Jordan gasped and his knees weakened. He sank toward the snow, but Benjamin used his other hand to hold the kid upright. He crept closer and thrust his face forward until their noses almost touched. "Your mother chose me, Jordan. Even knowing what I was. You, that was a mistake she learned to live with."

"You're wrong. She chose me twice," the boy screamed. "When she learned about me, and when she learned about you."

Benjamin's face turned scarlet. His lips peeled back over his teeth in a feral grin. "A mistake, Jordan. You're a mistake. Never forget that."

Joaquin knew then that he had to make a move. Rage was rattling the guy. He didn't like to lose. It was in his steely tone and in the plaintive wail beneath it. And in the sudden clenching of his hands in the boy's jacket as he threw the kid against the trunk of a turbine. He was pulling back, hand fisted, when Joaquin sprang forward.

Behind them came a great shuddering. It was a noise, but strong enough that it shook the ground. Like a sonic boom from the thrusters of a fighter plane, but the source was closer, grounded. The earth trembled. The towers wavered on their concrete foundations. And the blades of the turbines squealed. It was a sharp, metallic wrenching, as though the bolts holding the blades fast were pulling against their welded moorings.

"What the hell is that?" Benjamin asked, pulling back and looking deeper into the turbines.

"Wind," Jordan said.

"That happen a lot?"

"Probably."

It happened again. Longer. The earth vibrated with it. Joaquin felt a thumping under his feet, like a giant was walking the earth. And the towers, like masts on those old ships the Pilgrims had sailed to America, shook. There was creaking and a sharp splintering. It made the blood quicken inside Joaquin, but it also provided him with an opportunity. The shuddering was a distraction. It gave Benjamin a scare. Made him nervous. He let go of the kid's coat, and Jordan took a step backward. And then another. While Benjamin stared upward at the twirling blades of the closest turbine, Jordan continued to put space between him and his father so that he was slowly drawing closer to Joaquin.

And then the guy noticed, and he yelled at the boy to come back and he pushed his hand inside his parka and took out his gun. Under the light, Joaquin could see it well. The weapon that had killed his father. Dark metal, long barrel. Benjamin lifted it and pointed it at Jordan, and the kid froze.

"This won't do, Jordan. Your mom needs a statement. Like the grand finale at the end of a fireworks display. Shooting you won't do that."

Jordan didn't move, and Benjamin took a step in his direction.

"You asked me why I brought you here. It was more than just chance. It was serendipity. Everything else went to shit tonight, but not this. A bullet is boring, Jordan. I'm better than that at expressing myself. When she finds your body, I don't want her to cry. I want her stomach to crawl up her throat and choke her. I want her to scream. I want her to bleed. And a bullet won't do that, but Fillet of Jordan will."

He took another step, and Jordan shuffled backward.

"I had this planned before I left Georgia. There's something special about a wind farm, isn't there, Jordan?"

He raised his arm and gestured behind them. "I have a man who works for me. His job is to get here first and find out everything he can about the place. I don't mean points of interest, Jordan. I mean, where's the best place to dump a body? Where do accidents happen? You know what he told me about the wind farms?"

"That they're as exciting as the botanical gardens?"

"You're a funny guy, Jordan. No, he told me gruesome stories about this place. Slice 'em and dice 'em stories."

"Already heard them," Jordan said.

"But not your own. You want to hear how that one goes?"

"Does it have a surprise ending?"

"Am I boring you?"

"I'm on the edge of my seat," the kid said, and Joaquin admired his spunk.

"I'm choosing to believe that," Benjamin said. "Because I'm the story-teller." And he continued. "Wind shear. That's what this place is all about, collecting and using wind to power America. But wind shear causes updrafts and downdrafts and even backdrafts, none of which are very good. All of them kill. They bring down airplanes and suck firefighters into the flames. And all those drafts, they occur regularly right here in turbine country."

Joaquin looked beyond Jordan, beyond Benjamin. He had to shift his position, take a few steps away from the foundation of the turbine that was sheltering him. And then his gaze swept over the field, looking for shelter, for the covering of darkness, but it was too far away.

"I doubt it," Jordan said. "There have been accidents, but not a lot. Not every day."

"There are some dos and don'ts, of course," Benjamin agreed. "All those safety regulations we won't follow."

"You can't cause a backdraft to happen," Jordan said. "They're an act of nature."

But Benjamin was shaking his head. "I'm a planner, Jordan. Remember? Oh, I didn't know it would happen tonight, but opportunity is a beautiful thing. And this wind farm, it's a perfect symphony, isn't it?" He turned slightly and gestured behind him with his arm. The masts creaked. The blades spun overhead with deceptive calm. "All it takes is a sudden change in momentum. One small hesitation. No more than a hiccup." He stepped closer to Jordan. "I figure I can do that with a single bullet. And a boy your size, the draft will suck you right into the blades."

Jordan was silent.

"Good thinking, right?" Benjamin asked. His face beamed with pride. "Your mother will love it, and we have just enough time to get you in position before she arrives."

"She's not coming."

"Of course she is," Benjamin returned. "You have your cell phone with you, don't you, Jordan? Your mom has been following us, gaining on us for a while now. Don't you just love GPS?"

Jordan's response was visible. His body shook.

"I want her to watch you die, but I'll settle for watching her discover your body. Well, what's left of it. That's a lot for her to live with. I don't think she can do it."

The guy took another step, keeping the gun on Jordan, and Joaquin knew he was going to have to move fast. He had to leave the safety of the turbine and grab the kid. Keep moving. Find things to hide behind as they ran for the trees and the darkness within. That was the best plan he could come up with. Keep moving and get out of the light.

He slid along the base of the turbine, heard the nylon in his parka scrape against the concrete and his boots crunch in the snow, and then he was visible. Benjamin caught the movement and turned toward him, and Joaquin spoke.

"Run, Jordan. Run!"

Jordan froze for a moment, then looked over his shoulder at Joaquin, who was running toward him, and he was just putting his feet into motion as Joaquin grabbed his arm and pulled him along.

For the third time that night, Joaquin heard the crack of the gun and put more fire into his feet. He'd heard that being hit by a bullet was like taking a solid punch. It could knock him to the ground. He expected it, but it didn't happen. He had Jordan by the wrist. The boy tried to keep up, but Joaquin was taller, his legs longer, and he pulled the boy along with him.

Bullets hit the snow and sprayed it into the air. They pinged off the metal of the turbines. He heard another, heavier round that could have come from a cannon, it was so loud, but maybe it was a play of sound, as it echoed through the valley and bounced off the surrounding mountains. And then the wind shrieked and the earth shook, rolling beneath their feet so violently that Joaquin and the boy were knocked to their knees. He felt a force drag against his body, pulling him backward, peeling him off the earth, and he yelled to the kid.

"Keep moving. Stay down and crawl." And he didn't let go. Pieces of metal began falling around them, hitting the snow like rain. Small slivers of metal, some big enough that they fell on his back and shoulders like fists. It felt like the whole damn wind farm was coming apart.

39

Nicole left her cruiser on the side of the road, just short of the wind farm. The trail had been easy to follow. So easy that she knew Benjamin was expecting her. She called her position in to Lars, took her Colt Commando from its holster on the console, and shouldered into the night air.

With Benjamin, only bold would do. And if things hadn't changed, he was a bad shot unless the target was at point-blank range. So Nicole didn't try to hide her arrival. She slipped under the barbed-wire fence, following the trail left for her but not disturbing the prints. She noticed that there were three distinct sets—two close together, sometimes tangling; other times a drag pattern appeared. She knew these belonged to Jordan and Benjamin. The third set followed, parallel, and these puzzled her. They were unexpected, but she didn't break her stride. She walked at a clip, across the sloping field and toward the turbines, progressing at an angle that allowed her a greater field of vision and reaction time.

Three sets, as with Beatrice's murder. Two of them tangling, one following. As they were at the lake. There had to be some significance in that, but she couldn't find it. Not in that moment. Because she was a hunter after prey. She had come to kill, and this time she would follow through.

She was within fifty yards of the first turbines when she caught a blur of cobalt blue as a figure dashed from one concrete foundation to another, deeper into the farm.

She recognized the parka, the figure of the young man wearing it. Joaquin Esparza. But what was he doing here?

She quickened her steps. Released the safety on the Commando's trigger.

The closer she drew, the stronger the wind generated by the tilting blades overhead became. And because of it, she could hear nothing else. Until she reached the perimeter of the first masts.

"Good thinking, right?" Benjamin's voice, patting himself on the back for a job well done. "Your mother will love it . . ." And those words put a tic in her blood. The tone was absolute glee. Whatever Benjamin had planned, he knew it would cause Nicole the deepest grief. "I want her to watch you die . . ." The draft from the turbines became a force, and she pressed into it as she advanced. ". . . your body, what's left of it . . ."

She opened her angle, walking sideways, until three figures appeared, forty yards away. She'd hit center mass at sixty. Didn't matter, she told herself, that that had been at the range. She stopped, raised the rifle, and looked through the scope.

Jordan, alive, but standing in the line of fire.

Benjamin, gun drawn and pointed at her son.

Joaquin, hidden behind a concrete pillar but on the move.

Benjamin spoke again, a jangling of sharp words Nicole would not allow to pierce her concentration. There could be only her finger resting lightly on the trigger, the long, cold scope of her tunnel vision, and the target. No emotion.

Benjamin raised his arm, waved the gun, laughed. And she remembered the sound of it, when he lay beside her in bed, in the pursuit of dreams, confident, already a winner. And again, later, when he was looking into the barrel of her gun, confident, always confident and always ready to make a deal.

Another lifetime, she reminded herself. She'd made a decision then. She'd carve it in stone today. Jordan's life was nonnegotiable.

Her finger curled around the cold metal, and she waited. She was a good shot. Center mass at this distance was a guarantee. But she needed to see daylight between Jordan and Benjamin, and she silently urged her son to move, to trip, to fall to his knees and scramble to safety.

"Run, Jordan!" The words were caught by the wind and reached her ears distorted. It was Joaquin. He dashed forward as Benjamin turned to the sound of his voice, his gun tracking the bold figure running a jagged line through the snow. Too close. Too close to a man who had no respect for human life other than his own.

Jordan moved. He staggered forward, his feet gaining traction, his legs clambering through the heavy snow. Out of reach of Benjamin, but too slow. Too easily caught once Benjamin realized he'd lost his prize.

Benjamin fired, and the snow flew up in a geyser just left of Joaquin's feet. The young man dodged right but kept his aim steady. He was closing in on Jordan, putting himself between Benjamin and her son. And her mother's heart fluttered with relief but also trembled as she feared now for both boys.

They were still too close. Still in the sight as she held the Commando and looked down the barrel.

Benjamin turned as Joaquin passed and fired again. This time the bullet hit a turbine, the concrete shattering and spraying into the air.

Joaquin grabbed Jordan's arm and pulled him into a run.

Benjamin fired three more times, rapid, little thought and less aim, the bullets kicking up snow and ricocheting off the turbines. Nicole steadied the rifle against her shoulder, took a solid stance with Benjamin in her scope, then dialed back to perfect her aim.

And then the close shrieking of metal tore through the landscape, and pieces, some as big as her fist, fell from the sky. She lowered the Commando and took stock of the scene. Benjamin had hit a turbine. The bullets, the pummeling wind, were pulling apart the blades. Bolts and anchors flew from the pinnacles. Next would come the shredding of the blades themselves as they pulled apart from the nacelle. Then they would pitch through the air. One turbine, three blades. All hell.

She refocused. Peered down her sight.

And the earth shook beneath her feet, rolled the same way it did during a powerful earthquake. Nicole staggered. She held on to the Commando, but barely, and never took her eyes off Benjamin.

She wished she had.

Sheets of wind ripped down the slopes and through the valley. They created a churning, swirling dervish that blasted the turbines. The blades of the one damaged by Benjamin wobbled on their mast and fell forward as the tower shuddered and canted. Even from a distance, the wind pulled at Nicole's body, pushed her to the ground, scooped her up and pulled her toward the keening turbine. She fought it, and watched the sheer drafts pull Benjamin off his feet and up, up into the loosening blades. He was screaming, his mouth open and his lips peeled back over his teeth. Rage and terror. It took a moment for Nicole to realize, as his voice came back to her off the mountains, that it carried her name.

Death like this had happened here before. More than once. But she'd never witnessed it. She'd seen the remnants. She'd helped pick up the pieces. But she wouldn't tonight.

She turned away from what was left of Benjamin and found the trail of prints left behind by her son and Joaquin. Had they found shelter behind one of the concrete foundations? Were they clinging for life?

"Jordan! Joaquin!" she called. "Drop to your knees and head east." Away from the drafts and their undertow. To safety.

She crouched but remained on her feet, dashing through the snow, peering behind each of the turbines she passed, looking for Jordan, for the young man who had risked his life to save her son's. East, as she'd told them. Still, it was a long moment before she found them, well out of earshot. Joaquin still holding on to Jordan, pulling him along, laying low to the ground.

She had underestimated the young man.

The lighting in the wind farm made it almost as clear as day, and she could see their flushed cheeks and the worry etched into their features. Nicole quickened her stride, cut across the field using the pillars for cover as they did, and met them just beyond the last of the windmills. And though she knew Jordan was too old for it, she bundled him in her embrace and buried her nose in his hair, and he tolerated it.

She looked over his head at Joaquin. "He's dead," she told them.

Joaquin nodded. "He killed my father."

"You saw him do it?"

Jordan pushed against her hold, and she released him but kept him within reach.

"Yes. I followed him. My father. He didn't want me to, but I knew what he was planning. I knew I would never see him again."

"I'm sorry, Joaquin," she offered.

He considered her words and accepted them. "I know."

"What was the truth about Beatrice?" she asked. "Was she a medical miracle?"

"That and more," Joaquin said. "My father's super cell worked. Not once, but four times. Four different cancers, each aggressively worse than the one before it."

"What he did was wrong," she said, and Joaquin nodded.

"Beatrice died, but her sacrifice will save many people," he said. "Right now that's not enough for us, but maybe someday . . ." He looked over her shoulder, and Nicole turned to follow his gaze. Department cruisers were arriving. They left the Lake Road and plowed through the snowy field, bar lights rolling.

"Did he kill my sister?" He nodded behind them, toward Benjamin's body, fallen in the snow.

Nicole stepped closer and held his gaze. "No. It was Kenny King. He confessed, and we have enough physical evidence for a conviction." But if he hadn't gotten to her first, Charlene would have done the deed. Nicole was convinced that she was the watcher, hired along with Benjamin to squash the success of Nueva Vida. In the photo with Dr. Esparza, the woman had worn a Cossack and UGG boots. Benjamin wasn't the shooter; he was the brains. It made sense that he would marry up. Create a partnership that would advance his insatiable need for power. They would look for her next.

She shared her theory with Joaquin, that Benjamin and Charlene were hired to kill. One stone, two birds. There had never been a moment when either Beatrice or her father was meant to live through Nueva Vida.

"Sanders," he said. "I figured that out tonight, when she kept calling. Pharm companies like controlled advances. Big finds topple the giants."

"Your father knew."

"But not until this morning." He looked over his shoulder, but only briefly, and changed the subject. "He wanted to kill Jordan."

"And would have," Jordan said. "He's a *planner*. He was going to cause a backdraft that would suck me into the blades."

Nicole felt the tremble that went through his body. Her joints loosened, and liquid gathered in her eyes. She pulled Jordan close and lowered her face until she smelled the pine trees and snow in his hair. She held on to him until he squirmed, and then she faced him and spoke only the truth.

"And that's exactly what he did, but to himself. Now you never have to worry about him again," she promised. To Joaquin she said, "Thank you. You saved his life."

"I helped. I left a trail, and maybe I bought us some time."

"And you ran into the line of fire," Nicole said. "You grabbed Jordan and you got him to safety. You saved my son. Thank you."

He tried to shrug, clearly uncomfortable with the praise.

"No more dying. Bea was all about that. In the end, that's what my father wanted too." He looked into the field, where parts of Benjamin lay in the snow, though they could see none of the carnage from where they stood. "That really his father?"

Nicole nodded. "Poor judgment on my part." She ran a hand over Jordan's spiky hair. "But I wouldn't change it."

Joaquin's eyes darkened. His lips drew thin with grief.

"My father, he would have turned back the clock for Bea. He would have given it all up for her."

"In the end," Nicole said, "he did."